SMALL BONES

An utterly addictive crime thriller full of twists

KERRY BUCHANAN

Harvey & Birch book 2

G000017720

JOFFE
BOOKS

Joffe Books, London
www.joffebooks.com

First published in Great Britain in 2021

Cover art by Nebojsa Zorić

ISBN: 978-1-78931-843-2

PROLOGUE

It was the perfect night for burying a body, and he had the perfect place ready and waiting. Clouds scudded across the sky. There was no moon to give him away, and the lashing rain would keep most people indoors.

Besides, the garden was totally private, with a high wall on one side and thick hedges on two others. On the fourth side, the Victorian mansion loomed over him, its darkened windows like eyes. If he'd been a superstitious man, he might have thought it represented the judgement of generations of fine, upstanding citizens, glowering down at him.

But he wasn't, so his only emotion was gratitude that the people living there were heavy sleepers.

He didn't need a torch to find the spot. The ground had been levelled and flattened over the previous days so the builder could lay concrete slabs as a base. They were already in position, ready for pointing. Even on this moonless night, they showed up as a pale rectangle against the darker lawn around, but the sound of the rain bouncing off them would have told him where to go.

It wasn't hard to lift three of the slabs, and the soil beneath was easily dug, despite having been tamped down hard. It didn't need to be a deep grave. By the time the steel frame and glass had been constructed on the concrete base, there'd be little chance of any wild animals digging up the remains.

When he'd finished the hole, a mixture of sweat and rainwater dripped from his chin. He placed the small body inside, arranging the arms and legs as though the child was curled up in bed. Then, without wasting time on regrets, he covered the body with earth, stamped it down hard and re-laid the slabs. He made sure to clean the spade and replace it in the gardener's shed, exactly where he'd found it.

CHAPTER 1

Belfast, present day

Human finger bones can easily be mistaken for bits of clay pipe when you dig them out of the soil. Sue had heard that somewhere, maybe on *Time Team*.

She stared down at the broken clay pipe stem in her left hand, then at the thin, greyish lump in her right hand. They didn't really look alike at all. She'd tried to convince herself that the bone was animal in origin, the remains of someone's picnic lunch, but she knew she was deluding herself.

She'd been digging up bits of clay pipe all morning, along with broken willow-pattern cups and fragments of green bottles, but something about this little misshapen piece had stayed her hand before she could chuck it into the wheelbarrow with the rest of the rubbish.

She puffed out a breath. It *couldn't* be human. She knew this because the place she was digging was the site of the greenhouse her grandfather had built when she was a child. Storm Dennis had put the final nail in the greenhouse's coffin, skewing the frame into a twisted wreck and sending shards of glass scattering all over Sue's vegetable patch. She was clearing the ground now, to make way for the herb garden she'd designed on the back of an envelope.

Carrow Lodge had been in her family for roughly 150 years, built by Tobias Hearn in the late nineteenth century as a trophy house, flaunting the family's new fortune. But shipbuilding had been in decline in Northern Ireland since the *Titanic* hit an iceberg, so the money had dwindled away until all that was left was the decaying house and its wild gardens filled with ghosts.

It couldn't be human, she told herself again, determined not to let her mind drift into those dark recesses, the stinking cave of doubt and suspicion she'd managed to keep locked up all these years.

Sue slid the piece of bone into her coat pocket and massaged her aching lower back. The concrete slabs that had made up the base of the greenhouse were stacked neatly against the fence. They'd been well laid, but for as long as she could remember, there'd been an area in the corner where the floor canted into a slight hollow. Water had pooled there sometimes, when her grandfather had forgotten to turn the sprinkler off.

She drove the fork deep into the rich loam and twisted it with an expert flick, turning the soil with the ease of long practice. It stopped sharply, jarring her wrist. The tines of the fork had caught in something round, like an old football. She stooped to examine it a little closer. No, not a football.

Footballs didn't have eye sockets.

* * *

Coffee helped to revive her. She buried her nose in the mug and breathed deeply, letting the fumes sharpen her mind while the dark liquid flushed away the last numbing traces of shock.

Her first instinct had been to leave the scene exactly as she'd found it and call the police, as her years of training told her she should. She'd got as far as googling the non-emergency number, having decided it was hardly a 999 emergency, before the repercussions dawned on her.

That greenhouse had been a part of her teenage years, a magical place of twisting tomato plants with jewel-like fruits, and shiny purple aubergines. She'd often sat there in summer, watching spiders scuttle across the concrete slabs, chatting with her grandfather as he pruned and tied and watered his plants.

It wasn't that old. Sue remembered it being built when she was at school, but the garden, including the spot where the greenhouse had stood, had been in her family since the late 1800s. That meant that someone in her family, or someone close enough to her family to have free access to the garden, must have buried this body. Another thought struck her. *During her lifetime*, or surely the builders would have come across the body as they prepared the ground for the base?

A cloud drifted across the sun, and she shivered.

So, if she called the police, and if some forensic archaeologist raked over the soil, it was going to open a can of worms that Sue didn't feel able to deal with, not right now. She wasn't sure she'd ever be ready to deal with it, not even if she lived to be a hundred.

The coffee flooded her veins, firing up her determination to protect her family. Especially her father. Her fingers tightened on the handle of her mug and some of the liquid sloshed onto the table. She wiped it away with her sleeve and put the mug down.

No police. Not until she had no other choice.

She should just put the skull back where it had come from. Cover the whole thing up. Build a shed or something.

She bit her lower lip, thinking. She couldn't afford to buy a shed, or to replace the greenhouse. She and Dad were only just making ends meet as it was with her tiny savings and his Attendance Allowance. She'd given up a good job to look after him, but she'd never seen the need to save, always believing her dad would bail her out if she was in trouble. When she'd applied for power of attorney, shortly after his diagnosis, she'd been shocked to find that there was nothing left in his bank account.

This was wasting time. Yes, she'd prefer to leave this particular family secret buried, but at least she could ask a friend for help.

The clouds cleared and the room lit up with a golden glow of sunshine, dust motes dancing in the rays of light. She put the mug and cafetière aside to be washed later, then stood staring out of the window, trying to convince herself.

She sighed. She did need help, and she thought she knew who to ask.

CHAPTER 2

"Hello, Sue. How lovely to hear your voice. What can I do for you?"

Professor Mark Talbot had the sort of sunny nature that endeared him to his employees, past and present. The sound of his voice raised Sue's spirits and lightened the millstone around her neck.

"Mark, I need your help."

"Of course! Anything at all, dear lady."

That affected English accent had once set her teeth on edge, until she'd got to know him better. The Old Etonian act was camouflage. He'd grown up in a sooty two-up two-down in Leeds, but had won a scholarship to the local grammar school, where he'd promptly reinvented himself.

"Can I meet you for a coffee? I need to show you something."

"Certainly. I'm free this afternoon, if you are."

"Yes." Since she'd left the pathology lab, she'd had virtually no life beyond her own home, but Dad always took a long nap in the afternoon, allowing her to occasionally slip out. "Clements on Botanic? In an hour?"

"I'll see you there."

* * *

Clements was buzzing, as usual, with students and professional people. She'd picked it partially for the quality of its coffee, but mainly because it was so busy that it would be easy to be anonymous in here. The usual meeting place for her old work crowd was a little café just off the Falls Road, another reason for choosing somewhere well away from that area. The last thing she needed was a bunch of nosy pathology techs asking questions.

She ordered an Americano for herself and a latte for Mark, and splashed out on one of the enormous fifteens, a sticky cake filled with marshmallow and cherries, for them both to share. By the time her order was ready, Mark had shouldered his way through the crowd and inserted himself behind the last remaining table for two, discretely tucked away in a corner. She carried the tray over, awkward with the carrier bag swinging from her arm, and sat down facing him.

"Food first," he said. "Whatever it is that's worrying you will be less frightening once you've wrapped yourself around some sugar."

They ate and sipped their coffee in silence, letting the chatter of students and young professionals at the nearby tables wash over them like white noise. Sue was reassured that she couldn't decipher anything her neighbours were saying at the next table, which meant their own conversation should be equally private.

"I've been gardening," she began.

"Excellent. I read an article recently that said gardening is wonderful for your mental health, especially if you're growing food to eat. Are you?"

"Herbs," she said automatically. "But the patch I was turning over hasn't been used for cultivation in a long time — thirty years or so."

"Sounds like hard work."

"Not really. The ground was full of debris. You know the sort of thing. Bits of broken pot, old bottles, clay pipe stems. Remnants of other people's lives."

He nodded. She wanted to go on, but now the words wouldn't come. She couldn't think how to say what she needed to say, so she tiptoed around it. "Would you mind having a look at something for me?"

"Something you dug up? I'm not an archaeologist, you know."

"I know." She delved in her pocket and brought out two small objects. She handed him the first, one of the bits of clay pipe. He turned it over, a quizzical look on his face, so she handed him exhibit B. The finger bone.

That got his attention. He examined it closely, fishing his reading glasses out from an inside pocket, then he returned it to her.

"Have you any idea how many people think they've dug up a skeleton? I'm told the police get a few most months, especially in the summer when people are spending time in their gardens."

Her heart lifted, despite her reservations. "You don't think it's human, then?"

"It's quite badly damaged," he said slowly. "Some rodent or other has had a good go at it."

"That's not an answer."

"No, I know it isn't." Mark closed his eyes for a moment. "This is your family's garden you're digging up, I'm guessing. The one you inherited? You do realise that if you want me to take this further, it will almost certainly have to be done through official channels?"

She hadn't actually inherited the garden, not yet. But even people as close to her as Mark often forgot about her father.

"Yes, but I think it's a little late to leave it well alone, I'm afraid." Her mouth was dry. She wished she'd asked for a glass of water with her coffee, and now she needed the loo as well.

His eyes sharpened. "Why?"

Sue lifted the plastic-wrapped object from the capacious bag at her feet. With a wary glance around at the other tables, she slid the white plastic supermarket bag aside to expose the front of the skull with its blank eye sockets and small, surprisingly white teeth.

"Because I think I found the rest of the body," she said.

Mark's sharp intake of breath made her jump. She covered the skull up and shoved it into the bag, safely out of sight. No one had even glanced their way.

"What were you thinking, Sue? You can't just dig up evidence and cart it around like a bag of flour! You have to go to the police," he said. "This isn't something you can just pretend didn't happen. You must know that."

"I suppose I do, but it's complicated."

"Explain, then."

"Carrow Lodge has been in my family since forever," she said. He still looked blank. "My grandfather built a greenhouse on the spot where I found the—" she glanced around and lowered her voice — "the remains. No one has disturbed that spot in the last, what, thirty-odd years? Not until the damn greenhouse blew down in the storms last winter and I decided to turn it into a herb garden."

"Ah."

She'd known he would understand.

"You're worried your grandfather, or someone close to your family, might have buried the body?"

"Exactly."

He frowned. "Have you told—?"

"No!" It came out far louder than she'd intended, and this time a serious-faced girl who'd been typing on her laptop looked over. Sue hoped the pulse that thudded in her ears wasn't obvious to anyone else. "No," she said more quietly. "Dad's doing really well at the moment, and I can't risk anything that might upset him."

"A skeleton in the garden might just edge into that category," Mark said, with a return of his usual humour.

Sue started to giggle but caught herself before it became hysterical. "So, what do you advise?"

"I could have a closer look at the two, erm, exhibits you brought along today," he said. "I'm not a forensic anthropologist, which is what you really need, but I can probably take a stab at ageing and all that."

"Oh, would you?" It was as if a weight had been lifted from her.

"Of course."

"And keep it between just the two of us?"

"For now. But you must understand, Sue, that I work for the government. If I do something outside the law, I not only risk my own career, but I also bring the entire State Pathologist's Department into disrepute." He took a deep breath. "So, if this turns out to be a recent burial, I will have to report it. Or better still, you should report it yourself."

She nodded miserably. "All right."

CHAPTER 3

When she got home, Sue hoked around in the shed until she found the remains of a gazebo her parents had used for one whole summer. The last happy summer she remembered. The material was a sort of canvas with clear plastic windows. It would do to keep the weather off the site until Mark got back to her, at least.

She dragged it over to the partially dug herb garden and weighted it down with some of the slabs that had made up the floor of the greenhouse. Thank goodness her garden was so private, with no other houses overlooking it. This spot was hard enough to see from her own house, thanks to the hedge some ancestral Hearn had planted to separate the lawns and herbaceous borders from the more utilitarian vegetable garden. It had been kept under control in Grandfather's time, but now it grew wild, the top of it far above her head.

She scrubbed the dirt from beneath her nails and tried to imagine the wealthy, upright, strait-laced Hearns having such a dark secret in their past. *A skeleton in the cupboard*, she thought, and the hysteria bubbled up again. There was a secret, though, wasn't there? One she'd kept inside her all these years, too afraid to look for answers.

She pushed open the door to the kitchen, which was at basement level because the house was built on a hill, and went inside. The ancient, scrubbed pine table that must have been built in situ, since it was too big to have come in through any of the doors or windows, took up most of the floor space. It matched the solid-pine cupboards and dressers that could have come from a set for a BBC costume drama.

Carrow Lodge really needed a makeover. The furniture was antique, but not in a good way. The heavy, dark-oak sideboards in the rooms upstairs wouldn't raise much at auction. Perhaps in another couple of decades, they'd be back in fashion, but few people had the space for such massive pieces these days.

And the matching pair of chesterfields in the drawing room. They might have fetched good money if the leather hadn't been clawed by generations of house cats, and if the stuffing wasn't hanging out where mice had made a nest inside one winter.

Besides, the house didn't belong to her. Her father was no longer able to make decisions, and she'd been granted power of attorney, but it was his for as long as he lived, and that could be for years. For the sake of his dementia, she'd decided to put up with things the way they were. Doors that stuck, floorboards that creaked in the night, damp stains in the one bathroom and heating bills that had crippled her even when she was working full-time. It was still better than the confusion that would result from moving them both to somewhere more manageable.

Her phone vibrated and she glanced down at the screen. *Reminder: Dad dinner.*

She lifted a ready meal from the freezer, stabbed a fork into the plastic covering and popped it into the microwave. Lasagne, his favourite. Or it had been, when he'd been able to taste the difference. Now, he ate anything she served him as long as she remembered the glass of red wine with it.

The microwave pinged. She tipped the lasagne onto a plate, added a bit of salad and poured his wine into the special glass she kept just for him. It had a wide base and a short stem, making it hard to knock over. More like a brandy glass than a wine glass, but safer.

She carried the tray up to the ground floor and into the front room, pushing the door open with the skill of long experience. It scraped across the carpet, and she made a mental note to fetch a screwdriver later, to tighten the screws in the hinges.

"Hi, Dad. How're you feeling?"

He was hunched up in his chair, eyes closed. As she always did, Sue watched for the rise and fall of his chest, but when she saw it, she couldn't decide if she was relieved or disappointed.

The television flickered in the corner of the room, BBC News on a constant loop, with video footage of a plane crash somewhere followed by a presenter in a studio looking suitably solemn. Dad opened his eyes at the sound of her voice and smiled.

"Any good news on the box?" she asked.

"You're my good news," he answered. "Always were, from the moment I first saw you dancing."

For a fraction of a second, she'd thought he recognised her, but he was talking about Mum again.

"I've brought you your favourite," she said. "Sit up a bit, and you can have it on your knee, if you like?"

"TV dinner. What a treat. You don't usually let me get away with this, Monica."

"Yes, Dad. Special treat."

She tucked the napkin into the neck of his sweater and made the padded tray secure. The wine went onto the little table at his side, the one that held his packet of tissues and a tumbler of water that he never drank from. She took it away with her to freshen up, going through the motions. He probably never would drink it. He preferred wine, or Coke when he could get it.

When she'd first given up her job to care for him, Sue used to sit with him while he ate, but she was making less effort these days. He rarely noticed her presence, and when he did, he always called her Monica. It was distressing, but if she reminded him that Mum was dead, it only upset him. So now she took her own meals in the kitchen.

CHAPTER 4

Yussuf was typing away at a computer when Mark arrived in the bright, modern State Pathologist's Department building in the grounds of the Royal Victoria Hospital. He was nodding along to the beat of whatever he was listening to through his earphones. He didn't look up as Mark swept past into the lab, but he never missed a trick, so Mark knew his arrival would have been logged in Yussuf's massive brain.

The cocky East Ender had followed Mark from the London teaching hospital he'd worked in before he was offered the job here in Belfast. Despite his London accent, his massive Afro and his love of brightly coloured clothing, Yussuf had been accepted into the uptight, predominantly white Belfast social scene. He'd made friends and seemed to have less trouble than Mark with the rapid-fire Northern Irish speech.

Mark resisted the temptation to stop for his usual chat and strode on to the lab. Right now, he just needed a second look at that skull, with no one else around.

Once the door swung closed behind him, the place was quiet. He'd long since ceased to notice the smell of death, but with the way Yussuf kept it, the lab only smelled of disinfectant anyway.

He set down the plastic carrier bag on the nearest empty table and turned on the overhead lights, then put a gown, apron and gloves on. He wouldn't want to explain in a court of law how his DNA had ended up on a specimen.

The skull was bare bone with no soft tissue adhering to it, but even in the short glimpse he'd had of it in the café — how much contamination had it picked up there? — he'd absorbed details that he needed to examine further.

He started the audio recorder and spoke his findings aloud as he turned the skull over, rotating it in his hands.

"This is the skull of a juvenile, sex undetermined. No mandible present, but otherwise in excellent condition. Sutures not fused, confirming sub-adult. Upper teeth as follows. Central incisors, present both sides. Lateral incisors present both sides. Primary upper-left cuspid present, but absent from right-hand side with secondary beginning to emerge—"

The drone of his own voice helped him to focus. If this tape was ever produced as evidence, he needed to sound calm and professional.

"Age of subject tentatively estimated at between ten and twelve years," he concluded, then he tipped the skull to examine the feature that had first caught his eye. "Penetrating injury to the palatine process of the maxilla—" he carefully placed a probe into the hole — "traversing the suprasellar cistern. The shape of the injury and lack of fragmentation of surrounding bone suggests a sharp, narrow object such as a thin knife."

"You gotta be shitting me," Yussuf said from just behind him.

Mark jumped. He paused the recorder. "Meaning what, precisely, my dear boy?"

"Well, that's a life-terminating injury, right there, innit?"

"Your point being?"

"I ain't seen no police reports pass over my desk. No referrals. You doin' this on the side, Prof?"

Mark licked his lips behind the mask. Yussuf was completely trustworthy, loyal to the core, which was why he hadn't brought him in on this. If there were repercussions, they would only rebound on Mark himself, with his professional negligence insurance, and not on the poorly paid lab tech.

"Unless that's a specimen for teaching — and since I catalogued said specimens last year, and I don't recognise that kid's skull, I'm guessing it ain't — you gotta report it."

"I know," Mark said. "A friend dug it up in their garden, along with this." He fished the finger bone out of his pocket and gave it to his assistant.

Yussuf clicked his teeth as he examined it, then handed it back. "This is likely murder. You know that, right?"

"Yes."

"Asha's all right. You know, that DS we had in here last year with the Slasher case. You could give her a call?"

He'd tried to keep this low-key for Sue, but Yussuf was right, and Asha was a bit more sensible than some of the detectives he'd worked with over the years. More human.

"All right. I'll get her over here."

* * *

"Acting Detective Inspector Harvey."

The voice on the phone sounded distracted, and the change in rank threw Mark for a second. It was one thing taking a DS into his confidence, but a DI would take things much more seriously. Especially an acting DI with everything to lose and nothing to gain by keeping secrets.

"Hello?"

"Sorry," he said, flustered. "It's Professor Talbot here. State Pathologist's—"

"Prof! Good to hear from you." Still distracted. Maybe typing something as she spoke? "Do we have any open cases with you at the moment?"

"No. It's been pretty quiet on the crime front. I need to ask you a favour." The phone slipped in his hand. He wiped his palm on his shirt.

"That sounds mysterious. What sort of favour?"

"Could you come over here, do you think? No rush, not really, but if you come before Yussuf goes home, he can make you one of his special coffees?"

You sound as if you're begging. Man up, Mark.

"All right. It's, what, four-ish now? I've something I need to sign off here first. I can be with you in forty minutes. That soon enough?"

"Perfect."

He ended the call and said, without looking around, "Forty minutes. Have we got any of those Harar Arabica beans left?"

"Getting my grind on now."

"Yes. Thank you very much. That's an image I really needed planting in my brain."

When Asha buzzed to be let in, Yussuf brought her down the corridor, chattering the entire way. Mark had put the skull in a sterile plastic container and the finger bone, belatedly, in an evidence bag.

"What have you got for me that's too hush-hush to speak about on the phone?" she asked as she breezed in.

"Ah. Well. I acquired a skull that a friend dug up from the garden. I promised her I'd try to keep it low-key if I could."

That wasn't what he'd intended to say, but his carefully prepared speech had gone straight out of the window as soon as he saw the tall, confident, young Indian woman.

"Recent or historical? I assume it's human. You wouldn't have dragged me out here for a dog skull or something."

"It's human," he said grimly. "You'll need a forensic anthropologist to tell you more about the bones than that, and a forensic archaeologist to tell you how long it's been in the ground. I just do the pathology — and there's not much pathology for me to work with here, not without any soft tissues. But even I can tell you it was not a natural death. Glove up, and I'll show you."

He demonstrated the track of the weapon, explaining what she was seeing, and was reassured by her quick comprehension.

"Someone stabbed a child through the roof of his or her mouth. Could it have been accidental?"

"Possible, but unlikely. See the way the bone has been sliced through like that? This was a very sharp object, like a stiletto or some other thin knife."

Asha shuddered. "I saw enough of knives and the damage they can do last year. Are you able to give me any clue at all to when the crime was committed?"

"It must have been in the ground for at least thirty years. I can't tell from the bones, but the woman who discovered the skull owns the land it's on, so she knows the history of the site."

"And there might be more bones there?"

"I'd say it's highly likely. As soon as she found the skull, she stopped what she was doing and phoned me."

"She knew it was human then?"

"She should do," Mark said. "She was a path technician here for a number of years. If she can't recognise a human skull, no one can."

CHAPTER 5

Sue had a forkful of last night's reheated curry halfway to her mouth when her mobile shrilled, vibrating across the chipped marble counter where she'd left it. She lunged to stop the phone falling off the edge.

Mark's photo popped up on the screen. He must be using his personal mobile, not his work phone.

"Hi Mark. Any news?"

"Yes." His voice was brittle. "I'm afraid there is."

Sue tightened her grip on the phone, afraid she'd drop it with the way her hand trembled. "Tell me."

"Long story short, my dear, this is a police job. It's not going to be very pleasant. That's all I can say, for now. I'm sorry."

"Is there someone there with you?"

"Yes."

She swallowed, her tongue suddenly feeling too big for her mouth. "Police?"

"Yes."

"Oh."

"I expect they'll be with you fairly shortly." He rang off.

She tipped the curry into the brown food bin under the sink. Her appetite had fled, and the yellowy stuff looked like diarrhoea all of a sudden. She ran upstairs to the front room. Dad had fallen asleep with his meal half-eaten, but the wine glass was empty. She took the tray and glass away. He'd sleep for an hour or two, with luck, and hopefully no one would need to disturb him.

As she finished the washing up, the doorbell clanged. It was part of the same ancient pulley system that had once summoned servants from the basement kitchen to the family quarters upstairs.

She wiped her hands on her jeans to dry them, then swore. She'd have a pair of wet patches on her bum now. Living alone too long was leading to bad habits.

The police officer on her doorstep was young, dark-skinned, pretty in a hard-faced way and unsmiling. Beneath the uniform, draped with stab vest, radio and a heavy belt that looked as if it held everything including the kitchen sink, she'd probably be very slim. The PSNI uniform made everyone look bulky.

"Miss Hearn?" The officer flashed a warrant card, but Sue was too flustered to take it in. "I've been detailed to preserve the crime scene from any further damage," the officer said.

Sue bristled at her choice of words but managed to reply in a level voice. "Of course. Professor Talbot said someone would be here soon." She gestured inside. "This way, please. Would you mind keeping your voice down? It's just that my dad is sleeping, and I don't want to frighten him."

The policewoman's perfectly drawn eyebrows raised, then shot up even further as Sue locked the front door and pocketed the key. She didn't feel up to explaining her father's tendency to wander off and get lost.

"The easiest way to the garden is down here." She led the way downstairs to the kitchen, then slid her bare feet into her old gardening shoes and followed the police officer through the back door into the low, evening sun.

Seeing the garden through someone else's eyes made her realise just how overgrown it had become. The grass wasn't too bad — she wrestled the petrol mower into noisy life every so often and took the worst of the long grass down to an acceptable level — but the flowerbeds and shrubberies were wild and blowsy, roses hanging down from trellises.

The officer swore as her uniform jacket snagged on the thorns.

"Here. Let me help—"

But the woman wrenched herself free and continued down the gravel path. Well, it had been gravel, once. Now it was a slightly grittier bit of lawn with dandelion clocks sending their fluffy seeds floating in the breeze.

"It's down the back," Sue said, "through the gap in the hedge. I've covered the area to keep the weather off, and in case any animals . . ." She trailed off. The stripy green-and-white canvas had been chewed by mice or rats while it had been stored in the shed. And it must have been underneath a swallow's nest, too, because copious streaks of droppings had made an abstract artwork out of it.

The police officer tutted under her breath but loud enough for Sue to hear.

"That stuff will have contaminated the crime scene. You'll have to explain to the SOCOs that you put it there or they'll blame me."

Oddly enough, that little speech made Sue feel more charitable towards the young woman. Perhaps this was her first crime scene? She certainly seemed anxious to get things right.

"Can I get you a drink of anything? Hot or cold. I don't suppose you'd take alcohol, if you're on duty."

The policewoman's smile was like the sun coming out from behind a cloud. "I could kill for a cup of tea, if you have any. Nice, strong brew?"

They sat together on upturned steel buckets a safe distance from the burial site. That's what Sue had begun calling the patch of broken ground inside her own head. It made it seem more insubstantial.

"I didn't catch your name, when you showed me your card earlier," she said.

"Constable McAvoy," the young woman replied. "And you're Miss Hearn."

"Yes. Sue." Then she wished she'd stuck with "*yes*", because now it sounded as if she was trying to ingratiate herself. Which, to be fair, she probably was. "You're here to preserve the site, but I'm guessing there'll be more people coming soon?"

"Mm. SOCOs are on their way over. That's scene-of-crime officers, by the way. Shouldn't be too long. Is there a side gate into the garden, so they don't have to tramp through your house?"

"Not anymore. There used to be a path, but it's all brambles and overgrown hedge now, and the padlock to the gate was lost long before my time. There is a gate down there." She pointed past the vegetable patch towards the stone wall at the bottom of the garden. "And a public park across the road with parking spaces. They could leave their cars there and walk through this way, if I can get it open."

"Name of the road?" Constable McAvoy was all business now. Sue told her and she radioed it through to some impersonal voice.

They hadn't used the back gate for years, and weeds had grown up in front of it. The bolt was stiff with rust, squealing as Sue wiggled it open. Then the gate itself, more like a door, with wooden planks swollen from years of damp neglect, needed a shoulder to shift it. Once she'd finally managed to wrestle it open, pulling up most of the weeds by hand, she took a moment to catch her breath.

The park stretched out in front of her, quiet at this time on a weekday. A couple of women were pushing buggies along the path, and a man was throwing a ball across the grass for a chocolate Labrador. The SOCO team arrived in a grubby little van that belched smoke from its exhaust.

The pair of them struggled into SOCO suits in full view on the pavement, looking like a couple of extras from a low-budget disaster movie as they hopped from foot to foot. One was tiny, dwarfed by her baggy body suit. The other was tall, rotund and squeezed the seams of his. *The Two Ronnies,* she thought, *which makes the little one the stooge to the big one's clever gags.*

The smaller of the two marched over to the gate. "Susan Hearn, no?" Her Eastern European accent turned "Hearn" into "Heern".

"Yes. Sue Hearn," she replied and held out a hand before dropping it, embarrassed, as she realised the woman was wearing rubber gloves to prevent contamination.

"Jolanta Wiśniewska, which no one here can either pronounce or spell, so everyone calls me Jana. Where's the body?"

"Right through here, but—"

The diminutive woman marched past her into the garden. "Come, Marley. We don't have all day!"

The big man followed her, scowling, carrying heavy-looking bags of equipment.

Sue trailed after them down the gravel path to the site of the greenhouse. Constable McAvoy stood, hands behind her back and feet slightly apart as if she was on sentry duty. There was no sign of the empty tea mugs. "The resident placed the cover over the crime scene," she said, without looking at Sue. "I thought it better not to move it."

Oh well. Whatever truce they'd shared as they sipped their tea was clearly over.

"Quite right," Jana said, and Sue wasn't certain which of them she was addressing. The little SOCO glanced up at the evening sky, where clouds were beginning to gather in great purple-tinged piles.

"Okay, Marley. Let's set up the tent in case it rains, then we can see what's been hiding here."

Constable McAvoy, at a word from Jana, took Sue up to the house. She was glad. With the clouds had come a drop in temperature, and she was shivering in her thin blouse and jeans. The kitchen was warm all year round, with the oil-fired Aga radiating heat whether she needed it or not.

She put the kettle under the tap. "Another mug of tea?" No point in blaming the constable for her attitude. No doubt she had bosses who'd censure her if she made a wrong move that endangered any legal case that might come of this.

The thought chilled her all over again, despite the warmth of the room.

"Thanks. I can go and get the mugs?"

"It's okay." Sue opened the cupboard to reveal dozens of mismatched cups and mugs of all shapes and sizes. "I'll get them later. Where did you hide them, by the way?"

The officer looked embarrassed. "Under the hedge. Sorry."

"It's fine," Sue reassured her, thinking how bizarre the whole situation was. "I'm sure you had your reasons."

They sat at the big pine table and munched shop-bought biscuits from a tin while the Aga burbled happily, and expensively, in the background.

"It's my first week on the job," Constable McAvoy blurted out. "Well, not quite, but my first week since probation."

"I see." And she did. It explained the prickly attitude, the swing from cocky to anxious, the hidden mugs. The officer didn't know if it would be seen as inappropriate. *Colluding with the enemy.* Now, where had that thought come from?

"Did they cover this sort of scenario in your training?"

"What, preserving a crime scene? Yes."

"No, I meant keeping me company."

"Oh." McAvoy looked startled. "I should have gone to the station when the SOCOs got here." Her hand drifted towards the radio on her stab vest.

"I'm sure they'd prefer you here. If it turned out I'd been the one to bury the body, they'd probably rather someone kept an eye on me in case I destroyed evidence or whatever."

"Yes." McAvoy let out a breath. "I expect you're right. You're not, are you? The person who buried the body."

Sue shook her head, wondering if she'd ever been that naive. "No. The storm blew my greenhouse down. I was going to replace it until I saw the price of even quite a small greenhouse. Once I'd got over the shock, I decided a herb garden would go very well there instead."

McAvoy smiled. "Bit of an unpleasant surprise, then, when you tried to dig it up?"

"You could say that." Sue's hand tightened on the handle of the mug, and she forced herself to relax her grip. The impulse to say more, to explain to this stranger why she'd wanted to keep her discovery secret, her suspicions about who may or may not have buried the body in the first place, was almost overwhelming. Almost.

The doorbell broke her train of thought.

"I can get that, if you like?" the constable said.

"No. I'd better get it, in case Dad wakes up and finds a stranger in the house."

McAvoy looked confused.

"He has dementia. Strangers upset him."

"Ah."

Sue could virtually hear the penny drop as the constable remembered her locking the front door and pocketing the key.

CHAPTER 6

December 1992

The morning was not going well. Alistair had cut himself shaving and the bit of toilet paper he'd stuck to stem the bleeding had been insufficient for the job. He'd bled onto the pristine white of his shirt collar, and there'd been no time to change.

Still, today was the day he'd squeeze the worst of his debtors and make them squeal. That always cheered him up. His first visit, under the cover story of following up on a burglary lead, was to a small jeweller's shop in an alleyway in Belfast. The place was dingy and dark, the windows in need of cleaning, but the gleaming displays of watches, rings and necklaces glowed warm in the yellow electric light.

The jingling doorbell brought the jeweller from his little backroom, a welcoming smile on his face — a smile that froze as soon as he saw who the customer was.

"Morning, Andrew. Business good?"

The little man wrung his hands together. "Not good at all, I'm afraid, Mr King. Times are hard." He shrugged expressively. "Mostly watch repairs, these days."

"Really? Then if that's the case, why has this display changed since my last visit?" He pointed to the heavy gold chains, the sort a man might wear as a status symbol in certain circles, and the thick signet rings with inlaid black stones. "This is high-end stuff, Andrew. Big money."

"True. True. But there was a lot of outlay to buy those pieces, Mr King. A lot of outlay. Nothing in the way of readies left, you see."

Alistair shook his head sorrowfully. "That's a real shame, Andrew, because I'm sure time and skill went into making these pieces. I doubt if they'll be worth much when they're all melted together and mixed up with the ashes of the shop, and that's even if there's anyone left alive to look for them by then. That's the sort of thing that might happen if I'm forced to withdraw my protection."

The jeweller paled and put out a hand to steady himself against the counter. Alistair wondered idly what the state of the old man's ticker might be.

"But if you pay what you owe by the end of the week, I might consider leaving the rates the same for another couple of months before I put them up again." He pretended to think, even though he had the numbers clear in his head. "That's three grand, Andrew. Three grand by Friday lunchtime will buy you some breathing space."

The jeweller's chest rose and fell a couple of times. He finally managed to speak. "Three thousand pounds? How did it get to that?"

"Compound interest, my friend. And I'm only giving you to Friday because I like you. I think you're good for it, don't you? Because it would be an awful shame if you weren't."

He left the shop with a spring in his step and returned to his car, which he'd left on a yellow line with no fear of a parking ticket — the local traffic wardens wouldn't dare. He sank into the driver's seat and checked the notebook that lived in his inside jacket pocket.

The next name was less of a known quantity. A relatively new debtor whose addiction had led him into a debt he hadn't so far honoured. Alistair tsked to himself. He hated people who had no self-control. Still, this one was soft and ripe for plucking. *And who knows*, he thought, *perhaps there'll be a steady income once he realises he has to pay up or lose something he values.*

He pulled up outside the tall Victorian house, half hidden by trees. The gravel in the driveway crunched under his feet, deep and expensive. One day, he'd have a gravel driveway like this and a grand house of his own, as soon as he'd collected enough money to rebuild the derelict farm he'd inherited, the way he saw it in his mind's eye.

The front door, painted glossy blue, was at the top of a grand flight of stone steps. It had a polished brass knocker but no bell that he could see. He knocked, and the sound echoed as if there was a generous space behind the door.

The man who answered his knock was not the one he expected. This was an older man, perhaps in his fifties or sixties, well dressed, hair neat and with a pair of shrewd eyes beneath bushy grey eyebrows.

One of those eyebrows raised in query.

"I'm here to speak to Michael Hearn," Alistair said, wary of giving too much away. "Is he in?"

"Who is asking for him?"

"He might not recognise my name, but it involves a business transaction." He fished out one of the false cards he carried, representing him as a financial advisor. It was an impressive card with gold edging and fancy script.

The other man took it and turned it over in his fingers, frowning. "Michael isn't here at the moment, but I'm his father. If you'd like to leave a message for him, I'll be sure to pass it on."

"No, thank you. When is he likely to be in, do you think?"

"I really couldn't say." There was suspicion in those shrewd eyes now. Time to leave.

"Not to worry. Tell him I'll be sure to catch up with him sometime soon."

He walked to his car, aware of eyes boring into his back. He drove around the corner, then did a neat three-point turn and parked up on the opposite side of the road, a few houses along from the Hearns'.

The old man was sharp, too sharp. Perhaps Hearn Junior wasn't such a pluckable goose after all, if he was living with his parents. Alistair had been assured Michael was rolling in money, or he'd never have allowed the debt to build so quickly. Still, if he squeezed hard enough, some juice was bound to drip out in the end.

He flinched as a figure ran past his car, a leggy teenage girl with a school bag bouncing on her shoulders. She wore the uniform of a local grammar school. The blazer alone, according to the moans of the chief superintendent, who also had a daughter at the school, was the equivalent of a week's wages for a sergeant. Fucking kids. Thought the whole world owed them.

She turned into the driveway he'd just left and disappeared.

Pretty wee thing, mind. If she'd been a few years older, he might have been interested, but he was no pervert. Still, he wondered if the brown legs were natural or the result of fake tan. His breathing had deepened, and there was a tightness in his crotch that made him angry. Why did parents let their daughters out in such short skirts? Didn't they know the effect it had on normal, red-blooded males?

CHAPTER 7

Present day

The newcomer looked more like a journalist than a member of the PSNI. Sue opened the door a small distance but kept her foot behind it. "Yes?"

"Sue Hearn?" The Belfast accent clashed with the woman's appearance, which suggested origins somewhere in the Indian subcontinent. "Professor Talbot called me in. I'm Detective Inspector Asha Harvey." She held out a hand, and Sue took it without thinking. It felt small and fine-boned against her calloused fingers, but the grip was firm.

"Are you with the police?"

"Sorry, I should have said." She fished out a battered laminated card.

This time, Sue took the time to read what it said. It identified her as a sergeant, so the promotion must be recent. "Won't you come in?"

She locked the door behind them, as she always did, and the inspector didn't ask why or even change expression.

"I have to keep it locked," Sue said. "My father has dementia, and in the early days he sometimes wandered off. Do you mind if I check on him before I bring you out to the garden?"

The detective smiled. "Of course not, Sue. This is your home. You must do whatever you need to."

Hmm. Masterfully done, Sue thought. *You've been on a management course or three, I'll bet.*

She tapped on Dad's door, even though she wouldn't normally bother. He was lying with his eyes half-open, staring sightlessly at the ceiling, but his fingers drummed on the arm of his chair in time to the music he was listening to through his headphones. He didn't seem to notice her, so she left, closing the door gently behind her.

"Everything okay?"

"He's lost in opera. *Carmen*, I think." The tapping followed the distinctive rhythm of his favourite aria. "Constable McAvoy is down here."

The stylishly dressed detective made Sue feel shabby and old, a bit like the house, but that was no reason to be rude to her. As she led her into the kitchen, the young constable rose to her feet, reddening.

"Sorry, Sergeant. Miss Hearn very kindly made a pot of tea." She flushed. "I mean Inspector."

"Nothing to be sorry about. Any left in the pot?" The newcomer made herself at home on one of the spindle-backed chairs. "This is lovely. So homely, with the range. Does that run all the time?"

And next thing she knew, Sue was explaining how an Aga worked to a detective inspector, in her own kitchen, while a uniformed constable made them both a fresh pot of tea. Something about Asha Harvey's warm eyes made her feel comfortable, as if she wasn't being judged.

"It must get really hot in here in the summer."

"Yes, it does."

The inspector glanced over at the constable. "I take it SOCO are here. Who did we get?"

McAvoy seemed much more relaxed, too, now, as if she trusted the detective. "They sent us Jana and Marley, boss."

"Oh good. Jana. Just what I need." The constable laughed.

Sue was surprised when the detective asked her if she'd like to accompany them down the garden to see how the SOCOs were doing. She'd expected to be kept right away from the investigation, but there was something unconventional about the inspector. She followed gladly, prepared to take full advantage until someone more senior came along and ordered her away.

A white tent, a bit like the old gazebo in its youth, stood over the area where she'd found the bones. The side nearest to them was open a little, the two curtains pulled apart. The male SOCO was kneeling on the ground with his back to her, face close to the ground.

There were little yellow plastic markers dotted around with numbers on them, and the two officers had laid down raised plastic stepping-stones, presumably to keep their footwear from touching the ground and contaminating it.

"Found anything?" Asha asked.

Jana's face popped up from the other side of Marley. "Ash! My favourite copper. No, nothing except site debris on the surface, but we won't dig down. You need a sweet FA to do that."

A what?

"Forensic archaeologist," Asha said. "Jana has her very own dictionary of official terms, don't you, Jana?"

"Yep, but you always know what I mean, don't you? We're on the same wave-distance, you and me."

"In your dreams," Asha muttered.

The forensic archaeologist arrived soon after. It had been nearly four years since Sue left the State Pathologist's Department, and this man must have begun consulting for the police more recently than that, because she didn't recognise him. In fact, he barely looked old enough to shave, never mind hold a postgraduate degree.

She retreated to her upturned bucket to watch from a distance as the professionals rigged floodlights, run from a generator Marley lugged from the van on a sack-barrow. When he started it, the peace of her garden was shattered, but it settled down to a steady diesel thump-thump, and after a while, she managed to zone it out.

What it did do was drown out any conversation between the white-suited figures in the tent. Sue stuck it out for a while, then went inside to check on her dad, feeling guilty for having abandoned him for so long.

She needn't have worried. He was still in the same position, but he looked up this time as she came in. She'd added a curtained alcove to the room where she'd installed a chemical toilet for his use — the bathroom was upstairs, and he was none too steady on his feet. From the smell, he'd used it while she was gone, but had, as usual, forgotten to flush.

By the time she'd got him into his pyjamas, hands washed and teeth brushed, and sorted the toilet, it was far later than his usual bedtime. More guilt. He was slurring his words, a sure sign that his poor, damaged brain was exhausted.

Sue shut the door behind her, closed her eyes. A pressure headache was building. The best thing for it would be to get a good night's sleep, but how could she, while the police were digging up her garden looking for the rest of the skeleton?

She pushed herself upright and wandered down to the kitchen, brain still in overdrive.

She'd had time, before she met Mark for coffee, to examine the skull. She might not be a pathologist, but enough body parts had passed by her in her years at the mortuary for a fair bit of knowledge to seep in.

The skull had been small, the teeth very white, some of them still unerupted bumps in the bone of the upper jaw. That was no adult buried in her garden, of that she was certain. But what of the penetrating injury? Had *she* done that with her garden fork? She didn't think so. The tines had gone through one of the eye sockets, nowhere near the hard palate. She'd have felt it if she'd thrust the fork through bone, wouldn't she?

It was fully dark outside now, except for the arc lighting that cast the hedge into sharp relief. Every so often, a silhouetted figure would move around, but for all they cared, Sue might as well not be there at all.

Which was why, when the door creaked open and Asha came in, the hood of her white suit lowered and the mask dangling from a finger, Sue jumped as if she'd been goosed.

"Oh, I want one of those Aga things," Asha said. She hurried across and leaned her bum against the front bar. "Bliss!"

"Have you—?"

"Yes." Asha watched her with compassion in her eyes. "I'm afraid we've found the rest of the skeleton. I don't normally say this, but bearing in mind your prior experience, would you like to take a look?"

Sue climbed clumsily into one of the papery suits, tucked her hair inside the hood, and donned mask, safety goggles and gloves. Now she'd be anonymous, just like the real police.

The rain Jana had been afraid of had arrived in full force, driving into Sue's goggles until she felt she needed windscreen wipers. After the gloom of the garden, the inside of the tent was dazzling. It took her eyes a moment to adapt, to relate the excavation site to the level patch of soil she'd left earlier.

They'd uncovered the edge of a pelvis, the top of a humerus and part of a femur. Even to Sue's inexperienced eye, it looked as if the body had been placed on its side, knees tucked up to the chest in the foetal position, but she knew from her training that appearances could be deceptive.

It was quite a small skeleton. Definitely a child.

"Has anyone in your family ever gone missing, that you know of? Any apocryphal stories?"

Sue shook her head. "No child, no."

Another white-suited figure, kneeling at the edge of the grave cut, glanced sharply her way. "But an adult has?" he asked.

She wondered who this man was. He wasn't Marley — too slightly built. He was astute, too. He'd instantly picked up on something she'd rather have remained hidden.

"Well, yes . . ." she said slowly, dragging the words out. "My mother disappeared when I was a teenager. She was officially registered dead a few years later, when I was away at university."

The man stood up. He was tall but very slim, and to give that impression in a bulky scene-of-crime suit, he must be thin indeed.

"This is DC Aaron Birch," Asha said. "He and I will be working together on this case, Sue."

Sue nodded. "Do you have any idea how the body got here?"

"We were hoping you might be able to help us with that one," DC Birch said. "We'll need as much information as you can give us about the house and garden, who it belonged to before you moved here, and all the rest."

"But that can wait until tomorrow," Asha said quickly. "I'm sure you must be exhausted, Sue. It's been a long day. You should try to get some rest."

It was as if the words carried some sort of sedative within them. She fought down a yawn and nodded. "Thanks. Will there be someone here all night? Would you mind very much asking them not to go upstairs in the house in case they disturb Dad? There's a cloakroom off the kitchen, if anyone needs the loo or to wash hands—"

Asha pushed her gently out into the rain. "Stop worrying. No one will come into the house without asking you, not for the moment, anyhow. Just try to get some shut-eye."

And, much to her surprise, she did. Until the nightmares began.

CHAPTER 8

December 1992

Alistair tapped his front teeth with the pen he'd been using to make notes. According to the records, there were four people living in the big house with the gravelled driveway: the owner, William Hearn; his son Michael; daughter-in-law Monica; and granddaughter Susan, the girl who'd run past him the other day.

Plenty of leverage to use on the skinny runt who owed him money. He'd taken the pressure off for a few days until he'd worked out the dynamics of the household. This was no ordinary squeeze, but it had the potential to be a regular income if he played it right.

The woman was a teacher in a local primary school, the old man didn't seem to work — old money, wouldn't need to — and his son called himself an artist. The woman was his way in.

There she was now, with her handbag slung over her shoulder and a second bag in her hand, weighing her down a little to one side. School books, he guessed. She got into a small hatchback and drove off towards the school.

Once she'd passed him, he started the engine and followed a safe distance behind her. She was just parking neatly in a space when a boy bounced up to her, a skinny lad of maybe nine or ten. Alistair was no good with kids' ages. The boy lifted her heavy bag from the passenger seat, his face red with the effort, and carried it for her. *Little shit.* Just the sort Alistair had despised when he was at school, and there'd been plenty of them at his English boarding school. *Real little arse-licker, that one.*

He watched the two of them walk inside the school, then returned to Carrow Lodge. On the way, he passed William Hearn with a set of golf clubs. He was climbing into a red BMW alongside another man, both dressed in the latest fashion for gentlemen of the greens.

Alistair smiled in his rear-view mirror. Good. He'd be gone for a few hours, at least.

No one came to his knock this time, so he fished out his lock picks and opened the door himself.

He stepped into the ornately tiled entry hall and listened. Music played somewhere in the distance — classical. Opera? It was hard to be sure.

The two front rooms were empty, but the furnishings suggested no lack of money. Nothing new, but comfortable leather armchairs and faded Persian carpets. A grandfather clock ticked its sonorous rhythm at the foot of the stairs, echoing in the hallway.

Downstairs was a big kitchen, warm from the range that burned there, but there was no sign of any paperwork. He went back up and continued to the floor above, staying close to the edge of the steps so as not to creak any floorboards.

The music became louder the higher he went. How could anyone take pleasure from that wailing? He tried to strain his senses past the distracting sound, listening for movement. Nothing.

At the top of the last staircase, a door stood slightly ajar. This was where the music was coming from.

He pushed the door a little further open, just enough to see into the attic room. It was bare boards, no carpet or rugs, but flooded with light from big sloping roof windows. The only furniture was a cheap sofa bed, more modern than anything else he'd yet seen in the house, draped with throws and cushions. Lying on the bed, oblivious to everything around him, was Michael Hearn.

Alistair entered the room, no longer so cautious, but checking his surroundings by habit, memorising details. Several easels stood with part-completed paintings on them. More canvases were stacked against the walls where the ceiling came sloping down. Not one that he could see appeared finished.

A still life with a jug and some fading flowers was the most complete one there, and even that had no background, just bare canvas, as if the artist had painted the interesting bits and then got bored.

There was a partially painted portrait on one of the easels. A young woman with laughing eyes and a generous mouth. Her long, dark hair was swept back from her face, held in place by a flowery scarf. It was barely more than a sketch, but Michael Hearn had caught the essence of his wife. Perhaps he did have some talent after all.

The sleeping man stirred, mumbling something that Alistair couldn't quite catch, and turned over. The movement revealed an empty bottle and a clear plastic envelope with small blue pills in it that had been hidden under his body. Alistair took a closer look.

Not mine. Alistair didn't supply Valium, so the rat must be getting it somewhere else and mixing it with whiskey. At this rate, he wouldn't live long enough to pay his debts. On a low table next to the sofa were a few white grains and a rolled-up piece of paper. *Those* are *mine. And if he's mixing it with these, too, his brain must be fried.*

He turned to the portrait of Monica Hearn, drawn by the laughter in her eyes. He'd keep that. It wasn't finished, but then he wouldn't exactly be displaying it on his wall, would he?

There were a handful of paintbrushes, some in a jar of spirit, some drying up in clogs of oil paint. He took one and squeezed red paint from a tube onto the brush, then he put his head on one side, examining the picture on the other easel. It was a painting of a child playing on a beach. She was squatting down near the edge of the sea, a bucket in one hand, spade in the other, looking at something in the sand. It might have been Michael's own daughter as a toddler.

As he drew the red paint across the centre of the canvas, leaving a clear and unambiguous message, he hoped the painting did depict the idiot's daughter. That should spur him into action, if nothing else did.

* * *

The station was quiet at this time of day. Most people were in the canteen, swapping stories and exchanging dirty jokes. Alistair passed the black officer in the corridor, and her insolent smile made his fists curl, but he forced an answering grin to his face.

"Lonnie. How's things?"

"Good, thanks, Al. You?"

But by then, they were past each other, and he didn't feel the need to reply. He wondered how that woman was still hanging on here. It couldn't be easy, with the comments and catcalls, but she seemed to have a hide like a rhinoceros. He heard a door close behind him.

His own office, shared with one other detective and a couple of young uniforms they used as gofers, would be empty until at least half one. He closed the door behind him and went straight to his desk, unlocking the top right drawer. His little black book would be safer in there over the weekend than in his pocket, where Lorraine might find it and wonder. She loved to surprise him by taking his clothes to the dry cleaners, and he'd almost lost the book that way once already.

He'd just relocked the drawer when a movement at the corner of his eye made him sit up.

Yvonne Patterson. Blonde, big-boned, with a red face and a way of wearing her uniform as if she'd stolen it from a corpse. How long had she been there?

"Yvonne. What are you doing in here?" It was a perfectly good question: she wasn't part of his team, and he doubted if she'd ever make detective. Not sharp enough.

She hitched her bum onto the edge of a desk. "Looking for George. Have you seen him?"

"He's probably in the canteen," he replied, feeling his patience straining. "Can I give him a message when he gets back?" Whatever did she want with Aiken? He hadn't even known they knew each other. Still, poor Aiken, if Yvonne Patterson was after him. It was a standing joke in the ranks that she was on the prowl for a man.

"No, it's okay," she said vaguely and stood up again. "I'll try the canteen." Then she drifted out of the office and her heavy, flat-footed steps receded along the corridor. How much had she seen? Mind you, she was so dim she wouldn't think anything of it anyway. He shrugged away the worry and went out to his car.

* * *

Rain drove down while he waited in the school car park for his quarry. The wipers made a terrible noise as they fought to keep the windscreen clear, but he needed to see Monica Hearn in time to intercept her before she drove off.

All the same, he almost missed her. The tail lights went on in the little hatchback, swirling red spots in the rain. But then he was saved by the same little shit of a kid he'd seen that morning. He was trudging along the pavement with his schoolbag above his head to shelter his face from the driving rain, and the teacher must have spotted him at the same time.

The internal light came on as she got out and ran over to him. She seemed to be urging him, pointing towards her car. He nodded and grinned, then ran ahead of her towards the vehicle, which still had its engine running, puffing pale smoke from the exhaust.

Alistair was out of his own car in a flash. "Mrs Hearn!"

She spun like a startled deer and turned to face him. "Do I know you?"

"Not yet," he replied. "I'm a business associate of your husband. I'd like to give him a message."

She raised an eyebrow, those dark eyes of hers flashing with annoyance. "I'm sure Michael will be only too happy to speak to you if you call at the house."

"I've already been to the house," he said. "Your husband and protector seemed to be comatose under the influence of drugs and booze. You can tell him that if he doesn't repay me by the end of the week, there will be consequences." It was hard to concentrate with those dark eyes searching his face. "You have a very pretty daughter. She looks great in that uniform, but why do you let her run around in such a short skirt?"

And, just like that, the spark left her eyes, to be replaced by cold fury.

"If you ever threaten my family, I will track you down and make you regret that you ever met Michael, do you hear me?"

The car door hit him on the hip as she drove off in a swathe of gritty spray. The pain was excruciating but short-lived. By the time he'd blinked away tears and rain, the hatchback had disappeared.

Little spitfire! He'd enjoy getting to know her, if he got the chance.

* * *

Kernaghan was on the front desk when Alistair arrived back at the station, picking his nose and examining the result.

"Evening, boss. 'Bout ye?"

Alistair sighed. Aiken was the brains of this pair, but there wasn't much to choose between them when it came to manners. He checked there was no one else in the front office and that the connecting door was closed, then leaned over the desk.

"I might have a job for you two," he said in a low voice. "Friday or Saturday. Woman called Monica Hearn needs removing from her home and entertaining for a few days until her husband coughs up what he owes. Think you can manage that?"

"Yes, sir. She the one that lives in the big house off the Malone Road?"

"That's the one. Usual deal. Don't make a move on her until I give the go-ahead, and treat her with a proper respect. I might even drop in and exchange a few friendly words."

"Okay, boss. I'll tell George."

CHAPTER 9

December 1992

Rain hammered against the car windscreen and the squeaky wiper blades did little to shift it. Will hunched down in the passenger seat, wondering what new trouble he was in, while Miss Stewart talked to the strange man outside.

The glimpses he got through the window showed him a tall, heavily built man in a dark overcoat towering over his teacher, but Miss Stewart was the one doing the threatening by the sound of it. He felt a sneaky admiration for the man in the overcoat, because if she'd talked to him like that he'd be peeing his pants by now.

He hoked around inside his school bag until he found his homework book. Not too much to do. The usual spellings and some maths, but numbers came easily to him, so that wouldn't take him long. He shut the book.

At that moment, Miss leapt into the car, making him jump guiltily, even though he hadn't been doing anything. She slammed the car into gear and floored the accelerator. His head jerked back against the seat and his belly did a hiccup. She hadn't even closed her door. As the car hurtled off, the open door hit the man with a bang, but she didn't stop. If anything, she drove faster as the door closed itself.

Her knuckles were white where they gripped the wheel, and her jaw was clenched. He'd never seen her so angry before, never even dreamed she could be this cross.

"Do you know that man?" Miss Stewart snapped. She was dripping wet, her pale cream raincoat soaked through.

"No, Miss. Who is he?"

"No one," she said, but she sounded distracted. "William, if you see him again, especially anywhere near the school, I'd like you to tell me straight away. Can you do that for me?"

He let his breath out in a huff. "Yes, Miss. Will I tell Mick and Stella to watch out for him, too?"

She sighed. "No, William. We'll just keep it between you and me for now, shall we?"

"Okay, Miss," he said.

"I'll run you all the way home, since I've kept you so late. Can you give me directions to your house?"

That was one thing Will was good at. He only had to visit a place once, and he'd be able to find it again, even in the pouring rain. Directions to the house were piss-easy.

Miss Stewart came to the door with him, to explain to his parents why he was so late. Not that they'd have noticed. They weren't his real parents anyway, just foster parents. *Only in it for the money*, as his friend Mick would say. *My da says you're their fatted calf, me old mucker. Anything happens to you, and the money stops, right?*

Mick always knew what was going on. Will hadn't even known that Gillian and Kevin got money for looking after him. He'd always thought they did it out of the kindness of their hearts, but this revelation had explained a lot. Like the way he wasn't allowed to bring friends home from school, yet the other kids in the house were. And the way Timothy and Joseph got new clothes, but he only got hand-me-downs.

Still, they could be worse. At least he felt safe here, unlike the kids' home he'd been in before.

As soon as Miss Stewart's car was out of sight, Kevin gave him a shove. "Better get on with your homework, then. No tea until it's done."

Will worked on his lap in the room he shared with his foster brother, Timothy. He sat hunched over so he didn't bang his head on the upper bunk where Tim was reading a comic before tea. Joseph had a room to himself, being the eldest and taking his O levels next year. No one would dare to go into Joe's room without an invitation, not even Gillian.

When he'd finished, he put his books away and sank back onto his bed. If he closed his eyes, he could almost imagine he was in the cabin of a boat. He let himself rock a little from side to side as if the boat was moving to the waves.

"What're you doing?" Tim asked, leaning over the edge to stare at him with sleepy eyes. He'd had his thumb in his mouth. A shiny gloop of saliva dripped from it.

"I'm a pirate," Will said, opening one eye. "See? I lost my eyepatch is all."

Then he regretted it, because Tim's face crumpled. "Mum! William's teasing me!"

A door slammed somewhere downstairs and Gillian's voice screeched, "William! What have I told you? If you bully Timothy again, there will be repercussions!"

Will wondered, not for the first time, what "repercussions" were. He'd worked out that they weren't padded things on sofas, but he'd no idea beyond that.

He rolled over, turning away from Tim, and pretended to be asleep.

* * *

Will sat cross-legged on the wooden floor of the assembly hall, letting the principal's voice wash over him. His gaze drifted over towards Miss Stewart. Her face was lined and her lips were tight with worry. She caught him looking and flashed him a smile, but her heart didn't seem to be in it.

How do you ask your teacher if she's okay when you're only ten years old? Will's life experience hadn't provided any examples of people asking if he was okay, at least not where the person actually wanted to know the answer, so he had nothing to go on. Still, she'd always been kind to him, so he gave it his best shot.

"Miss?" he asked later when she bent over his desk to correct a spelling.

"Yes, Will?"

"Are you worrying about something? Was it that man last night? The one you were telling off?"

Her eyes widened, the pupils contracting as if she was scared. "Why would you ask that, Will?"

He shrugged, wishing he'd never asked. "No reason, Miss. Sorry."

Her face softened. "I am worried, as it happens, but it's nothing to do with the school, or with any of you, so you needn't let it bother you as well. Now, what about this one." She pointed to the word "*recieve*" in his careful handwriting in the spellings book. "Can you remember the rule for i and e together?"

"Yes, Miss."

"And?"

"I before e, except after . . . oh." He rubbed out the i and the e and changed them around.

Miss Stewart patted him on the back and moved on to the next desk, but Will still worried about her.

Maybe that's why he followed her home that evening.

Will's route home passed the end of her street anyway. She only lived about a half-hour's walk from the school, so he'd sometimes see her ahead of him if it was a dry day. She was slowed down by the heavy carrier bag with all their homework to mark, so he had no difficulty keeping up.

The streetlights were just beginning to pop into life when it happened.

One moment he was trudging along in her wake, listening to the click-clack of her heels on the tarmac pavement, the next she was gone.

He stopped, eyes searching the shadows. The big houses on this street had tall hedges along the roadside; their driveways were shadowy caves. He quickened his pace until he reached the place where she must have been when the sound of her steps stopped. Had he heard a startled squeak at the same time? He couldn't be sure. He'd been lost in thoughts of pirates and hadn't really been concentrating.

He found her bag straight away. She had dropped it at the side of a driveway, scattering the school exercise books in a fan of pale grey against damp tarmac under a hedge that smelled of dog piss. He started to scoop the books up, knowing how upset she'd be at where they'd landed, when an engine started up close by.

Very close by.

Headlights came on in the driveway, twin spotlights that blinded him. He threw an arm up to shield his eyes.

The engine raced, tyres squealed and instinct took over. He threw himself sideways and rolled as the car passed inches from his feet. Loose gravel peppered his bare legs, then the car was gone, leaving the smell of rubber and exhaust hanging in the air.

He lay, panting, until his skin began to prickle painfully. Nettles. *Fucking nettles!*

He got shakily to his feet and looked around, but there was no one else there, not anymore. He'd only had a glimpse inside the car, barely enough to see the driver's hard eyes and close-cropped, red hair, but he was certain Miss Stewart had been in there. The house that the driveway led to was dark and he could smell the damp from here. No one lived here. It would be the perfect place for an ambush if you knew Miss Stewart's route home, and that would be easy enough to find out.

What to do. Should he go back to the school? There'd probably be no one there by now, except maybe cleaners. Tell Gillian and Kevin? He almost laughed aloud. The thought of the police crossed his mind very briefly but didn't settle. He'd been brought up with a healthy fear of anyone in a uniform, and the police were top of the list of People to Stay Away From.

He knew where Miss Stewart lived. She was married and had a daughter who went to the big school just out of town. He'd see her sometimes, nose in a book usually, as she waited for the school bus, and occasionally she'd be in the front of the car when Miss Stewart stopped to give him a lift in wet weather. She seemed nice. There must be a husband, too, he guessed — a man, at least.

He should let them know.

Glad that he'd made a decision, he scooped up the fallen books — some of them had tyre tracks across the covers, and one was ripped across the middle, the pages all twisted and torn. He glanced at the name on the cover and smiled. Ryan Doherty. Couldn't have happened to a better kid. He still had scabs on his knees from the last time Ryan had tripped him up in the playground.

CHAPTER 10

December 1992

Miss Stewart's house was one of the big old ones with a driveway winding between trees. Steps led up to a grand front door, painted dark blue and decorated with a handle and knocker in dull, gold-coloured metal.

Will couldn't reach the knocker, so he banged on the door with his fist. The heavy wood absorbed the sound, and he was sure no one inside would be able to hear it. He went back down to see if there was any way around to the other side of the house, but if there was, it was overgrown.

He stood, unsure what to do next, when a curtain twitched in a window on the ground floor. Someone must have heard him, then.

The front door opened, and an old man glowered down at him. He saw the school badge on Will's sweater and his face softened. "Hello. Who are you?"

"Will. Who are you?"

"I'm Will, too," the old man said. "But most people call me William. William Hearn. What can I do for you, young Will?"

"It's Miss." He held out Miss Stewart's bag. "I think something happened to her."

The man was down the steps in a heartbeat, moving well for someone so old. He held out a hand, and Will passed the bag to him. Mr Hearn searched it and came out with a purse embroidered with flowers. Will recognised it as the one his teacher used when she paid her share of the book club money.

"Where did you find this?"

"In a driveway." Will pointed back the way he'd come. He didn't know street names, but he could find his way pretty much anywhere.

"Can you take me there?"

"Yes." He hadn't meant to sound so offended, but Mr Hearn didn't seem to mind.

"I'll get my coat. Hold on a moment."

He disappeared inside, then reappeared wearing a shabby overcoat that reminded Will of Detective Columbo, who Gillian watched on TV. Will led the way to the driveway where he'd nearly been run over.

"It was here," he said. "I was walking behind Miss, when her shoes stopped making a noise. I thought she might have fallen, you know, in those heels she wears, so I ran after her, but she'd gone."

Mr Hearn produced a torch from his pocket. The yellowy beam lit up the tarmac and the dilapidated house, paint peeling from its lopsided front porch. He pointed the beam at the edge of the drive, where a flattened patch of nettles marked Will's dive to safety. Will scratched at the stings, which he'd almost forgotten about, and they burned again as if he'd just got them.

"There was a car here," the old man said. He showed Will the way the dark moss on the damp driveway had been squashed down in two lines, and where it had been churned up as the car raced forwards.

"Yeah," Will said. "It nearly ran me down."

The torch pointed at his face. "They drove at you?"

"Yeah. I was picking up the books. Miss wouldn't want them getting all dirty."

The torch played down his bare legs, and he realised he was bleeding from tiny cuts where the gravel had scraped him.

"Was Miss inside the car?"

"I don't know." He rubbed a bruise on his hip that he'd only just noticed. "I jumped for it, so I couldn't see, but I can't think where else she'd be."

"And did you see the driver?"

"Yes. Sort of. Red hair, really short. Scary eyes. I *think* there was someone else in the back, but I couldn't be sure." Then, wondering why the old man hadn't suggested it himself. "Are you going to call the police?"

"Yes, I am." He searched Will's face, as if he was reading his thoughts. "Where do you live, Will? I should probably take you home, or your mum'll be worrying about you."

Will looked away, embarrassed. "Don't have a mum. Gillian won't notice if I'm late, unless I miss my tea."

"Nevertheless, young man, I think home is the best place for you right now."

They walked side by side in silence until Will couldn't bear it anymore. "What do you think happened to her?"

"Oh, she must have bumped into some friends on her way home and gone with them," Mr Hearn said. It was a lie, probably to make him feel better, but even Tim could lie better than that.

They reached the semi-detached house he lived in, but Will didn't want the old man coming to the door. He turned, trying to think of a way to say it without upsetting him, but Mr Hearn just nodded. "Off you go, then. Make sure you get that homework done, or Miss will be after you tomorrow!"

But she wasn't. Miss Stewart wasn't in school the next day, and it seemed no one had bothered to tell the school she wouldn't be coming, because the head, Mr Barrie, sat with them for the first hour until a breathless supply teacher turned up to take his place.

Will couldn't keep his eyes from the window, expecting to see police cars turning up, but there was no sign of anything out of the ordinary at all.

Except for the black Volvo that parked outside until just after break. It had one person in it, but Will couldn't see inside because of the way the sun reflected from the glass.

He wandered over to the school fence to take a closer look, but as soon as he got close, the engine started up and the car moved off.

Miss Stewart didn't come back, and the police didn't appear. The weather turned nasty over the weekend and on Monday she still wasn't back. Perhaps she was sick. No one would think to tell the kids, and he wasn't about to ask a teacher, not with all the flak he'd get.

"Maybe she's moved away," Stella said. "You know. Elopped, or whatever they call it."

Mick snorted. "Elopped? What's that when it's at home?"

They were inside, crowded together in a corner while rain drummed on the roof of their mobile classroom and sheeted down the window. Will watched as water droplets joined up like rivers, fascinated by the patterns they made.

"She means eloped," he said. "She got it from one of those romance stories."

Stella shoved him so hard he banged his nose on the glass. "What was that for?"

"I don't read romance," she snarled. "I read it in a magazine, actually."

"A woman's magazine," Mick sniggered, dodging away before she could punch him. "Reading the problem page, were you?"

"It's back," Will said quietly. The black Volvo cruised to a halt the other side of the road from the school, not far from where he'd seen it the first time. The other two pushed their faces up to the window, then rubbed the condensation away with their sleeves.

A tall figure got out of the driver's side and stared straight at them, or at least that's what it felt like. He was too far away to be certain, but Will was nearly sure it was the same man Miss had been telling off before she disappeared. It was something about the way he stood, as if he was in charge of everything. Like the army officers you saw in war films, all square shoulders and stiff upper-lip.

Then the rain must have got too much for him, because he got back in the car, but he didn't drive off.

Will glanced at the classroom assistant who was supposed to be keeping an eye on them while the teachers ate their lunch. It was Mrs Connors, and she was about as dim as the torch he used to read under his blankets at night.

"Cover for me," he said to the others, then made a bent-double sprint for the door.

The rain was pelting down. He was blinded as soon as he pushed through the door, but he knew where he was going. He chose a route that would keep him out of sight from most of the windows — as if anyone would even see him in this downpour — and that brought him to a little side gate. From there, he could come up on the parked Volvo from behind.

The plan worked. There was only one man inside this time, and he had his eyes fixed on the school. Will ducked down below the windows, then straightened up next to the driver's window, secure in the knowledge that his friends were watching out for him from their classroom.

The man was so intent on the school that it took him a moment to notice the dripping boy at his window. Then, he spun his head and for one long moment, they looked into each other's eyes. It was the same man.

Will thought he'd drive off again, like he had before, but instead the man opened the car door, giving Will a blow to the chest that winded him.

Once again, his instincts saved him. He ran as if the devil himself were in pursuit, breath coming in harsh gasps, swerving in through the gate, skidding on the waterlogged grass.

He crashed through the doors into the building and kept running, imagining the breath of the man on the back of his neck, but when he glanced over his shoulder, he was alone.

It took ages for his breathing to return to normal, so he hid out in the boys' toilets, drying himself with loo roll. His sweater and trousers were soaking. He waited until the noise of feet outside marked the end of lunch. Then he followed the new supply teacher to his classroom.

"Sorry, sir. I was running a message for Mr Barrie," he said. The Primary Sevens were given a bit more freedom than the younger classes, so the teacher just smiled and nodded Will back to his seat.

"What happened after I legged it?" he whispered to Mick while Sir was writing on the board.

"Nothing," Mick whispered. "He stood watching you run, then he got in the car and drove off."

"He didn't chase me, then?"

Mick shook his head, one eye on the teacher. "No. The speed you went, mate, there'd have been no chance anyway!"

CHAPTER 11

December 1992

On Friday morning, Michael Hearn answered Alistair's knock on the blue front door. Michael looked ill, his face drawn and pale, eyes red-rimmed. A dark stain, possibly red wine, decorated the front of his crumpled shirt and he smelled faintly of vomit.

"Where is she?" he asked. "What have you done with her?"

Alistair kept his face smooth, hiding his surprise. Aiken and Kernaghan shouldn't have taken her yet. A cold chill tightened the skin of his face.

"I told you I'd get the fucking money!" Hearn was almost crying, leaning against the door jamb as if that was all that was holding him up. "You said I had time. Where is she? Where's my Monica?"

Alistair's brain worked like lightning. Monica Hearn had disappeared. Hearn was assuming he'd taken her, after his threats. Perhaps she'd upped and left him! His heart gave a little leap, then settled down. He wasn't going to lose the money just because of a pair of dark eyes. Still, this could work in his favour.

"Pay me what you owe, and then we'll see about the woman. And remember, you still have a daughter—"

The door slammed, but he was already walking away. He would put Aiken and Kernaghan onto finding Monica Hearn. How hard could it be to find a prim schoolteacher in Belfast?

He drove to the school and sat outside, giving himself time to think. He could see into her classroom, the mobile nearest the fence, but there was a man teaching in it, not her.

The weekend went by and still no sign of her. Alistair started to watch Carrow Lodge and the school, without really knowing why. If he had a bit of spare time, or was taking a lunch break, he'd drive by and observe from a distance. He was parked outside the school that rainy Monday, when the little shit sneaked up on him. He got out of the car to give chase, but the wee bastard was like a whippet, lean and fast, and now rain was dripping down his collar. He couldn't come back here, not after he'd been noticed. Nosy little sod. Wouldn't put it past him to have taken his registration number.

But he couldn't help himself returning to that quiet, leafy street day after day, watching Carrow Lodge until he knew all their routines. It had become an obsession. Something about those dark eyes haunted him. He watched the old man walking to the shop for bread and milk — no more golf these days, it seemed. There was no recognition in the man's eyes when he passed King's car, but he must have remembered him.

They'd built up a bit of background for Monica Hearn now, and even checked out her family, but she was an only child and both parents were in a nursing home in Ballycastle, where she came from. Not too far from his own farm. Kernaghan had gone to speak with them, but neither had heard from her, and the staff confirmed that story. Resources for the search were limited, because this was an unofficial inquiry. If word got out to the powers that be that he was searching for a missing woman, questions would be asked, and he couldn't afford those.

If he hadn't taken Monica Hearn and his men couldn't find any trace of her using public transport or a taxi, then maybe someone else had abducted her? But who?

He ran through the local gangs in his head, but none of them would dream of taking on King, would they? Unless there was a new operator in the area, trying to make an impression by interfering in King's game. But how would they know about his interest in the Hearn house?

Alistair was about to give up for the day and drive back to the station, when a figure appeared in his rear-view mirror, all knock-knees and untidy hair. That blasted kid again. Every time he turned around, there was that skinny little sod, getting in the way. He was the reason it had all started to go wrong.

The boy turned into the Hearns' driveway, scuffing the gravel with his toes as he walked. Alistair lost sight of the brat behind the tall hedge, and he was just considering getting out of the car for a recce when the boy reappeared, socks at half-mast.

Alistair was pretty sure he couldn't be seen, parked in the shadows, but the boy shot one startled look in his direction before setting off the way he'd come. Alistair watched him until he turned off the wide, tree-lined road. He'd either gone to ground in a driveway or found a turnoff, but there'd been nothing like that on the map he'd studied back at the station.

He started the car and turned it around, cruising slowly along as he searched for where the boy had gone.

There. A narrow lane, so overgrown by trees and bushes from the gardens either side of it that it was almost invisible. There was a speck of green light at the far end, so it must open out somewhere. He consulted his mental map and grimaced. The park.

He found a road that took him the same direction and finally turned left then left again. The park opened out to his right, an expanse of green with tarmacked paths criss-crossing it. The only people in sight were a woman with a pram, far out in the park, and a cyclist moving away, towards the city centre.

And the boy, trailing fingers along the fence as he walked, apparently unaware that he was being observed. Then the boy glanced over his shoulder and quickened his pace.

CHAPTER 12

December 1992

After his close shave, Will became wary. He really wanted to know what had happened to Miss Stewart, so he decided to go to her house again after school that afternoon.

As he passed the driveway where she'd disappeared, he half expected to find police tape fluttering in the breeze. The tyre tracks didn't look particularly unusual in daylight, almost as if nothing had happened here. He shuddered and sped up.

The big house looked just the same. He knocked again with his knuckles, and again the sound was dead, muffled. This time, no one twitched a curtain. He was about to give up and walk home, wondering if Miss Stewart would be in the telephone directory, but then the door opened.

It was a younger man this time. Thin, with hands that shook and eyes that were haunted. His clothes had been made for someone fatter, too.

He looked Will up and down, blinking, as if he was struggling to focus.

"Is Miss Stewart in?" Will asked, wishing he'd planned better.

The man swallowed, and his eyes darted around as if searching the undergrowth for hidden enemies. "Miss Stewart?" Then he seemed to gather himself with an effort. "Oh, you mean Monica. No. She's not here."

He was starting to close the door, so Will blurted out, "I'm in her class. At St Peter's. When's she coming back?"

The strange man's face crumpled, and to Will's disgust, he began to cry, the tears flooding down his cheeks as the rain had down the classroom windows. "I don't know," he sobbed, and took a rasping breath. "I don't know if she'll ever be back. Now go away!"

This time, he slammed the door. Will was left shaking, breathing as hard as if he'd just run a race. *What was that all about?*

He trudged slowly down the driveway, then stopped. On the other side of the road, parked in the shadows of a lime tree, was a black Volvo. He'd been kicking himself for not getting the registration number last time, while he had the chance, but there was no way he was going anywhere near the car again.

The quickest route home would take him right past it, but he turned and walked the other way, ears straining for the sound of an engine starting up. He ducked down the first alley he came to and followed it to the opposite end, where it opened out into a broad, one-way road with parking spaces along the far side. Beyond that was a park.

He knew this place. He'd been here before, when he was very young, and he was pretty sure he knew the way to Gillian and Kevin's from here. He strode out, now he was away from the car, letting the rhythm of his feet clear his mind so he could think through what had been going on over the last few days.

He was passing a gate in a stone wall when the sound of an engine broke into his thoughts. He glanced back to see the black Volvo, or one exactly like it, turning towards him from another side road further along. *Shit!* There was nowhere to hide. Open grass on one side, with no one else about, and a massive wall on the other.

He tried the gate, but it was locked. He gave it a good kick, in case it was just stuck, but only hurt his toe. *Fuck!* He ran a few paces then stopped as the car pulled up alongside him. The driver was at the other side, but he must have had electric windows, because the one nearest Will slid down. It was the same man. Tall, heavily built, wearing sunglasses even though it was close to dusk. He had dark leather gloves on, too, and still wore the overcoat. Between the front seats sat a black, rectangular box with a telephone on top of it.

Jeez, he has a carphone?

"Will, isn't it?" the man said. He didn't sound scary. He had a funny accent, like the people from the TV. Will decided not to answer.

"I'm a friend of your teacher, Monica Hearn. Miss Stewart. Would you like me to take you to her?"

He was so convincing that Will was almost reaching a hand to open the car door and climb in, but then he remembered himself. "No thanks," he said. "But you can tell her I was asking after her." That was the sort of thing adults said to each other.

The driver gave a thin-lipped smile and put the handbrake on. Will swallowed.

The driver's door opened, and the man got out, but he kept his distance. "There's no need to run this time, Will," he said, somehow making it sound as if he thought Will had been an idiot for being afraid. The nicer he sounded, the more alarm bells were ringing.

But what were his options? He couldn't outrun a car. His mouth was dry, and the strap of his school bag was damp from the sweat on his palms.

Then a creaking sound brought him spinning around. It was the garden gate he'd kicked a moment ago, and in the gap stood the old man, Mr Hearn, breathing heavily as though he'd been running.

Relief flooded him, and he smiled. "Nice talking to you," he said to the car driver, recovering his cheekiness now he had a friend at his back. "But I'm meeting someone at the house. Bye!"

He edged away as he spoke, towards the gate.

The driver wasn't looking at him anymore. Instead, his eyes were locked on the old man's.

"Leave the lad alone," Mr Hearn said, but his voice shook. "He knows nothing."

"Really?"

Will jumped. How had the stranger moved so quietly? He was almost close enough to touch, and there'd been no rustle of clothing or sound of footfall. He backed away, but the old man was blocking the gate, and now Will was between the two of them.

"Where is she?" Mr Hearn asked. "Have you hurt her?"

The stranger smiled again, but there was no humour there. Will didn't think humour would come easy to those thin lips. "Not yet, but the clock is ticking. Do you have the money?"

"I told you we'd get it. I have most of it. I'm selling my shares in the company, but it takes time."

"You don't have time. I told you what would happen if you didn't pay up, didn't I? Do you really want to be responsible? And I believe you have a granddaughter. Pretty child, and clever, too, by all accounts. Looks lovely in that school uniform, with her pretty blazer and her Marillion school bag. Shame, really, if anything were to happen to her, don't you think?"

Will gasped. He'd not understood a thing they were on about until then, but there was no mistaking a death threat.

Those hard eyes suddenly focused on Will again. A gloved hand shot out, grabbed Will by his shoulder and jerked him forwards. Held there, with his face buried in the thick woollen overcoat, he could neither see nor hear. He could barely breathe.

He pummelled the man and kicked, but something hit him on the side of his head, and suddenly the night sky was whirling in front of his face. He was lying on his back on the damp pavement, and someone was playing the drums inside his skull.

Hearing came back next.

"Leave him alone! I'll vouch for the boy. He won't tell, will you, Will? Will? Tell the man."

Will you will . . . you will, Will. The words echoed to and fro, but he couldn't move his lips to reply.

Then he was jerked upright. Held there, half-strangled by his own collar. Boke rose up, burning his throat, but he swallowed it down.

"I don't leave loose ends," the stranger was saying. "Consider this one a warning. If you want your daughter-in-law home, you'll have the money by tomorrow at six. If not? Well. It'd be a pity. She's a good-looking woman, Monica."

Will blinked as something flashed in the orange street-light. Something long and thin and shiny. It rose up like a firework above him, then his head was jerked back and he lost sight of it.

The blow, when it came, was just a pin-prick. A nettle-sting. Then he was falling, but he couldn't feel the ground. Couldn't move. Couldn't feel anything.

Old Mr Hearn's face loomed above him, crying. Sobbing. "I'm sorry, Will. So sorry."

Then the lips were all he could see, still moving. Still talking, but there was no sound.

CHAPTER 13

Present day

It was well past midnight and Asha's eyes were gritty with lack of sleep. Jana and Marley had finished doing whatever they did and had packed away their kit in the van. Maggie, the forensic anthropologist, had brought her team of three along, including a young forensic archaeologist Asha hadn't met before. Between them, they'd efficiently excavated and then removed the skeleton, packing the fragile-looking bones in padding for transport to the lab.

Maggie straightened, easing her back. "An interesting case. The Prof sent the skull and a finger bone over earlier, so I've already had a look at them, but it'll be useful to check the rest of the bones for defensive cuts and all that."

"Do you have any idea of a time period yet?" DC Birch asked. Always eager, Aaron, but a good detective for all that. And tough, too. He'd been to hell and back last year, on their last case together, and yet here he was, on full operational duty. Maggie nodded to the archaeologist, Dan, who perked up at being asked a question.

"Tentatively, I put it at twenty to thirty years in the ground, judging by the soil layers," Dan said. "It's a difficult period: traditional carbon dating won't fly, because it's too recent, but there are some newish techniques based on the Suess effect and the bomb effect . . ." He rambled on in technical detail about carbon in teeth and decay-resistant proxy via pupal cases.

Asha had taken an online course on forensic archaeology and anthropology with Future Learn, a free online education programme, just for her own interest, but she enjoyed watching Aaron's eyes glaze over.

"Twenty to thirty years," Aaron repeated, as soon as there was a gap in the flow. "Could still have family alive then, and the murderer might well be alive, too. What d'you think, Ash?"

"Yes. We need to find out who this is. Aaron, could you get onto the mispers records for a period from, say, 1985 to 2005? A child of around ten to twelve years, according to the Prof." She turned to Maggie. "Would you agree with that?"

The anthropologist nodded. "There or thereabouts. As soon as I know more, I'll tell you."

"I won't hold you back then, because the sooner you can come up with a tighter timeline, the sooner we can find out who this wee man, or wee lassie, is."

"I'll try to get you a gender as soon as I can," Maggie said, "but I'll need to run DNA analysis on the teeth, and that can take a while."

Dan opened his mouth to speak, but Asha got there first.

"Dan, I'll need your report as soon as possible, please. A preliminary one will do for starters. When can you have it on my desk?"

That worked. Asha had thought it might. Maggie and her team were staggering down the path towards their vehicles before Aaron had his overalls packed away. She could get used to this promotion, but if she was going to make it permanent, she'd have to clear up this case in as short a time as possible.

"Stuck up git, that archaeologist," Aaron muttered. "Trying to blind us with bullshit."

"Yeah. These academic types are all the same. They can really get up your nose with their know-it-all, privileged attitude."

He had his back to her, bending down over his bag, but the ear she could see had reddened. Aaron had a first-class degree in psychology and criminology, whereas she'd joined the force straight from school, after her A levels.

"I'll get onto mispers first thing," he said. "Although I don't suppose there's any rush if the wee pet's been lying there all these years."

"While you're doing that, I'll make a start on the disappearance of Sue Hearn's mother. She was a teenager when her mother disappeared, and her father probably won't be able to help at all."

Aaron raised an eyebrow.

"Apparently he has dementia. It's possible he'll remember something that far back, but don't count on it, and besides—"

"Wouldn't hold up in a court of law anyway."

"Probably not, if he's considered incapable of making legal decisions. Still, every tiny piece of the puzzle helps us get an idea of the whole."

* * *

The next morning, Asha went to the big Victorian house on her own. She'd left an elderly sergeant, Lonnie Jacob, working her way through missing persons because Aaron was in court that day, giving evidence on a case of fuel laundering. They'd agreed that she'd ask the preliminary questions, and if she could gain any information about Sue's missing mother, she'd pass it on to him when he was free to follow it up.

In full daylight, the building looked sleepy and comfortable. It had been built with a buttery-coloured stone rarely seen in Belfast, probably imported at great cost. The imposing entrance, up a long flight of steps, was flanked by mock-Doric columns and the hefty front door had once been painted dark blue. The paint was beginning to peel in places, showing several layers of red and green beneath and bare wood near the handle.

There was a bronze knocker moulded into a lion's head, but someone had added a cheap plastic bell-push to the frame, so she pressed that instead. No sound from within.

Just as she lifted the knocker, the door opened, pulling her off-balance. She caught hold of the frame for support.

"Oh, I'm sorry!" Sue looked as if she hadn't slept at all. "I saw you arrive, but I was in with Dad and I couldn't come straight away."

"It's all right," Asha reassured her. "I should probably have rung ahead, but I was in the area, so I thought I'd call in. Would you rather I came back later?"

"No, not at all. But would you mind very much making your own way down to the kitchen? I shan't be long. You could put some coffee or tea on if you feel like it."

Sue hurried into the front room, swinging the door to behind her. It didn't quite close, catching on the carpet. Through the narrow gap, Asha saw a skinny man trying to rise from a low seat. In that flash, she realised his pyjama trousers were around his ankles and the seat was a toilet of some sort.

She strode to the stairs and clattered down them with no attempt at quiet. If Sue thought she'd been spying on her father while he was on the loo, it would get their chat off to a poor start.

The kitchen was rather worn-looking, with its unfashionable furniture and the pine table marked by decades of hard use. This place must once have been bustling with servants: a fat cook with a bonnet and apron kneading bread while a maid cut up vegetables and a boy watched over a cooking range in the big alcove that now held the Aga.

There was a cafetière sitting on the countertop and jars of ground coffee beside it. She filled the heavy-based kettle from the tap and placed it on one of the hotplates, lifting the lid carefully in case of burns, then sat down and waited for it to boil.

Sue moved quietly. Asha had closed her eyes for a moment, enjoying the warmth, before she felt the presence of someone else in the room.

"You can't be in a much of a hurry," Sue said. "It'll take all day for the kettle to boil on that side. The left-hand side is the boiling plate, the other is for simmering." There was a clatter, then a splash, then another clatter as she sorted it out. "And it'd never have boiled at all with all that water in it," she added.

"Sorry."

Sue smiled. "It's okay. How would you know, if you've never used one?"

It was good coffee. Asha took an appreciative sip, then pulled her notebook out from her jacket pocket.

"Mind if I ask you a few questions?"

"No. I expected it, but I'm not sure how much help I'll be."

"Start by telling me everything you can about this house, and the garden. Who owned it when, who did what in the garden, when did you move in here?"

Sue bit her lower lip. "The house was built by my three-times great grandfather, Tobias Hearn, and the family has lived here ever since."

"When did you start living here?"

"I never really stopped. Mum brought me home from hospital after I was born, and I've lived here ever since." She smiled. "That makes forty-three years and counting."

"Did your parents own Carrow Lodge then?"

"No. We all lived here with my grandfather, William Hearn. Mum was a primary school teacher and Dad was an artist. I don't think they could have afforded food for us all, never mind the rent on a house, or even a flat. Grandfather was a good man. He looked after us."

"What did he do? William Hearn, I mean."

"He didn't work when I knew him. The family owned shares in one of the shipbuilding companies, and there was still money coming in from those, so he didn't need a proper job. He was on a lot of committees, I remember. Social housing, workers' rights, policing, you name it."

Interesting. There should be plenty about William Hearn in public records. Another project for Aaron.

"What about the garden?"

"That's been just the way it is for as long as I can remember. The only change in my lifetime was the greenhouse. My grandfather built that when I was at grammar school. It was the same year—" She stopped, took a deep breath and went on. "This is something I've learned not to talk about. To anyone. He built it the same year my mum disappeared."

Asha let the silence hang, hoping for more. She didn't want to lead the witness, and this felt important.

Sue sighed. "I do understand that you're going to need to know everything, even the uncomfortable things. I've read enough crime fiction to have an idea of what it's going to be like, but it doesn't mean I have to enjoy it. What do you need to know?"

"What year did your mum disappear?"

"1992. I was in my early teens and doing well at school until it happened; then everything went wrong that year and I bombed."

"Everything?"

"Yes. Mum disappeared, and no one seemed to be doing anything about it. I tried to go to the police, but Grandfather stopped me. I've never seen him so angry. I think it was the closest he'd ever come to hitting me."

"That must have been very frightening. The teenage years are difficult for any girl, but you had so much more to deal with."

Sue shot her a look that said, *Don't try to be my friend.* Asha shifted tactics.

"Tell me about the day she disappeared."

"That's what was so strange. I didn't find out she was missing for several days. We'd been rehearsing for a choir competition, so I'd been at school late every evening, then staying with a friend. I was at her house more than my own for a couple of weeks. It was only when I came home and found everything in turmoil that I knew there was something wrong."

Sue stopped, as if lost in the memory.

"No one would tell me what had happened. Dad was like a zombie. He sat there, rocking backwards and forwards, but wouldn't speak. Grandfather was stomping around. And there was no sign of Mum anywhere. I ran upstairs to her room, but it was empty. The bed hadn't been made, and that was what freaked me out most, I think."

Asha made an encouraging noise. Sue stared at her with haunted eyes.

"Mum was very strict about some things, and making the bed was one of them. It had to be done every morning and had to be just right. Seeing the sheets and blankets lying all scrunched up on Dad's side just broke me up."

"Did they ever tell you anything?"

"No. I even asked at the school — she was a teacher — but they said she'd taken sick leave. It was the end of term, just going into the Christmas holidays, when everything is chaotic. The principal sounded really cross. Mum used to play the piano for the Christmas show, and she did the stage set, too."

Asha was desperate to ask why the police hadn't been informed, why Sue's grandfather had been so angry about the prospect, but she thought she might learn more from this stream of consciousness than from formal questions. Those could come later. But there was one question that needed to be asked.

"This was the early nineties, before the Good Friday Agreement. Looking back now as an adult, do you think there's any possibility she could have been abducted by a paramilitary organisation?"

Sue shook her head. "No! My family, we were never, ever involved in anything political." She took a deep breath. "I think, if it had been anything like that, even I would have had some clue, but there was nothing to suggest it."

Still, Asha thought, it was a line of inquiry that needed to be pursued for elimination if nothing else. "And you never saw her again?"

"Never. None of us ever spoke about her, either. It was like a sort of taboo. Now, as a middle-aged woman, I can't believe I didn't do more, but at the time it seemed impossible. Dad was a total wreck."

She stopped, frowning.

"I think he must have been on something. Looking back, I recognise the signs, but I'd led such a sheltered childhood that drugs weren't really in my mind at all then. Besides, this was Dad. No teenager expects their dad to be a druggie." She gave a wan smile. "At least, not one from the sheltered middle classes."

That set up a whole new train of thought. If drugs had been involved in the mother's disappearance, there were several avenues Asha could investigate.

Then she mentally shook herself. How did the disappearance of a primary school teacher in the 1990s relate to the child's skeleton in the garden? The sooner she had a date for those bones, the happier she'd be.

"And nothing was ever done about her absence. Didn't the school kick up a fuss?"

"Not that I ever heard of. I was afraid to ask about it."

"Do you have any paperwork regarding your mum? Birth certificate, marriage certificate, any photos?"

Sue looked startled. "I've never really looked. If there is anything, it will either be in Grandfather's old study or boxed up in the attic. After she disappeared, Dad took down all the photos of her. I've no idea what he did with them, but it made me wonder if she'd run off with another man and he was too embarrassed to admit it. You're very welcome to look."

How had Sue resisted the temptation to look for clues to her mother's disappearance? Had the old man been such a powerful influence in her life that she'd just fallen in with his wishes, even after his death?

William Hearn's study was on the first floor. It reminded Asha of a museum, and she doubted if it had been redecorated since the house had first been built. The walls were lined with bookshelves, mostly leather-bound spines in neat rows, with a few modern hardbacks and a scattering of paperbacks.

The furniture was polished dark wood and leather, but badly worn. Mice must have taken up residence at some point, judging by the scraps of chewed bindings. There was a faint musty smell, too, and no air currents.

It's a time capsule, she thought.

The heavy, leather-topped desk sat in a corner, positioned so anyone sitting at it would be silhouetted against the window. Old-fashioned power-play. She imagined Tobias Hearn in his inner sanctum, giving orders to underlings from that desk, but now a fine layer of dust covered everything.

"It's all a bit of a mess," Sue said. "I really should clear this room out sometime."

A bell tinkled somewhere, so faint Asha wasn't sure if she'd heard it or not, but Sue must have been tuned in to the sound.

"That's Dad. Are you okay to search here on your own?"

"If you're sure you don't mind?"

Sue smiled. "Not at all. Go ahead."

CHAPTER 14

Sue ran down the corridor to the front room. There'd been an urgency to the bell that her finely tuned hearing had picked up.

She opened the door to find her father sprawled out on the floor, face down. He had an SOS app built into his watch that alerted her if he had a fall, but it hadn't gone off this time. Bloody tech.

She dropped to her knees beside him and tried to lift him. As thin as he was, he'd once been a big man and she could barely raise his shoulders off the ground. He turned his face to her, and she was sickened to see the way his lips dragged down on one side, a string of drool hanging there. One eyelid was drooping, too.

"Oh, Dad!"

He mumbled a reply, but he was slurring too badly for her to be able to understand. He'd had minor strokes before, but nothing like this.

"I'm calling an ambulance," she said.

He shouted a meaningless jumble of sounds and tried to grab for her, but he was positioned the wrong way, so his hand just flailed the air.

"I know, but you've had another stroke, Dad. I need help."

Then she remembered the detective.

"Inspector Harvey! Help!"

The other woman was there so fast Sue wondered if she'd already been on her way. Maybe detectives had an inbuilt extra sense for emergencies?

"What do you need me to do?"

"Help me get him into his chair, then I'm calling an ambulance."

Together, they got him onto his back, with difficulty, as he was fighting them, so they gave up on the chair and just propped him up with cushions on the floor. Sue stayed sitting with him while Asha called the ambulance, and she was glad when she heard the professional way the woman spoke on the phone. She'd have ended up in tears if she'd tried to speak to anyone.

The next while passed in a blur, waiting for the ambulance while Dad drifted in and out of awareness. He'd seem to sleep, head lolling and snores sawing away, then he'd wake again and start trying to speak.

"Should we call again? The ambulance is taking a long time."

Asha shook her head. "They'll be here as soon as they can. It's still rush hour between here and the hospital."

As she spoke, an ambulance turned into the drive, blue lights flashing but no siren. A couple of green-clad paramedics came up the steps. By the time they reached the door, she had it open.

"This way. He's just in here."

Dad was awake and furious, moaning and spitting, but the female paramedic was wonderful. She spoke to him like a real person, not a helpless patient, and his struggles eased as she explained everything she did while her partner wrote it all down.

"I'm afraid we'll be bringing you into the hospital for a proper check-up, Mr Hearn. They might well keep you in for observation, but we won't know until a doctor's had a look at you." She turned to Sue. "Are you his next of kin?"

"Yes. Daughter." That was all she could manage to say, because she was finding it hard to breathe.

"Would you like to come in the ambulance with him? Or you could prepare him a bag of clothes and essentials and follow us there if you'd rather?"

They needed her to make a decision? She froze, unable to think.

"You go with him," Asha said. "I'll pack a bag and throw in anything that looks useful." She held out a small, white piece of card with the PSNI logo on it. "Here's my mobile number. Do you have your phone on you?"

After their conversation about Mum's disappearance earlier, Sue's emotions were all over the place. It reminded her of her primary school days, when Mum would wipe her nose and check if she'd been to the toilet before she left to walk to school.

She patted her pocket. "Got it. He'll need his meds. They're in the cupboard above the sink, in the kitchen."

"Good. Text me if you think of anything else he might need. Now, go!"

And she did, strapping herself into the spare seat in the back of the ambulance once they'd wheeled Dad out on a stretcher. With the doors closed, it was like a cave, the small dark-tinted windows covered by slatted blinds. It was a tiny world, disconnected from everywhere else.

They swayed and roared through the dregs of morning rush hour traffic. Sue leaned forward to stare through the little window to the cab. Through the windscreen, all she could see were oncoming cars directly in front and brake lights off to the left. She sat back, mouth dry, as the ambulance filtered back into the correct lane.

They pulled up at the hospital and joined a queue of ambulance gurneys in a corridor, each one with its attendant green-clad paramedics. The man stayed with them while the woman headed off to book them in.

Sue took Dad's hand. "I'm here, Dad," she said, not sure if he could hear her. His eyes were closed, cheeks sunken and grey as if he was even older than his seventy years. His breath rasped in his throat and the long, artistic fingers were limp in her grasp, but when she tried to release him to let a young nurse pass, he gripped her tight.

"Your mum—"

At least, that's what she thought he said.

"What, Dad? Something about Mum?"

"Monica."

Oh God, he'd got confused again.

"Monica . . . because of me." He was slurring, but she was so attuned to his speech, she could just about follow him.

"I thought you didn't know what had happened to her."

He shook his head, distressed. "Don't know . . . must be dead . . . my fault."

Her mouth was totally dry now. The hospital sounds and smells faded away until there was just her and Dad, in their own bubble.

"Dad, what did you do? Why was it your fault?"

His eyes opened, but he was staring straight through her, into the past. Sue remembered the confusion of that time, the fear, the hushed voices — and the looks of loathing her grandfather had sent towards her father. Now, she might be on the edge of understanding why.

"*I* should have paid, not her," he said with absolute clarity. Then there was a breath of cool air as the outside door swung open, a tapping of heels, and DI Harvey was at her side.

"I brought everything I could think of. Is there anyone you'd like me to phone? Anyone who needs to know?"

The spell was broken. Dad's eyes drifted closed. His chest rose and fell and then was still. Sue gripped his hand tighter.

"Dad! Dad, can you hear me?"

The paramedic was there in a flash, pushing her aside. He shouted something, and nurses appeared from all over, along with an exhausted-looking young doctor, her stethoscope banging on her chest as she ran.

Dad's stretcher was rushed past the queue. Sue tried to follow, but her way was barred by a plump nurse in a dark-blue uniform.

"I'm sorry," she said. "Are you the next of kin?"

"His daughter," Asha said for her. Sue couldn't find enough air to speak. Her chest hurt as if she'd run a mile in icy fog.

"I'm sorry," the nurse repeated. "But you can't go into Resuscitation with him. There's a private waiting room across the hall with a kettle and comfy chairs. I promise someone will come and get you as soon as we know anything."

"I'll look after her." Asha shepherded Sue into the small room with worn plastic armchairs in generic hospital pink and blue. "Do you want to go through the bag I brought and see if there's anything I missed?"

Sue roused herself. The detective was being kind, but she needed to be alone right now, to think over Dad's words. Had he even known what he was saying? It all made sense in a dull, miserable way. It fitted into her kaleidoscopic memories of the time.

Should she mention it to the detective?

Not yet. See if Dad pulls through. You can ask him more about it then.

". . . or coffee?" Asha was saying. She was peering dubiously into a mug. "I suppose if I fill these with boiling water and soak them, they might be safe enough to use."

Sue pulled herself back to the present with an effort. "Let me. It'll help if I have something to do with my hands."

In the end, they did it together, then sat and drank instant black coffee (because the milk smelled iffy), perched on the dreadful armchairs.

"Has this happened before?"

Sue shook her head. "Not as bad as this. He's had unexplained falls and vague periods. TIAs." She couldn't remember what TIA stood for. "You know, minor strokes that sort themselves out. He's on anti-clotting drugs, statins, you name it." She took a sip of the coffee and twisted her face in disgust. "It's a horrible disease, dementia. Robs you of your memories and causes so many other problems."

She found herself explaining vascular dementia, just for something to say, anything to prevent herself blurting out what Dad had said. The detective sergeant was a good listener. She asked the right questions and made sympathetic noises.

"Are you sure you don't need to be anywhere?" Sue had swung from wanting to be alone to needing the company of this pretty Indian woman with her deep brown eyes and kind smile.

Asha shook her head. "I phoned in on my way over here and explained the situation. If they need me for anything, they'll know where to find me."

The door opened and the plump nurse stuck her head around it. "Just to let you know, your father is stable for now."

Sue almost spilled the cold coffee on her jeans as she stood up. The detective took the half-empty mug from her.

"Can I see him?"

The nurse smiled. "Of course. We'll be keeping him in, but the ward doesn't have a bed ready for him just yet, so he'll be here with us for a wee while." The Northern Irish expression sounded off in the nurse's English accent. Like someone from *Coronation Street* trying to sound Irish.

* * *

He looked shrunken, somehow, on the hospital bed. He wore a gown that had slipped down to reveal pale shoulders freckled with age spots, and every breath rasped, loud in the quiet cubicle.

"Dad? Can you hear me?"

His eyelids flickered, but his breathing pattern didn't change.

"He's sleeping," the nurse said. "Strokes really take it out of you. We'll not know how much damage has been done until we get the scan results, which shouldn't take too long."

"He's had a scan?"

"Yes, as soon as we had him stable enough. He had a CT to start with, but depending on the results, he'll probably need an MRI as well. That might not be until tomorrow." She lifted the clipboard from the end of the bed. "Can I just take a few details from you, while he's resting?"

At some point, the detective's phone rang, and she left the cubicle to answer it. Sue wasn't sure if she wanted her to stay or not. Her father might say something more about the past.

Selfish cow. None of that matters, now. Only Dad getting better.

Or dying. That was the small voice that whispered in the night. *If he dies, you'll be free.*

Asha came in briefly to apologise.

"I'm sorry, I have to go. Is there anyone I can call to come and keep you company?"

"No, thanks. There's no one except me and Dad. I'll be fine on my own with him." Then, as the detective was leaving, she added, "Thank you."

Asha smiled, and the curtain swung across behind her, closing Sue and Dad away from the rest of the world. She sat on the hard chair, drawing it close so she could hold his hand. It was cool and dry. Unresponsive.

"Just so's you know, Dad, I'm here with you. I'll stay with you as long as they'll let me. You're going to get better and come home with me." *Or into a home, anyway. What if he's paralysed? Incontinent? Can you really handle all that? Could he cope with you wiping his arse for him?* She nearly did that as it was, but he was usually physically able to do most things himself, so long as she reminded him.

The eyelids flickered again. Opened.

"Monica."

"No, Dad. It's me. Sue. Susan."

"Monica. I miss her so much. Should have been me, not her."

"What happened to her, Dad?"

He rasped a deeper breath, and his eyes swivelled vaguely in her direction. "The man was bad through and through.

81

A killer. How was I to know he was a killer? A man in his position?"

It was the most he'd said to her about the past, ever. She doubted if anyone else would have been able to follow the indistinct words, but she was still glad she was alone to hear them.

"What position, Dad?"

"Who'd suspect him? It would have been our word against his, and everyone trusts a peeler, don't they?"

CHAPTER 15

Asha hurried to the station. The preliminary forensic report was in, and she wanted to read it herself, drawing her own conclusions instead of being led into someone else's by hearing it second-hand over the phone.

She was almost at her office when a familiar acidic voice called her name. "Acting Detective Inspector Harvey. A word, if you please." It was phrased as an order. Asha turned and retraced her steps to Patterson's office. The Chief loved to ambush officers as they rushed by; that was probably why she always left her door slightly ajar.

Patterson didn't look up as she entered, instead fiddling with papers on her huge, polished-wood desk. The designer suits Patterson favoured should have made her appear powerful, but she wore them as if they were charity shop rejects. Maybe it was her slouching posture. But despite that, and the brassy blonde hair, the Chief always gave Asha the impression of robotic efficiency and attention to detail. She never missed a trick.

"Ma'am?"

"This historical burial you're dealing with is a good case to ease you in to your temporary promotion, a chance to shine. Talk me through your strategies."

"It's a child's skeleton, ma'am, and it was definitely murder, sometime in the last thirty years or so, but that's about all we have so far. I was on my way to see if the forensics report was in."

Patterson seemed oblivious to the hint. "I'm sure you're aware that as a female officer in a senior role, all eyes will be upon you and, by extension, upon me as your commanding officer. Your every action will be judged and compared to those of the male of the species, so do try to make sure you show a strong, independent front. You'll be on your own out there, so I don't want to hear about you screaming for help at every turn."

"Yes, ma'am. Strong and independent."

"Well, why are you wasting time here? Go and chase up that forensics report. I'd like this case cleared up quickly and cleanly."

Asha fled.

Aaron was sitting on her desk, swinging his feet like a schoolboy. He'd loosened his tie, undone his top button and thrown his suit jacket over a chair.

"Thought you'd be in court all day," she said, searching her desk for the report. He must have been looking through it, because it was laid across her in-tray rather than neatly inside it.

"Pleaded guilty," he said, succinctly. "Read."

She sat in her comfortable swivel chair, a gift to herself to celebrate her temporary promotion to DI. The report ran to several pages of closely typed text. Maggie and Dan must have been up all night working on this.

She scanned it quickly first, then settled down to read it more slowly. Aaron knew her well enough not to interrupt.

"Healed fractures in some of the fingers," she muttered. "And mild rickets. Don't see much of that these days, not even as long ago as the nineties." She turned the page. "And the dates match. Interesting."

Aaron straightened up. He was bursting to ask what she meant about dates, but he knew to wait until she'd finished.

Finally, she flipped the last page over, back to the cover. "So, we have a child aged about ten to eleven years old. Prof was bang on about that. No sex yet for the skeleton, but the report says they died somewhere between late October 1992, when the ground was cleared for the greenhouse, and mid January 1993, when the greenhouse was completed. So he or she was buried at around the same time that Sue Hearn's mother went missing — she shared the house with her husband and father-in-law, and Sue herself, of course. According to this, the pupal larvae are typical of colder weather, so wintertime, and Monica Hearn disappeared just before Christmas 1992, according to her daughter."

"But what's the connection? Beyond the coincidence of date and place, of course. How much do we know about Monica Hearn?"

"Not enough. I was just about to begin a search of William Hearn's study — that's Sue's grandfather — when Michael Hearn had a stroke. I wonder if Sue would mind if we went back with one of the SOCOs. That room didn't look as if it had been disturbed in years."

"You seemed to be bonding nicely with her last night," he said, smiling. "Why don't you ask her?"

"Great idea, while her dad's hanging on by thin spi-der-silk. That would undo everything we've achieved. No. It'll have to wait until he either dies, which would be a shame if it's before we question him, or he gets better."

There was a tap on the door, and it opened straight away. Sergeant Jacob waddled in, a sheaf of papers in each hand. Lonnie Jacob, still one of the very few black officers in the ranks of the PSNI, could be awkward, stubborn, out-spoken and downright obstructive, but Asha liked her. And respected her. She'd helped make it possible for women like Asha to find their way into this force and had given her the courage to see it through.

Besides, the elderly sergeant knew more about the PSNI, and the old RUC, than almost any other serving officer. According to rumour, that was the only reason she was still working here, long after most officers would have retired, and with an office of her own. She knew something about everyone, all the way up to the very top.

Even the bigots would bring her doughnuts sometimes.

"What have you got for us, Lonnie?"

Lonnie waved the thicker pile. "Mispers records for children between the ages of four and fourteen from the period 1980 to 2005. Except for these." She raised the smaller sheaf. "Which are from 1988 to 1993."

How the hell did the woman get to hear these things? She'd only just read the report herself. She glanced at Aaron, who shrugged and shook his head.

"Thank you, Sergeant," she said. "Any of them leaping out at you?"

"Nope. The ones in that time period look to be either too old or too young, unless the boffins got the child's age wrong."

Then she turned and waddled out. It would be easy to underestimate Lonnie if you didn't know her. Many new officers had, and then regretted it.

Asha pored over the reports with Aaron, hoping against her experience that the sergeant would be wrong. There had been eleven unresolved mispers for that period, but none fitted their skeleton.

"The dating of the skeleton is the weak point," she said. "We'd better look at the years either side."

But there were only two that came anywhere near the description of the child buried in Sue's garden. Both were, according to the reports, too tall to be the dead child, and they were from the extreme outer boundaries of the times they'd set for their search.

Aaron leaned back in his chair. "What if the kid had been abducted and kept somewhere for years? It'd be a really old missing persons report, but he'd have died and been buried later on."

"I think Lonnie must have had the same thought," Asha said. "She extended the search criteria to cover that possibility."

"So, we could be looking at a child who went missing from somewhere else, maybe over the border, or even from across the water, and was killed here in Belfast?"

"Or a child who slid between the cracks. What if no one reported his or her disappearance? Maybe no one missed them, even."

Aaron, bless his innocence, looked outraged. "How could anyone not notice if their kid goes missing?"

"Plenty of reasons. Mum was a user and out of it most of the time? Abusive family, afraid to report the disappearance in case they were charged?" She was remembering the healed fractures.

"But surely someone would have reported it? I mean, it was the nineties, for God's sake. They had computers in the nineties and an internet of sorts. There were probably even mobile phones."

"Sue's mum's disappearance wasn't reported," Asha said, mildly. "And she was a fine, upstanding citizen. A teacher, no less."

Aaron subsided a little. "You're right. I should make a start on social security records, kids who were under the social care system throughout that period."

"Lonnie might help you," Asha said. "And you're right, we should also extend the search to mispers from other places, not just Northern Ireland. While you're doing that, I'll concentrate on the missing teacher."

Her first port of call was Monica Hearn's official records. Birth, marriage, death. Not that she expected to find a death certificate, but if she did, it would be a pleasant surprise. She sent the requests away, then looked up the school Monica had taught in. St Peter's Primary. It was almost thirty years since she had disappeared, but the school's records could give her a clue. Or inspiration, anyway. She tapped the number into her mobile.

The call was picked up by an unfriendly secretary, and identifying herself as an acting detective inspector didn't thaw the woman's attitude — Asha didn't think the woman would be flustered by the chief constable on the phone, never mind a lowly DI. Still, she managed to arrange an appointment to meet the current principal, Maureen Snow, the next morning. She felt she'd achieved quite a lot with that.

Asha tapped her fingers on the desk. She'd set the wheels in motion, but until the results started to come in, there'd be nothing new for her to do. A restlessness had taken over her. She wanted to do something, to go somewhere and ask questions. She could call the hospital and ask after Sue's father, but they wouldn't tell her anything.

Her mobile rang in her hand, number not recognised.

"Hello? Is that Detective Inspector Harvey?"

"Yes. Sue? Is everything all right?"

There was a sound like someone choking, then a tannoy announcement that drowned out all else and made Asha move her phone a bit further from her ear, then Sue's voice came back on.

"Dad's stable, but they're keeping him in for more tests and observation. I'm going to get a taxi home, but I think I need to speak to you, fairly urgently. Can you meet me at home?"

Asha smiled, knowing it would sound in her voice. "Better than that, I'll come and collect you. We can chat on the way."

CHAPTER 16

Sue had aged in the hours since Asha last saw her. She stooped as she walked to the car, feet dragging, and the face turned towards her once she had her seatbelt buckled was pale.

Asha allowed her time to recover herself, staying quiet as she navigated the afternoon traffic between the Royal Victoria Hospital and the old house in South Belfast. Sue sat with her hands clasped between her thighs, despite the warmth of the day.

"Dad was talking, lost in the past. He kept on thinking I was my mum."

Asha stayed quiet, letting her work out what she needed to say.

"He said a lot of things that made no sense, but then he said . . ." She looked away from Asha, out of the window. "He said that it should have been him, not her, but that he'd no way of knowing the man was a killer. Bad through and through, he said." She twisted her fingers together in her lap. "Then he said something else. Something I'm not sure makes any sense at all. I don't know if it's a hallucination from his condition, because he does get them, but he seemed lucid enough to me."

What? Asha wanted to say, but she let the silence drag out. They were nearly at Sue's house. If she didn't say it soon, the moment would be lost.

"He said that someone in his position should be better, or something like that. Then he said you should be able to trust a policeman." She glanced at Asha. "It's probably a delusion. He has them all the time, and he'll know there have been police in the house, so his poor diseased mind might have built up a story that fits the pieces. It's what happens in dementia, sometimes. The brain fills in the gaps with anything that rings true."

"You don't really believe that, do you? You think he's actually remembering."

"I do. God help me, Detective, I do."

They pulled up at Carrow Lodge in a spray of gravel, and Sue sat staring out of the windscreen, as if she couldn't find the energy to move. The building loomed, the windows like sightless eyes staring down at them. Even Asha, not normally prone to atmosphere, shuddered.

"Give me your key, and I'll open up and put the lights on," she said. "A hot drink in your own home will make you feel better." *Make both of us feel better.* She was under no illusions about cases of police involvement in crime, both past and present, but this would need to be handled very carefully. There were procedures to follow.

Sue reached obediently into her bag and fetched out a set of keys with a Hawaiian dancing girl, incongruously, as the key ring. She picked out two, a Yale-type and a big, old-fashioned key, and passed them over.

The doorway was in deep shadow, and Asha's eyes hadn't adjusted from the bright sunlight, but there was no mistaking the vertical line of darker shadow at the edge.

She advanced cautiously, holding the heavy bunch like a cosh, and took up a position to one side of the door. There was no sign of damage to the door itself, but the big lock beneath the handle had some fine scratches that might have been new. It was hard to be certain.

She nudged the door inwards with her foot. It swung silently on oiled hinges and revealed a long hallway barred with rectangles of light from the rooms on either side.

That was odd. Asha had been the last to leave, and she'd closed every door on her way out.

The click of the car door opening sounded over her racing pulse. She flapped a hand at Sue, telling her to stay put, and stepped inside.

Old houses breathe. The wood ticks as it expands and contracts. Asha let herself absorb those sounds until they became background noise, then listened for anything that didn't belong.

Nothing.

But was that nothing because the house was empty, or nothing because someone was holding their breath, hoping she'd go away?

This is where I should shout, "Police!" It's also where I should call it in.

But she didn't. *Strong and independent*, Patterson had said. *You'll be on your own out there.* And she was.

She moved along the edge of the hall, where the floorboards were less likely to creak, until she could see inside the first room on the right, a sitting room that looked as if it hadn't been used for years.

Unless they were hiding behind the door, that room appeared to be empty. She peered into the door on her side of the corridor, Michael Hearn's room. It was so cluttered with his effects and the syringe wrappings left behind by the paramedics that she'd have been hard-pressed to tell if anyone had been through there. She dipped inside, ready for anything, but the room was empty.

Now she had to decide if she would go downstairs, to the kitchen and out into the garden, or upstairs towards the bedrooms and William Hearn's study.

Something creaked on the floor above.

All her copper instincts screamed at her to get out, to radio for backup, anything but go up those stairs.

The sensible thing would be to go outside and radio for assistance, but while she was there, whoever was hiding upstairs could nip down into the basement kitchen and out the back way. There'd be no one out there now SOCO and the specialists had finished.

She trod the first step. Then the second. The third one creaked beneath her foot, and she froze.

Adrenaline rushed through her system, making her light-headed. This was insane. She reached into her pocket for her mobile, turning to retrace her steps, when a scraping sound from above made her flinch.

Something struck her on the back of the head. Pain flared through her skull. The floor rushed up to meet her, and the worn, faded carpet pressed against her cheek like a caress. A body at the bottom of the stairs. *The perfect murder scene,* she thought, as she drifted down into a sea of blackness. All it needed was blood to complete the picture.

Ah, there it is. A dark pool spread across the carpet like oil, catching at her nose with its metallic scent until she floated away on it. Someone was calling her name. She wanted to tell them to go away, but the words wouldn't come.

Time ceased to exist.

A siren sounded somewhere nearby, so loud it set off fireworks behind her eyes.

Fingers probed her head, none too gently, and she cried out with the pain of it. Then bile filled her throat and she knew she was going to vomit, but she couldn't move. Was she paralysed?

Choking. Burning. *Fuck!*

Ice flooded her veins, a lagoon of cool liquid working through her. She followed its track through her circulation, willing it to reach her poor head, and then it did. She floated away a second time, forgetting where she was, what she was doing here, even who she was.

Every so often, she'd drift up into awareness. A glimpse of sky, trees waving in the breeze. Anxious voices, some she recognised, some she didn't. The inside of an ambulance, and the compression of a blood-pressure cuff on her arm. Bright lights, probing.

The next time she opened her eyes, she was in a hospital bed with machines bleeping both nearby and in the distance. She knew where she was, but it was a struggle to remember who she was. Or how she'd got here.

She tried to sit up, but failed the first attempt, so she decided it wasn't worth the effort.

An arm came around her shoulders, supporting her. The bed hummed as the top part lifted to make a back rest.

"That will do for now," said a female voice. Confident, sure of herself. "We don't want her throwing up again, but if she does, there are basins on the table. I think she's awake now, but she might not feel much like speaking."

"Okay. Thank you." Asha felt a smile trying to turn the corners of her mouth as the voice triggered memories. *Aaron.*

The door swished open and then closed, letting in the momentary buzz of a busy ward outside. Asha kept her eyes closed and waited. Aaron wouldn't stay quiet for long. He was incapable of it.

"How are you feeling?"

"Like I've been ten rounds with Carl Frampton," she croaked.

"What happened?"

"I was hoping you'd tell me." She concentrated on keeping her voice even, keeping the panic down. "I can't remember anything at all."

A shadow darkened the room. She opened her eyes, then blinked against the pain and closed them again. In that flash, she'd seen concern in Aaron's face, the lines around the eyes that hadn't been there earlier, when . . . when . . .

* * *

She awoke again, disturbed by commotion in the ward as visitors flooded in, chattering expectantly. How much time had she lost?

She blinked the sleepiness from her eyes. It seemed too much trouble to raise a hand and rub them, so she settled for blurry vision.

"You're awake, then?" If she hadn't been, that hard, sharp voice would have guaranteed instant alertness. Detective Chief Superintendent Yvonne Patterson, queen of stating the obvious.

"I understand your memory has been affected?"

Asha felt under no obligation to answer a stupid question. She waited for a sensible one.

"What's the last thing you remember?"

Ah. She'd been trying not to think about that. There wasn't any one memory she could latch on to, just a jumble of scenes and snatches of conversation. She worked moisture into her mouth to speak, but didn't get the chance.

"Do you remember going into the Hearn house?"

Hearn. Hearn. The name sounded familiar.

"Susan Hearn and her father Michael live there." Patterson was becoming impatient, but that wasn't going to make the memories return any faster.

A rustle of clothing as the Chief stood up. Asha supposed she should be honoured that the big boss had taken the trouble to come see her in person, but she really wasn't. She was uncomfortable, wary and a little scared.

"I can see you're not ready to answer questions yet, but I can assure you that I will need answers, and soon, so I suggest you work hard to remember the missing time period." Her leather-soled, flat shoes tap-tapped over to the door. "There's more than a thirty-year-old murder and misper at stake here, Detective. We have a contemporary misper to deal with, and the clock is ticking."

CHAPTER 17

Sue woke to darkness so complete she thought she'd gone blind. She tried to move, but as soon as she lifted her head, it hit something hard.

Her heart kicked painfully in her chest as panic flooded her. She lashed out with hands and feet, but in every direction there were hard surfaces, and her shoes made a dull booming noise as they hit the ceiling.

She stilled, exhausted. Her breath rasped, far too fast, in the tiny space. She closed her eyes, for all the good it did, and made herself slow her breathing right down. If she really was in a tiny space, she needed to conserve oxygen.

Good. Now, gently, feel all around. She used her left hand to touch the surfaces. She was lying on something rough but yielding, like an old-fashioned woollen blanket. It was too thin to provide much padding, but at least it meant whoever had put her here was thinking of her comfort.

Her heart started to race again. Who had put her here? Why couldn't she remember?

Calm.

The sides and ceiling were textured, not cold but not warm either. Some sort of wood. Plywood? She rapped the top with her knuckles, and it sounded dull, as if the wood was quite thick. *Or buried deep underground.* The sides and head end were the same, and by stretching her toes she could touch the foot end. No reason to doubt it would be any different.

As far as size went — and the panic really wasn't easy to control — it was not much bigger in any dimension than her own body, except for length. At five-foot six, Sue was average for a woman, but this would surely have taken a six-foot-plus human.

Six feet long, six feet deep, said her treacherous inner voice.

No. The sound isn't right for there to be soil piled above me. There must be a space around this box. There had to be.

She tried to work out how she'd got here, but the last clear image she had was of watching the young detective disappearing into her house. She'd got out of the car to follow her, but Asha had signalled her to stay put, so she'd dithered halfway between the car and the house, eyes glued to the open door as Asha slipped inside.

What next? Think, woman!

She'd heard a noise. Something heavy landing with a dull thud and then bouncing. It sounded as if it had fallen onto the hall floor, but it must have hit something else first. Or someone.

She'd called Asha's name. She remembered looking up at the big front door with its faded, peeling paint and being too scared to go any further. Gravel had crunched to her left. She'd spun around, but been dazzled by the sunlight filtering through the trees, her attacker only a silhouette towering over her.

As if her thoughts had power, a pale strip of light appeared along the edge of her prison. Several strips, all faint. They confirmed her fear. The box was shaped very much like a coffin.

Sue strained her ears, but the wood was too thick. Was there someone there? She tried to imagine where she was. Inside a building? Or had night fallen while she'd been unconscious? There was no sense of movement.

Then something hit the outside with a clang that sent vibrations through her spine. It sounded as if the box had been hit with an axe. Or a spade. A second loud noise, like a metal door slamming — van doors, perhaps — then nothing until an engine started up, a deep diesel rumble that rattled her inside the box.

This time, the panic wouldn't be controlled. She screamed and hammered on the ceiling and walls, throwing herself at them. She shuffled down to the bottom, bent her knees as far as she could and kicked hard. The walls felt solid, but she'd be damned if she was going to give up.

Again. Another kick. She screamed like she'd seen wrestlers do on the television — a primal roar, a battle cry — and something gave with a screech.

Tears burned in her eyes. One more try. She could do this.

Wood splintered as nails ripped free, and more light flooded in. The bottom of the box hung like a flap. *A cat flap*, she thought inconsequentially. Now for the hard part.

She rolled onto her front and thrust upwards with her bottom, using her thigh muscles. Over the growling engine noise, something squealed. The nails were sliding through the wood.

The van must have turned a sharp corner, because she was thrown sideways, but the adrenaline was flowing now, and she was almost free.

The base separated from the walls and roof, but it was painfully slow and she was tiring. Another sharp bend threw her the other way, and the force of momentum achieved what she'd failed to do, ripping out the last few nails on that side of the box.

Sue crawled out from the wreckage, bruised and bleeding, blinking in the dim light. She'd been right about the van. A Transit, with wooden shelves along one side. Tools littered the floor, including a pickaxe and shovel. She didn't want to think about what they were for.

One side of the van had a sliding door, but if she used that to escape, the driver would surely see her in his wing mirror. The back doors would be better.

She crawled over to them, too disoriented and battered to even think about standing, but there were sheets of ply fixed over the inside, so she couldn't get at the release mechanism, if there was one. She ran her fingers over the surface, looking for any sort of button or handle, but there was nothing.

At least it was a van full of tools. A hefty claw hammer hung from a pair of nails on the wall. She unhooked it on the third attempt, as the van swung around another corner, throwing her off-balance.

The plywood sheet resisted, but she was close to freedom now, and she wasn't giving up for anything. A pry bar would have been better, but she couldn't see one, and the pickaxe was just too massive.

Finally, she loosened a corner and hauled it away from the metal door frame. Shit! Wrong door! The lock mechanism must be on the other side.

Her fingernails were torn and bleeding, and her arms felt like cooked pasta, but there was no choice. Whoever had stuffed her in that box, she was a hundred per cent certain they hadn't done it to keep her safe.

The second panel came away with a banshee's screech. She fell backwards and landed on the remains of her box. Sharp pain pierced her side, but she had no time to waste.

The van changed gear and slowed down. They could be at their destination already, and here she was, still trapped like a rat. She tried every part of the mechanisms, but the door remained stubbornly closed.

A sharp braking action sent her backwards again, but she bounced up onto her feet like a gymnast, not caring about another bruise.

There. At the bottom right of the door, a little black lever. She tugged at it and the door swung open, pulling her with it. The van accelerated again.

Her feet hit the tarmac, but she was spinning in the air, her hand wrenched from its grip on the door. She hit the ground hard, air forced from her lungs in a single blast.

Exhaust smoke descended on her like smog, and through a haze of tears she watched the van drive away, one door swinging, onto a dual carriageway.

It was the West Link, the inner-city log-jam road loathed by commuters into Belfast, but the road appeared quiet now. That had to mean very early morning, or there'd be traffic on the move.

Her momentum had deposited her against the kerb, in among dried mud, bits of car and discarded drinks cans. How long before the driver noticed that door swinging? Not long, but he'd have to take the next exit and circle around to look for her.

No time to lick her wounds. She needed to get moving. She pushed herself upright, trying to block out the pain, and turned her face towards the rising sun. She couldn't quite straighten up. Something stabbed her in the side every time she tried.

The Millfield campus of the Belfast Met must be nearby, but too far to run in her condition. There were no convenient shops or houses around here, and the streets seemed curiously empty.

Her watch was missing from her wrist, but the air had a feel of night about it and the streetlights were lit. How long had she been unconscious in that box?

Her head ached and her throat whistled with every breath. She staggered across four lanes of a road that would normally be busy and drifted along a wire mesh fence, far too tall to climb. She trudged on, trying to go faster, but it was like one of those nightmares where however hard you try, the destination gets no closer.

Then the fence dipped away from her and she staggered sideways into a high, steel security gate that clanged as her shoulder collided with it.

She clutched at it with fingers that had almost forgotten how to bend and shook it. Locked, obviously.

An engine sounded in the distance, deep and throaty. He was coming for her!

The gate had heavy hinges protruding on this side, so she jammed the tip of her battered shoe into it and lunged upwards. Her fingers closed on the upper hinge, and the other hand gripped the wire mesh. The top didn't seem so far away now. One desperate lunge and her left hand caught the top of the gate.

The engine drew closer. It was coming from the direction of the city, where she expected the van to loop back.

The tendons in her wrist pulled sharply, and fire darted down her side, focusing on an area just beneath her ribs, then she was up. She got one elbow, then the other hooked over the top and swung a leg.

She made it on the third attempt, shaking hard. She hauled her chest and then her tummy onto the top, then gravity took over and she fell.

CHAPTER 18

Aaron waited around the corner until Patterson's heavy steps faded down the corridor towards the lifts. The cup of drinks-machine coffee was burning his fingers, but he'd rather blister than face the Chief right now.

As soon as he was sure the coast was clear, he slipped inside Asha's room. She looked just as pale and drawn as she had earlier, but the fist nearest him was tightly clenched, and beneath the sheets a foot tapped.

She turned towards him, and her eyes were clear, if shadowed. "Aaron! I hoped you'd be back. You need to tell me everything that's happened. Now."

He sat on the plastic chair and took a sip of the watery mud they sold as coffee. "Where will I start?"

"I don't know. You tell me! The Chief said something about a thirty-year-old murder and misper, and a contemporary misper. I feel as if I can almost remember, but not quite. If you start at the beginning, I'm hoping you'll trigger the memories. Go."

"Okay. We were called out to a skeleton some poor woman had dug up in her garden. Sue Hearn." Asha nodded carefully, so he went on. "It was a child of about ten or eleven, murdered: a stab up into the roof of the mouth. The house has been in the woman's family forever, and the bones must have been buried before a greenhouse was built above them around thirty years ago by her grandfather. With me so far?

"The first misper is Sue Hearn's mother, who went AWOL around the same time the child was buried. She was never reported as missing for some reason, but Sue's father, Michael Hearn, has dementia, and any other family members who'd have been around at that time are long gone."

"So, who is the other misper?"

"Ah. That's where it gets tricky." There was no easy way to say this. "Sue's dad had a stroke. You picked Sue up from hospital and drove her home. We have your car on CCTV all the way to Carrow Lodge, and we found it in her driveway, passenger door open, no one inside. You're lucky a passer-by saw it and called it in so soon, or this might have had a different ending."

"The front door was open," Asha said, remembering. "The house door. I told Sue to stay in the car."

"Her handbag was in the car, in the passenger footwell, but no sign of her." He took another sip of the muck in the paper cup. "Please tell me you didn't go inside on your own without calling for assistance."

"No-win situation." Or that's what he thought she'd mumbled. "Damned if I do, damned if I don't," she expanded, leaving him even more confused. She sighed. "I went inside, checked the two ground-floor front rooms, but that's all I can remember."

"It's still more than you could remember a few minutes ago. Well done!"

She shot him a slit-eyed look that said, *If you patronise me, prepare to die.*

"What else do you remember? Is it just the part where someone hit you on the head that you can't recall?"

"As you told me the series of events, I remembered them, but before that, everything was a blank."

He nodded. "That happened to me once after a rugby concussion. I forgot everything until someone told me, then everything came back complete. Like people's names. I had no idea, but if I heard the name, I'd remember where I knew them from, if I'd kissed them, where they lived, what pets they had, you name it."

She snorted, then winced. "Please, Aaron. Don't make me laugh." Her face crumpled. "I've just remembered something else. I was supposed to meet the principal of Monica Hearn's primary school tomorrow at ten."

"I'll phone her first thing and rearrange it for when you're out of hospital. Perhaps we should be prioritising Sue Hearn though, rather than a cold case. Meanwhile, make sure you do as you're told and rest. We need you firing on all cylinders," he said. "How do you feel?"

"Like lukewarm shit being stirred in a pan."

"Oh good. I'll go and chase the doctor to let you out then, shall I?"

The doctor was pleasant but stubborn. Miss Harvey (Aaron was glad she wasn't in earshot) would need to remain overnight under observation. As soon as her concussion began to subside, and once they were certain she hadn't incurred any further damage, she could possibly be allowed to go, but she'd need total rest for at least a week.

Aaron nodded, but he knew what Asha would say about the prospect of a week's rest.

He broke the news to her, surprised when she didn't argue or give him a row for not arguing on her behalf. She must really be feeling rotten.

He left her in peace to sleep off the headache and went to the station. In the corridor, he passed Aiken and Kernaghan, two ageing uniformed constables who fancied themselves as the station comedy duo, but only at the expense of others. They were bullies, the pair of them.

He could have turned towards the stairs, but it was late, he was knackered and he was damned if a pair of racist, sexist RUC anachronisms would make him take the stairs when the lift was right there, so he kept going.

Neither of them spoke until he was past them, then Aiken sniggered. "Got his funeral face on. Paki slut must be dead."

He kept going. It had been said loud enough for them to be fairly sure he'd heard, but quietly enough that he could pretend he hadn't.

"Any bloke that went into a dangerous situation without backup would have been disciplined, but with all this *equality*," Kernaghan slurred the word, "she'll probably be the next DCI."

The lift pinged and Aaron stepped inside. Only as the car ascended, and he filled his lungs with the scent of old fag smoke, stale urine and vomit that no amount of cleaning was able to shift, did he relax. He uncurled his fists, which had been so tightly clenched that his nails had dug into his palms.

"You look as if you need a good, strong, put-hairs-on-your-chest coffee." Lonnie's accent was a strange mixture of her own rich Jamaican heritage and an acquired Belfast edge. She rarely failed to bring a smile to his face.

"If you're offering to drink the coffee with me, Sergeant, I'm yours." Tension oozed out of his shoulders, down his arms and into his fingers, where he could shake it out.

"I'll have a pot on the go before you've emptied your in-tray."

Aaron's internal radar gave a soft ping. Lonnie didn't waste words, so there must be something of interest on his desk. He trotted off obediently to the open-plan office he shared with a handful of other junior detectives.

The name "*in-tray*" was a misnomer. Few people had them these days, but there was a brown cardboard file sitting on his desk, a bit tattered, and faded in a one-inch strip along the edge where someone had left it sitting in full sunlight beneath other files. He snatched it up and leafed through it.

The front page had a photograph clipped to it. A young boy stared warily at the camera. He had floppy brown hair, cut short around the back and sides in classic nineties curtains, and a sprinkling of freckles across his nose and cheeks.

You couldn't tell from the photo if he was tall or short, but he looked as if he could do with a good feed. The cheekbones were sharp, and the bit of his upper body the photographer had caught showed defined collarbones beneath a faded T-shirt.

Aaron lifted the photo and read the first few lines. It was a missing persons report, but judging by the thinness of the file, it hadn't gone very far. He skimmed through it. William Lee, ten years old when he'd disappeared from his foster parents' home in January 1993. Whoever had been working the case — the signature was an illegible scrawl — had made a note that the kid had probably run away. And that seemed to have been the final conclusion. There were a couple of typed-up statements from the foster parents, one from the boy's social worker, but nothing that gave any real detail. No reason for him to run.

He carried the file down the corridor, quickening his pace as the smell of coffee reached him, and took Lonnie's spare chair, the one that tried to tip the unwary onto the ground with its missing wheel, while she splashed milk and a couple of sugar cubes into his chipped mug.

"Well?" she asked, putting the mug near his elbow.

"Could be. But we'd need to track down the natural parents to confirm with a DNA profile."

"Yes," Lonnie said. "I thought you'd say that, so I did some digging. Turns out his da was killed in a knife fight in 1997 and his ma dropped off the radar around the same time. There was no DNA database in 1992, but I'll keep looking in case there's anything later than that for either of them. In the meantime, read on."

What had he missed? Ah. A younger half-sister, also in care. Same mother, Shannon Lee, but different father. There was a name, but no mention of her social worker or whether she'd been fostered out or even adopted.

Lonnie slid a single piece of paper across to him.

"Louise Lee, born 5 May 1985. Adopted by a Mr and Mrs McCoubrey of Larne when she was six months old.

Same surname as William, so both kids must have taken their mother's name."

"Lonnie, you're a wonder."

She pointed to a wrinkled cheek. He got up and planted a kiss on it.

"Now go home and rest. Plenty to do in the morning."

He wasn't about to argue.

CHAPTER 19

This time, Sue thought she was dying. She couldn't get a breath. Her lungs felt like a vacuum, a black hole inside her chest. As her vision began to fade, the engine noise grew louder and a low-slung sport car roared past, heading towards the West Link.

It wasn't him!

Not that she was safe, far from it. She managed a painful breath, then another, and the spots in her vision receded.

She crawled away from the fence on all fours, then staggered to her feet and managed a shambling run that jarred her aching side with every step. There were buildings up ahead, and the glint of sun on windows in a car park. If she could get around a corner she'd be out of sight of the road, at least.

The car park was nearly empty. Only three or four cars sat there, and most had a sheen of fine water droplets covering them. Dew.

Hope abandoned her. This was the Millfield campus, part of a college of further education, so there'd be little activity here for hours yet until staff and students started to crawl in.

It was the last straw. She sank down onto the grass at the edge of the path, the adrenaline leaving her in a rush. There was the entrance, not thirty paces from her, but there was no sign of life inside.

"Are you all right? Do you need help?"

It was a female voice, with an Asian lilt. For a moment Sue thought it was Asha speaking, but then she raised her head and looked into a pair of worried brown eyes beneath a black hijab. The woman was about Sue's own age, and she carried a supermarket bag bulging with files and folders that was surely about to burst and scatter its contents everywhere.

"Yes," she said, thinking that surely it must be obvious she needed help. "Do you have a phone? Can you call the police?"

The other woman looked surprised and a little relieved. "Yes, of course. Would you like to speak to them yourself?"

Sue tried to smile, but her face had forgotten how. "If you get through. My name's Sue Hearn."

"Oh!" Comprehension dawned. "You've been on the news. Here, I have a blanket in the car boot. I can wrap you in it. Would you like to sit inside the car? I can put the heater on. You're frozen."

The sudden kindness was too much. She tried to speak, but only a wordless moan made it out, then she was gasping and sobbing, and couldn't see for tears that burned in her eyes like acid.

Dimly, she heard the woman's voice. She must have dialled 999, because she asked for police and an ambulance. Her voice was like music, so sweet and kind. Sue thought they could be friends, once this was over.

After that, there was the touch of another human's arm around her shoulders, the soft feel of thin, silky fabric against her cheek as she buried her face in the other woman's shoulder, her senses filled by the warm scent of spice.

When the emergency services arrived, they had to pry her from her rescuer's arms.

"Stay with me!"

"I will."

And she did. She stayed at her side, holding her hand when she could, when the paramedics allowed her, and talking to her all the time, reassuring, telling her what was happening.

The ambulance journey would have been unbearable if it hadn't been for that beautiful voice and the warmth of the dry, soft hand gripping Sue's bruised fingers. Each turn, each acceleration, sent her pulse racing. With the tinted windows, she could have been back inside that van again.

CHAPTER 20

Asha gave Aaron enough time to have left the hospital, then tried to stand. The room spun and she sat back down sharply. Maybe she wasn't quite ready to leave yet. She sank back onto the bed and closed her eyes, just for a few minutes, it seemed, but woke to the kerfuffle of a nurses' shift change, the perfect cover to allow her to sneak out unnoticed.

This time when she stood up, the dizziness wasn't quite as bad. She pulled the blind aside and peered out at a morning sky across the city rooftops. She must have slept for a few hours at least, and the rest had done her good.

Her clothes were neatly folded in her bedside locker. Bending down to pull them out brought on a whole world of pain and nausea, but she was determined. She leaned against the bed to keep herself from falling over as she pulled on trousers that seemed tighter than she remembered, despite her having boked her guts up and eaten nothing. Thank God she'd worn a loose-necked, stretchy blouse at least, and slip-on pumps.

Once she was decent, she tucked her phone and car keys in her pocket, wondering where the vehicle was. Probably with SOCO, getting checked out for evidence. *Damn. I should have cleared out the back seat. I'll never hear the end of it when they find all the empty carry-out wrappers.*

The nurse's station was at the other end of the modern, wide corridor and if there was anyone at it, they were too short to see over the top. She let herself out of the automatic doors and walked carefully towards the lifts.

This new wing was a maze of corridors leading in every direction, and wards that shared the same number but were identified by different letters. She passed a couple of sets of stairs, but the thought of bouncing her head down them was beyond imagining, so she persisted until she found a lift. It said "*Beds Only*" on the doors. *Well, tough.* She was supposed be in a bed, so surely she had every right to use a bed lift.

Outside, the early morning sky was leaden with low clouds and the air filled with the scent of rain. She expected everything to have changed, but nothing had. There was the multi-storey, which was sadly lacking a vehicle for her. There had to be a taxi rank somewhere, but it was probably at the front of the old hospital, a long walk from here.

Time stretched out, a blur of gently placed feet so as not to jar her fragile head and neck, but finally she reached the front, a 1960s construction of glass and concrete. And no taxis. What was that company Aaron always went on about? Uber? He had some sort of app on his phone, but she never really used taxis and had no clue how to call one.

Luckily there was a payphone just inside the front doors, labelled with the name of a local taxi company. She ordered a ride but drew a blank when she was asked for an address, so she gave the first one that popped into her head. Sue Hearn's house.

* * *

Police tape fluttered across the driveway. As she paid her fare with her phone, grateful for contactless since she had little cash, the driver gave her an odd look.

"Sure you'll be all right? You don't look too good."

She mustered a smile but knew it would be pathetic. "I'll be fine. Thank you."

"All right. You know your own business, but . . ." He reached into an open locker in front of his gear stick and drew out a rectangle of card. "Just in case. That's my number. If you need another lift, or anything at all, just call." He looked about fifteen and the spots on his chin were threatening to join up and form an army to march down his neck and onto his chest, but the watery eyes held nothing but concern.

This smile was a bit better. "I will. Thank you again."

He watched her in his mirror as he drove away, so she gave him a wave and he waved back. Once he'd turned the corner, she lifted the tape so she wouldn't have to duck too low and went inside.

Only as she tried the front door did it occur to her that she was being stupid. If SOCO had finished their work, the house would have been secured, and she didn't have the keys. She paused on the top step and looked back, remembering Sue as she tried to get out of the car. Asha had driven her here, taken responsibility for her, and she'd been abducted.

A wave of dizziness washed over her, and she grabbed the door handle for balance. It turned in her hand and the door opened, letting out the slightly musty smell of an unoccupied house.

She pushed it wider. *Why* hadn't she called for assistance? To impress Patterson? She glanced at her mobile. The charge bar was a tiny red line, but at least she had signal. She swallowed and stepped inside.

There were no bars of light across the carpet on this occasion. The inner doors were all shut, and there was little illumination, except from a landing window higher up the stairs. She padded down the corridor, trying to remember every detail that had changed, because she'd need it for her report later.

At the bottom of the stairs, a dark stain made a shadow on the carpet, and she remembered the smell, the dust in her lungs before she lost consciousness. What had hit her? She was prepared to swear that no one could have come down the stairs fast enough and silently enough to hit her directly with anything, so it must have been thrown. Or dropped.

She tilted her head back to look up the stairwell, then squeaked as a ghostly white face stared down at her from the upper landing.

"Oh, so the dead are walking now, are they?" asked Jana, her voice muffled by her full protective suit and mask. "They're carrying their beds and appearing to many, no?"

"Just to you, Jana. You made me jump."

"Yep. I have that effect on women." She tilted her head sideways. "I don't think you should be out of your bed yet. What brainless doc let you loose? Or did you run?"

"What have you found up there? Anything?"

"Thanks to you and your hard head, yes. I think you disturbed him before he could get everything. Want to come up and see?"

The stairs were steep and turned several corners with landings before they reached Jana's level, the level of William Hearn's study. "Maybe later. Can't you come down here and tell me?"

"Okay. One second." Jana turned away and bellowed, "Marley! You keep on working. I'm going to check the kitchen again. Maybe you missed prints on the kettle or the coffee pot, no?"

Marley made some indignant reply that Asha was glad she couldn't hear. Jana flew down the stairs as if she had wings on her feet, incongruous in the baggy white suit. At the bottom, she stripped the mask and gloves off.

"We've already done these floors and the basement, but the owner has good coffee, I noticed. What you say we test it out? In the interests of science, heh?"

Asha didn't think Sue would mind, somehow, and the thought of the rich, strong liquid was a powerful temptation. "Do you happen to have any painkillers on you?"

Jana shook her head. "*Nie*, but I think Marley keeps some in the van. You put the kettle on, I'll look for them."

She returned with a battered packet of co-codamol, but when Asha held out her hand for them, she pulled them away. "What did the hospital give you when they discharged you?"

Asha licked her lips, eyes glued to the packet. "I think they had me on morphine, or whatever the equivalent is. Something in a drip, anyway. But they took that off during the night, and I've had nothing since. Give."

"That could have been liquid paracetamol. What time did the drip come out?"

"Are you my mother, now? I don't know what time. Hours ago!"

Jana handed them over and Asha popped two into her hand before the other woman could change her mind.

The coffee made a difference, too. It soaked through her like the morphine had, easing the tension that had been building up since she'd seen the empty driveway.

"So, what have you found? Any sign of violence outside?"

"There was a . . . what do you call it? A sciffle?"

"Scuffle."

"Yes. That. The gravel was disturbed, so I think she put up a fight. No blood, though."

That would have to be enough, for now. If he'd wanted her dead, he'd have killed her then and there. Or she. There was no certainty the attacker was male, although Sue's father's words suggested they probably were.

"How's the head now?"

"Sore. I'll live. Any idea what hit me?"

"I show you." She fished around inside the protective suit and emerged with a phone. "I took pictures before we sent it away." She swiped through to the one she wanted and handed the phone to Asha.

It took a moment to work out what she was seeing. It was a bronze bust of a clean-shaven man with a determined-looking mouth and short hair. He could have been a modern film actor if it hadn't been for the little plaque at the base that said "*Sir Isaac Newton*".

Jana was shaking with laughter. "You were felled by gravity, and by the man who discovered it at the same time! How good is that?"

The bust looked heavy. There was a ruler next to it for scale, and it was big. More than two feet tall. Asha touched the back of her head gingerly, realising that she'd been lucky. Her assailant might not have wanted to kill Sue, but he sure as hell hadn't had any reservations about killing a detective.

Jana's phone rang in her hand, and she squinted at the screen. "Ah, it's your boy wonder. Want that I tell him you're here?"

"No!" Better that Aaron thought she was still safely tucked up in a hospital bed.

"Okay. Your death sentence." She swiped to accept the call.

Asha closed her eyes, trying to listen, but Jana's voice seemed to be echoing like a bad phone line. Then one phrase cut through her stupor.

"Is the Hearn woman okay?"

Asha sat up too sharply and the room tilted. "They've found Sue?"

There was a squawk from the phone and Jana gave her a wry smile. "*Tak*, she's here. Maybe you come pick her up before she falls over, huh?" She ended the call. "So much for secrecy. He heard your voice, and he says he's on his way."

115

CHAPTER 21

"What the fuck do you mean, 'you lost her'?" King gripped the phone, knuckles white. "Why the hell did you take her in the first place?"

"Kerny panicked, sir. She was going towards the house, and he thought she'd seen him, so he hit her."

"Of course he did." That ape had less intelligence than a trained monkey. "*Did* she see him?"

"Don't know, but he thought he'd killed her, so he went and fetched the van and we shoved her in a crate. We were going to fetch the other one and bury them both over the border, but there was too much activity. Dog walkers and all. We thought it better to cut our losses and take the one we had, but then she escaped somehow."

Pulsing blood boomed in his ear as he fought to control his anger, to keep his voice calm. "What crate?"

"The one we used to bring the stuff in, you know? Antiques for your place. With extras."

"You used a crate that once had cocaine in it? What if they test her clothes? Fucking hell. You two aren't fit to be let out alone. Where did you lose her?"

"On the West Link," Aiken said stiffly. "At least, that's when I noticed the back door swinging open. By the time we got off the road and retraced our route, there was no sign of her. We did find the remains of the crate, though, and cleared those up off the road."

King closed his eyes. *Give me strength.* "Oh, well done." His mind raced. Bloody Hearn women. If he'd known just how much trouble that girl was going to be in the future, he'd have got rid of her back in the nineties.

And what the hell had happened to her mother? He ground his teeth in frustration at that thirty-year-old mystery. Monica Hearn's disappearance had been the beginning of the end for his protection schemes. Word got around that he'd killed a woman even when her family was willing to pay up, and suddenly businesses were folding all around him. People sold up rather than risk losing someone.

There were rules, a delicate balance between trust and fear. You pay up, no one gets hurt. As soon as that trust was lost, it became impossible to get it back. He'd long suspected that whoever took Monica Hearn had done it for that exact reason: to discredit him and undermine his reputation. And word seemed to have reached the powerful, too. He'd never intended to retire as a DCI.

Not that it had done him much damage in the long run, not with the other branch of his business. It was no bad thing for his dealers and direct customers to fear him. His clients had started to pay up pretty promptly after Monica Hearn disappeared, with fewer delays and excuses.

"Do you know where the Hearn woman is now?" he asked.

"Kerny's checking with the local hospitals, boss. I drove by her place, but there's Forensics crawling all over it."

"Tell me at least that you managed to search the house before Kernaghan panicked."

"You wouldn't believe that place. Like a fecking public library, bookshelves everywhere. I searched the desk and cabinets, and checked the shelves for anything that looked like a diary, but there was nothing. I was nearly finished when I heard the car arrive. If the old man left anything behind, it's not in there."

King let out a breath. He'd never trusted Michael Hearn's father not to go on investigating. There'd been something unsettling about him, some inner drive that might have led him to dig deeper, to try to find his daughter-in-law. But the threat to his granddaughter must have been enough to keep him in line after all.

"Do you know, I'm getting really fed up with those two detectives. I want to know how much they've discovered."

"Want us to try to find out?"

If only he'd still been on the force. He still had some contacts, people he could squeeze for information — after all, secrets were as good as hard cash when it came to calling in favours, even though blackmail was a dirty word these days. If people didn't want their actions used against them, they should control their impulses better. Like he did.

But Aiken, and Kernaghan even more so, were blunt instruments. Still, sometimes a blunt instrument is all you need.

"Yes. Give it a few days for the dust to settle, then grab them, find out what they know, then shut them up for good. If you manage it without any fanfare, there'll be a nice, fat sum appearing in your offshore accounts."

"Yes, sir. Leave it to us." The call ended.

It had all been going so well, that winter of '92. There'd been chaos across the province, with terrorist groups practically holding the government to ransom. Perfect conditions for an enterprising young copper to branch out and make a bit of money on the side. His career had been in the ascendency in the force, *and* he'd been making a mint on the side.

Then that Hearn woman had disappeared.

After that, his own career had stalled. He'd been in line for a promotion, but for some reason it hadn't happened. The chief superintendent in those days, a loud-mouthed man called Church, had promised to sponsor him, to act as a referee, but then, with no warning, he'd taken early retirement.

The next round of promotions had been blocked, and not even whispers in the right ears had solved the problem. It had been hinted that there were too many rumours attached to him, that people didn't want to work with him.

But Yvonne Patterson had moved steadily upwards, and that had really stung. By the time he was ready to throw in the towel and take the early retirement package being offered to long-serving officers, she was already well above him. And now she was chief superintendent. How the shit does rise to the surface.

He'd wondered, on occasion, if she might have had a hand in his fate, but every time he tried to imagine her as some Machiavellian character in the background, manipulating people, he just couldn't wrap his mind around it. She was too straightforward, a real time-serving career officer.

But *someone* had taken Monica Hearn. He stared out at the view across the North Channel towards Scotland. Lorraine was due back soon, but he had time to think before she swept in, smelling of expensive perfume and fresh air. Even the thought of her warmed him, made him smile. Then his jaw clenched. Nothing could be allowed to threaten his life here. Nothing. He'd worked hard for it, and he deserved it.

CHAPTER 22

The hospital room was warm, the sheets light on Sue's bruised body. The last few hours felt like a blur, with nurses and doctors and radiographers all taking their turn to examine her.

The faint commotion from outside was comforting in its way. Just knowing there were people out there, lots of people doing their best to keep her safe and make her well, was reassuring.

Because she felt far from well. The pain in her side that she'd thought had come from her climb turned out to have been a ragged wound caused by falling onto one of the long nails holding her coffin together.

The door swung open to allow a nurse in to do some routine observations. As it closed, she noticed a dark-uniformed figure sitting in a chair just outside the door. Did she merit a police guard? She couldn't decide if that was reassuring or worrying.

The first visitor she was aware of was Asha. She came in quietly and sat down next to the bed. Sue put out a hand and the detective grasped it.

"Oh, Sue. I am so sorry."

"Why? Unless you're the one who abducted me." She was surprised at her own stab at humour. "What happened to you? I heard a loud bang."

Asha smiled, but it was strained. "I was a victim of gravity. Someone dropped your bust of Sir Isaac Newton on my head, apparently."

"Oh."

"It's all right. Both Sir Isaac and I will go on to fight another day." She frowned and fiddled with a lock of hair. "Do you remember anything that happened to you, and are you up to talking about it yet?"

"I've been going over and over it in my head the whole time, but there are blanks."

"I know the feeling. Hopefully the memories will return."

"I'm not sure. I think I might have been knocked out at some point, because there's just a big empty space between standing at the door of my house and waking up in a coffin."

The detective's head shot up, and she winced. "A coffin?"

"Well. A wooden box not much bigger than a coffin, anyway. The lid was nailed down."

"Okay, I think we should get a record of this. Would you mind if I brought someone in to make notes? My own head still feels as if a blacksmith is using it as an anvil, and I doubt yours is any better."

"That's fine, but I don't know how much sense I'll make."

So, with the uniformed constable from the corridor drafted in to write everything down, Sue began to talk.

"You pushed my front door open, and I knew it should have been locked." She thought about it for a moment. "But you'd been the last one out, so I was wondering if you'd left it open by mistake. That's why I was getting out of the car. You gestured to me to stay put, so I sat down, but then I thought, *No, this is my house.* So I got out and went towards the door."

She shook her head, frustrated. "That's all I remember. I don't know if I went inside, or what I did."

"What do you remember next?"

"I woke up in total darkness and tried to sit up, but I was inside a box." She went on to describe everything that had happened. When she came to the part where she'd scaled the gate into the Millfield campus, she stumbled to a halt. All the desperation and defeat flooded back. She tried to speak, but the words wouldn't come.

"It's all right," Asha said. "Take a moment and have a sip of water. We have most of the story of what happened next from the woman who helped you. She refused to leave your side until she was certain you were safe, and she asked me to call her as soon as you were strong enough to see her."

Sue smiled at the memory of those doe-like brown eyes. "She was wonderful. She made me feel safe and I don't even know her name."

"She's been up here twice already today," the constable said, without looking up, "but I told her no visitors until you'd been interviewed."

"That will probably do for now. Constable, could you see if she's still out there and bring her in? If you feel strong enough, Sue?"

Sue nodded. "I'd like to see her."

As soon as the door closed behind the uniform, Asha bent low and whispered, "Do you remember what you told me in the car? About your mum's disappearance, and your father's suspicions?"

"Yes." Sue's heart sank. She wasn't sure she wanted reminding of that right now.

"Good. Let's keep it between you and me for now, shall we? I need to do some digging, and I don't want to set anyone's alarm bells jingling."

CHAPTER 23

It was late evening as she left the hospital for the second time that day, but still full daylight at this time of year. Asha breathed in the damp air — it must have been raining while she was inside — and stretched. The cool breeze cleared her mind a little, but she still felt fuzzy, slightly out of focus. Some of it was probably the concussion, but it felt as if a dark shadow loomed over her, watching and listening, waiting for her to make another wrong move.

How much weight should she attach to the words of a sick man with dementia? She had taken them seriously because of the way Sue had spoken. She clearly believed him, and she knew her father and his disease better than anyone.

If it was true, if there *was* someone from the PSNI involved, then certain facts became a little more understandable.

Like the reason Monica Hearn's disappearance had never been reported to the police. Or had it been reported and then squashed? She'd get Lonnie onto that. She was good at ferreting out things others preferred to remain hidden, and she could keep secrets, too.

And Aaron? If she brought him into the circle of secrecy, she'd be putting him at risk. He wasn't many years younger than her, but he had a fraction of her experience, and his enthusiasm could blind him to danger on occasion. Last year he'd had to be airlifted from the icy waters of Lough Neagh after an investigation brought him too close to a violent perp. They'd nearly lost him.

As if she'd called his name aloud, his tall, rangy figure appeared at the top of the steps to the car park. He waved and grinned.

"Thought you might want another lift."

She settled into the passenger seat of his Golf and closed her eyes. It smelled of aftershave and soap, and the faintest hint of spice.

"How's Michael Hearn?" she asked, as he folded himself into the driver's seat.

"Still not well enough to be interviewed. It's pretty touch-and-go for him right now so they're checking on him regularly. None of the staff have noticed anyone suspicious hanging around. Whoever took Sue doesn't seem to be interested in getting to him." There was a pause. "Where do you want to go?"

"Home," she said, without opening her eyes. "No rush."

He drove with a smooth efficiency that spoke of police advanced driving training. He was a fast driver, but he was the only driver with whom she could relax in the passenger seat.

"I didn't get the chance to tell you on the way over, but while you were playing catch with Isaac Newton, Lonnie managed to identify our skeleton," he said.

Asha opened her eyes and sat up.

"We think he's called William Lee, aged ten when he disappeared in January 1993. He was in care, and his foster parents assumed he'd run away. There was a misper report, but it had been misfiled. Lonnie used her usual magic to track it down."

"Who investigated, back in the day?" She thought she'd managed to keep her voice level, but Aaron shot her a suspicious look.

"Not sure. The signature was illegible. Is it important?"

"Probably not."

He nodded, distracted. "Will had a half-sister, and I've made an appointment to meet her tomorrow morning. She lives up in Larne."

"DNA."

"Exactly."

"Did you cancel that appointment with the school principal?"

"Yes. I said you'd be in touch to rearrange."

"I think I'll go first thing tomorrow if I can arrange it, now Sue is found. I've a feeling everything ties together. Whoever killed that little boy, William, may well have been responsible for Monica Hearn's disappearance, and if he or she has noticed us poking around now, that might be what triggered the attack on Sue." *And me.*

"Fair enough." He nudged the car into a lucky space right outside the tall Victorian building that housed her two-bedroom flat. The thought of all those dimly lit stairs up to the top floor suddenly felt overwhelming.

"I'm coming up with you," Aaron said in a voice that brooked no argument. "And I'm checking every corner and cupboard for signs of an intruder. Keys."

The flat was empty, except for the tropical fish that darted around the aquarium in the sitting room. She dropped a pinch of food into the tank and sank down onto the leather sofa. All strength had fled from her limbs.

She must have dozed, because Aaron woke her when he put a mug of tea on the table at her elbow. He'd put some chocolate digestives on a plate, too, and clutched a second steaming mug in his hand.

"You'd make someone a wonderful husband," she muttered.

"Is that a proposal?"

"Nope."

"Thought not. I'm staying the night, though. I don't think you should be left alone so soon after a head injury, so

I'm not taking no for an answer on this one. I can sleep on the sofa, once I've chiselled you off it."

"Okay." The relief surprised her. She hated fuss, and hated sharing her personal space with anyone, but the thought of big, sensible Aaron sleeping within call warmed her. "If you really want to sleep on the sofa, that's fine by me. It'll save me having to change the sheets on the spare bed."

He grinned at her, looking more boyish than ever. "Spare bed it is, then."

* * *

She awoke the next morning feeling refreshed, and with only a vague throbbing behind the eyes to remind her to take it easy. Aaron appeared while she was making coffee. He looked surprisingly fresh, too, considering. They sat companionably at her breakfast table and munched on toast and marmalade.

"Your car's still in Impound," he said.

"Thought it might be. If you give me a lift in, I can sign out a pool car if mine hasn't been released yet."

He gave her a considering look. "If we arrive together, there will be gossip. You know that, don't you?"

She leaned back in her chair. "Yep. The rumours will be rife, which means anyone who cares to eavesdrop will think you're staying with me, which might help prevent any unwelcome visitors. And . . ." She sighed. "Jana might just get the message, at last. Win-win, for me."

"Won't do my street cred any harm, either."

CHAPTER 24

They did get a few slanted looks as they walked across the car park together. Asha was tempted to give Aaron a peck on the cheek, but that might be stretching their working relationship a bit too far.

She stopped off at Aaron's desk to glance through the missing boy's file, making a mental note of the key facts. "You're not planning to bring that with you to show the sister, are you?"

"No. I took scans of all the pages, just in case I needed to show her a photo of her half-brother, but I thought I should leave the actual file here."

Asha glanced around, but there was nobody nearby to hear them. "Wise man. Don't tell anyone about the scans, either. They're a bit sensitive about files walking out of the building as it is."

* * *

Asha managed to sweet-talk the frosty school secretary into arranging a meeting for 10 a.m. She spent a bit of time on her report then went down to the garage and signed out a fairly new Skoda saloon. She settled into the comfortable seat, plugging in her phone so she'd have Apple Maps on the car's screen, typed in the address for St Peter's, and set off.

Monica wouldn't have had much of a commute into work. The primary school was about a mile or so away from Carrow Lodge, along quiet, tree-lined residential avenues. When she pulled up in the car park, she was disappointed to see a gleaming new building that couldn't be more than a few years old. She'd hoped to get a feel for the place where Monica worked, but there'd be nothing left of it in this pristine structure.

She put her "*Police Business*" notice on the dash and abandoned the car where it was blocking in the least number of staff vehicles.

As she stood outside the porch, a soft, persistent drizzle soaked through her light jacket. Finally, the door lock buzzed and she went through to be met by a plump, elderly woman who scowled at her. This must be the guardian at the gate who'd tried to repel her on the phone.

"Detective Inspector Harvey for my ten o'clock appointment with Miss Snow." It was already well after ten. She'd been kept waiting outside for at least five minutes in the rain, but she refused to let the woman see that she was irritated.

Maureen Snow was refreshingly young and very pretty, with dark chestnut hair in a ponytail. She must be good, to be a principal at such a young age.

"Inspector Harvey." She held out a slim hand with long, pale fingers and Asha shook it politely. "Please, have a seat. Ruby will bring us a tray, won't you, dear?"

The flash of resentment in the secretary's eyes told Asha plenty about the power struggle this principal must face every single day as she tried to rule staff members who were probably mostly old enough to be her mother.

As she'd feared, Maureen Snow could tell her little about the school as it had been thirty years ago.

"There are photo albums in the library," she offered. "And I can probably lay my hands on the records of staff and pupils from those days, but they'll need digging out of storage. Our retired caretaker is storing boxes and boxes of memorabilia in his garden shed, but I've no idea what he's kept." She smiled disarmingly. "I doubt if he's heard of GDPR, and my predecessor let him do pretty much anything he wanted. I know I'll need to do something about it soon, but for now it's doing no harm, so I leave him be. I'll give you his number and tell him you'll be contacting him, if you like."

"That would be great. I don't suppose any of your current staff would have been around in those days, would they?"

The door opened to admit the secretary, who was carrying a tray with two mugs of builder-strength tea and a plate of dry, plain biscuits.

"Miss Boyle here might have been working in the school then. What year did you start at St Peter's, Ruby?"

The tray rattled as it was set down. Ruby Boyle straightened, glaring from one to the other. "In 1981."

"Excellent. Perhaps Ruby can answer some of your questions in that case. I'll just go and phone Brendan to tell him you're coming, then I'll look for those albums." She left them alone.

Ruby crossed her arms over her chest, and Asha mentally sagged. Her head hurt too much for confrontation.

"Miss Boyle, do you have time to answer a couple of questions? I know how busy you must be, running a big place like this. I'm sure the phone never stops!" Was she laying it on too thick?

The older woman, however, smiled and sat down in the chair her superior had just vacated. "Indeed. This place will fall apart when I go. No one knows where everything is like I do."

"I'm so glad you're able to help me. Do you remember a Monica Hearn who used to teach here, back in the late eighties, early nineties?" She wasn't going to lead the witness to a date. Ruby needed to remember on her own.

The frown wasn't promising, then the chubby face cleared. "You mean Miss Stewart? I think Hearn might have been her married name, but a lot of teachers go by their maiden names. Saves them from weekend calls from unhappy parents who look them up in the directory."

Asha made a note. She should have thought of that.

"Can you remember when Miss Stewart left the school?"

The face opposite her creased in a smile. "I remember she left an unholy mess behind her. Costumes for the Christmas play not done, scenery half-painted and homework books never returned."

"She left suddenly, then?"

"Here one day, gone the next," Ruby said. "Extended sick leave, the husband said, but there was never a doctor's note. Left him for some other man, I reckon. He was no great shakes, always pale and thin and never met your eyes. I'd have kicked the dust from my heels and never looked back, if it was me." Another frown. "Why are you asking now, after all these years? Never saw any of your lot here when she went off."

"Oh, just sorting out a few details for another case. I'd like to track down Miss Stewart if I can, in case she can help us with some background." She was about to ask about Will, then the door opened and Maureen Snow came in with an armful of scrapbooks, which she placed on the low table in front of Asha.

"These are from the opening of the new school building. We had a display showing the old and new alongside each other. There are some photos from the time you're interested in."

Asha lifted the topmost book and it fell open to a posed picture of uniformed children in neat rows, the ones at the back no doubt standing on benches. At one end of the back row stood a teacher, one eye on her charges as she tried to smile at the camera. The legend at the bottom told her this was the Primary Seven class of 1995.

"What year did Miss Stewart teach?"

"P7," Ruby replied, with a sideways glance at the principal.

130

A few pages back, she found the photo for the P7 class in 1992. Miss Stewart was a slim woman in her late thirties or early forties wearing a calf-length skirt and a jacket with the padded shoulders and raised collar beloved of the eighties. Asha glanced at the rows of faces, then took a closer look at one of the boys sitting cross-legged at the front. There was something familiar about that face and those wary eyes. She'd need to check the file at the station.

* * *

Brendan O'Hare, the caretaker, walked with a Zimmer frame, but the button eyes in his sallow face were alive with intelligence.

"This way, Detective," he said. She followed him down the narrow hallway of the housing executive terraced house, through the tiny galley kitchen and out into the back yard.

"Garden shed" was too grand a name for the corrugated lean-to, and Asha's heart sank. No documents would have survived the first rainfall in that leaky, unstable structure. Still, she was here now.

Then he wrestled the door open and she saw the stacked plastic crates, all with lids clipped down and sealed with tape. Each one bore a label in neat, round writing.

"What year are you interested in?"

The records for staff and students for 1992 and 1993 were all in the same box. She lifted it onto the top of a pile, but he tapped her on the arm.

"Come on into the house. We can share a wee pot o' tay while you look."

"A cup o' tay is just what I need. Thank you."

Brendan's treasure trove was fairly random. There were bits of the children's artwork and writing, complete with drawing-pin holes where they'd been displayed in the school, as well as bits of music. More importantly to Asha, he'd kept some of the class registers, including the one for Miss Stewart's P7 class, with the dates and names neatly inscribed in her flowing script right up to 10 December 1992, after which date a variety of different hands seemed to have taken over from her. Supply teachers, Asha supposed.

She ran a finger down the names and stopped halfway down. *Lee, William*. His attendance was almost perfect until 18 December, when he was marked absent. He seemed to have remained absent for what was left of that term and into the next. In fact, after that date, there was no trace of him in the school records at all.

CHAPTER 25

Louise McCoubrey was an attractive, dark-haired woman in her mid-thirties with the same wary eyes as her half-brother. She looked confident in designer jeans and a branded top. Her hair, make-up and nails were immaculate, if understated, and she smiled when she opened the door to Aaron. He was on time, almost to the minute, for the appointment he'd made over the phone.

"Detective Constable Birch? Can I see your ID, please?" She took her time examining it. "Would you like to come in, or is this something I can answer on the doorstep?"

She was polite but businesslike, as if she hated to waste time, especially her own.

"I think it would be better if I came inside, if you don't mind," he said. "It won't take long, but I do need to ask you a couple of questions."

She raised one perfectly plucked eyebrow, then turned and led the way into her smart townhouse. It was one of a select number on a new development on the outskirts of Larne, designed to look like classical architecture but really just a respectable front for speedily built, wood-framed buildings with MDF floors.

The open-plan kitchen was crisp, clean and scarily tidy. Aaron was afraid to touch any of the shiny surfaces in case he left a handprint behind. Each stainless-steel chair at the dining table was set to the same precise distance and a bowl of freshly picked roses filled the air with scent. She didn't ask him to sit down.

"I'm afraid some of the questions I need to ask are of a personal nature," he began, and then regretted it. Now she'd think he wanted to know about her sex life. This was why Asha usually did the interviewing. Did Louise McCoubrey even know she was adopted? *Shit!* The room was too warm, and a dribble of sweat trickled down his neck.

"What do you know about your family history?" he asked, as a neutral introduction.

She looked surprised. "Not a lot. I was adopted as a baby, you see."

Thank God for that. "Yes. Do you know anything about your birth parents?"

She looked scandalised. "Why would I? John and Lily are my parents, as far as I'm concerned. Why would I want to track down some druggie who wasn't fit to raise a child, or some brood of yobbos—" Aaron hadn't heard that term in a while — "who run around in street gangs or whatever. They'd probably love to sponge off me if they discovered they had a sister with money. No thank you."

This wasn't going well. And the sun was glaring in through the French windows, making the room even hotter.

Better just get it over with before I embarrass myself and swoon from the heat.

"Your mother had another child before you. Your half-brother, by the name of William."

"Well, he can go fuck himself," she snapped, producing a packet of Gauloises cigarettes. Aaron recognised them because the Chief occasionally smoked them when she thought no one was watching.

"I'm afraid we think he might be dead, and that it wasn't an accident or suicide."

She spent too long lighting up, not looking at him. The flickering lighter flame cast her cheekbones into hard planes.

"We found human remains, and we think they might be your brother's, but the only way to be sure is—"

"A DNA sample from me," she said in a tight voice. "I watch TV and read books. I know what you're here for now, and the answer is no."

"Oh."

"Don't look so hurt. Puppy eyes don't work on me."

"It's just a cheek swab. It's not invasive or painful." He was trying to get a handle on why she was so determined.

"I know that. And I also know that once you have my DNA on your database, it'll be there for ever, whether I like it or not. If it turns up at some crime scene, I'll be flagged up in your system, someone will remember that my brother was murdered and I'll be listed as a person of interest. I know how these things work."

She'd been watching too much of the wrong sort of TV by the sound of it.

"That's simply not true," he said, mentally crossing his fingers in case he was wrong. Security of personal data was a hot topic in the popular media, but he was fairly sure he was right. "Retention of biometric data only applies when it's taken as evidence in a criminal prosecution, and there's no question of that in your case." He smiled. Asha told him over and again that his smile could melt granite.

Louise McCoubrey pulled out a chair. It squealed as she dragged the metal legs across the ceramic tiled floor. She sat down, and only then did Aaron notice the slight tremor in her hand. Comprehension dawned. She didn't want her DNA to be analysed because she was afraid it might already be on record somewhere. Which meant that Miss Snow White here might have drifted at some point in her past.

He changed tack. "I give you my word that any sample you provide will only be used to compare with DNA from the skeleton, and it won't go anywhere else. Not into a database, not anywhere." He met her gaze. *Just give me the damn*

sample, and if it matches, I can get a warrant for a formal one later.
"Do you trust me?"

She was taking a drag of her cigarette, and nearly choked on it. "Kid, I trust no one!" Then she blew out the smoke in a long stream from her nose. "But you can have your damn sample on two conditions. One." She held up a finger with a long acrylic nail. "Everything you said is true, and two—" a second finger — "you don't tell me if it was my brother or not. I don't need that sort of shit hanging over me."

"Deal. I just happen to have a kit here with me."

"Of course you do."

Back in his car with the precious swab safely tucked inside an evidence bag, clearly labelled for his attention only, he used the hands-free to call the Prof's extension in the forensic pathology lab.

"I have a favour to ask."

"Ask away, dear boy. If we can help you, we will."

"I think we've found a close familial relative of our victim, if we've identified him correctly. Am I right in thinking you can carry out DNA testing?"

"I can request DNA testing," Mark said warily. "But I don't do it myself."

"And can you keep the results contained in a single file, so they don't go onto any databases anywhere?"

"I suppose so. You do know what you're doing? I mean, you're not up to anything beyond the pale, are you?"

What did that even mean? "Nothing illegal, but the only way I could get this DNA was to promise it wouldn't get onto any databases. I don't like breaking my promises." Besides, there'd been a hard edge to Louise McCoubrey that made him wonder if she was still active in crime. Worth having a nosy into her affairs, once this was all over.

"All right. Send it over in a package and I'll have it run as a John Doe, as the Yanks say."

"Better make that a Jane Doe. I'll drop it off myself on my way to the station. What time will you be there until?"

* * *

136

The Prof's assistant was at the front desk, tapping away on a computer keyboard and humming tunelessly. He didn't look up as Aaron walked past but buzzed the swing doors just as he approached them, so he didn't need to even alter his stride. Smart lad, that.

Talbot was in one of the offices. His voice drifted down the corridor, dictating into a voice recorder, by the sound of it. Aaron followed the sound to a modern room with a couple of padded armchairs in front of a desk. The Prof looked up as he came in and gestured to the chairs without interrupting his dictation. It was all technical stuff that went over Aaron's head. He recognised the odd phrase that he'd seen in path reports before, but he closed his eyes and let the plummy English accent wash over him. It was like sitting through a Latin Mass, with the foreign words that he didn't understand but which had their own poetry. Except for the smell. Instead of incense, the Prof's office smelled faintly of formalin and cleaning chemicals.

He handed the plastic envelope over. "How long do these profiles take?"

"If I was processing this as an official forensic sample, which means it would be added to the database, I could have it back in a few hours. But the unofficial way will take one to three days. Are you sure you don't want me to put it through officially?"

Aaron sighed. "Of course I do, but I gave my word. This is, I hope, the half-sister of the boy under the greenhouse. She's pretty nervous about having her DNA on record."

"Interesting. Which side is she related to?"

"Maternal. Same mother, different father. Both were taken into care, but the girl was adopted as a baby, and the boy went into the foster system. She claims she has no knowledge of her birth family, but I wouldn't have classed her as a totally reliable witness. Sergeant Jacob is also searching through the database in case we happen to have any DNA on record for either parent. I'll get her to give you a call if she finds anything, will I?"

"That would be good. Being able to cross-check samples always helps in a court case. Let's hope the profiles prove a relationship so we can have a name for the poor lad at last. Now, dear boy, tell me what else is going on."

Asha had always said the Prof could be trusted, so he filled in Mark Talbot with everything they knew about the remains, the missing woman from the same period and now her daughter, abducted while Asha was nursing a concussion in hospital.

"Oh, God. Poor Sue."

Shit. He'd forgotten they knew each other.

"She's doing okay, by all accounts," Aaron said uncomfortably. "They're letting her out today or tomorrow."

"Do you know what the attacker was doing in the house?"

"Searching the study, apparently. It belonged to Sue's grandfather, William Hearn. Asha was about to search it when Sue's father took ill, and she never got back to it. I guess she must have interrupted him."

"I wonder if he found what he was looking for."

"Hopefully not. SOCO have packaged up every piece of paper, diary and file they could find and sent them over to be checked. The place is like a public library, though, so they left all the books there. The evidence locker wouldn't have room for all those books, anyway. Now a copper's been attacked, the Chief is baying for blood. I'm a bit worried Asha and I'll be taken off the case and it'll be handed over to someone more senior, especially now she's been injured in action."

Talbot nodded, sympathetic. He'd probably had interesting cases taken off him in the past, too. Forensic pathology had a lot in common with the force in many ways, with its hierarchical structure.

"Then you'd better make yourselves indispensable, hadn't you?"

Aaron left the mortuary and headed to the station, passing the impounded vehicle compound on his way. Asha's car looked sad and lonely. Hopefully SOCO would have the contents of the study ready to examine by now. He needed to check it pronto, before the high-ups removed him from the case. If they were to break this wide open, his gut told him, the clues would be buried in the past, and from what Asha had said, the old man's study was like a time capsule.

He logged in to his computer and checked if the evidence had been processed. Half of it had, which meant Jana or Marley might still be down there. If he was quick, he could catch them before they left.

Marley was just signing off on the last sack of paperwork.

"Hi, Marley. Did you find anything useful in there?"

The older man shrugged and tried to push past Aaron towards the exit. He wasn't known for his enthusiasm, but this was borderline rude. Aaron didn't move. "Come on. We're on the same team. Give me a clue."

A big sigh, blown out between nicotine-stained teeth. "Not a lot. Someone knew what they were about. Surfaces wiped clean." He stared into Aaron's face without blinking. Looked as if that was all he was getting.

"Okay. Thanks. I'll read the report."

Marley gave him a lopsided smile that was more of a grimace and pushed on past. Aaron let him go.

Up in the communal office, he sat down, fingers tapping on the desk. His eyes settled on the mouse, which was sitting where most computer mice sat, to the right of the keyboard. Aaron was left-handed.

He moved it to where it belonged and woke up his computer. The login screen appeared as normal. Anyone using his machine would have put their own username and password in, so he clicked in the empty upper box.

Magic. The dropdown menu listed the last few usernames, and his own was not at the top of the list. Instead, the top name was G. A. Aiken. The initials had always caused amusement among the Catholic officers because they spelled GAA, the Nationalist sports league, and Aiken was known to march with bowler hat, sword and sash every season.

So, the local shit-stirrer was trying to nose around his case, was he? Not that he'd have got anything that way

— trust Aiken to not understand computers. The only important evidence was . . .

He opened the bottom drawer. The slim file for the missing boy had been sitting on top. Thank God. It was still there.

He lifted it out and opened it, knowing before his eyes had time to focus that it was even slimmer than it had been.

The statements from the foster family were missing.

CHAPTER 26

Asha trudged along the corridor towards the office Aaron shared with a couple of other DCs and some of the uniforms. She stuck her head around the door, but his chair was empty. The monitor was awake and displaying the PSNI logo. His car was in the car park, so she knew he was in the building somewhere, and he couldn't be far away.

She tracked him down by ear, following the muffled sound of his voice until she opened the door to Lonnie's tiny office, where he was having a rant.

"It's outrageous," he was saying. "They're a pair of dinosaurs and they should have been pensioned off years ago, but this is the last straw!"

"What is?" she asked as she closed the door behind herself and leaned against it. "And I suggest you keep your voice down before someone comes along to listen in."

Aaron flapped a cardboard folder at her. "I left the file for William Lee's disappearance in my desk drawer, and someone's been at it while I was out. And they've tried to access my computer files, except they're as thick as pig shit so they got nothing there, luckily."

"You know who it is?"

"Yeah. Aiken. But he was too stupid to realise it's just a terminal, so if he accesses it using his login, all he'll get is his own files."

Asha sat down more abruptly than she meant to, scattering a pile of paperwork from the corner of Lonnie's desk. "What's missing from the file?"

"Statements from the foster parents, Gillian and Kevin McCarron."

"Shit. Tell me we at least still have the front page with the boy's photo?"

Aaron gave a reluctant smile. "We've more than that. Don't forget I scanned all the pages, so we still have copies of everything, just not the originals."

"Clever boy," Lonnie said, as if he was a poodle who'd just managed to stand on its hind legs.

Asha fished in her bag and pulled out the class photo. "Show me that photo, Aaron. I need to see if this is the same boy."

Aaron tugged the photo free from its paperclip and handed it over, coming to look over her shoulder as she compared the two.

It was the same boy, she was sure of it. So, there was a link between their skeleton and their missing person, right there. William Lee had been in Monica Hearn's class at St Peter's.

"We need that DNA, Aaron. How long will it take?"

He didn't quite meet her eye. "Two or three days, the Prof says."

"Really? I thought we could get results much faster these days?"

"Yes, we can, but I had to ask him to do it unofficially. That takes a bit longer."

Give me strength. "Why does Mark need to run this unofficially, exactly?"

He swallowed. "Because I promised Louise McCoubrey I'd keep it off any official databases." His eyes darted to meet hers, then away again. "Honestly, boss, it was the only way I was going to get it at all."

"Okay. Leave it with me. That way, you have plausible deniability."

"If she ever found out—"

"She won't."

Asha went to her own office and checked her computer. There was no evidence anyone had been tampering with it, and her desk and files seemed just as she'd left them, although it felt like weeks ago. She sank into her chair and lifted the phone to her ear.

Partway through dialling the Prof's number, her tired brain registered a soft extra click in the receiver. She paused, considering. First Aaron's computer, then statements missing and now a potential listener on her office landline?

The receiver landed in its cradle with more of a clatter than she'd intended. Hopefully whoever had been listening had had their eardrums assaulted. The thought made her smile, then the repercussions crashed over her. If they were listening to the landline, her mobile could be unsafe, too, and her email. She had to assume Sue's father had been right in what he'd said. Someone who'd been an ordinary policeman thirty years ago might be quite influential by now, if they were still in the force. If they were ordering phone taps on fellow officers, they could be very high up indeed.

She dragged herself down to the car park. Nothing for it but a face-to-face chat with the Prof. A glance at her watch showed it was after six in the evening. Would he even be there?

A quick drive-by, she promised herself. *If his car's not there, I'll go straight home and to bed. If it is, I'll pop in.*

The Prof's beaten-up Peugeot estate was covered in so many rust spots it looked as if the army had been using it for target practice. Asha pulled up next to it, but not too close. From the look of it, Mark wasn't too careful opening doors, and she couldn't face taunts about women drivers if she returned to the carpool with a dented door.

She rang the bell and waited. There was no one in view inside, and the entrance hall was in darkness. On the third attempt, the door buzzed open and she walked through, only to be baffled by the next automatic doors, which were also closed tight. As she approached them, hand raised to buzz, they swung open.

"Down here!" Mark's voice rang out. "I'm in the middle of something, but come on down."

He was gloved, masked and gowned, and in the process of weighing some dark-coloured internal organ using stainless-steel scales. There was no one else there that she could see.

"On your own tonight?"

He gave her a quizzical look. "Yussuf has gone over to London for a funeral. Some aunt, or maybe a cousin he calls Auntie. I couldn't quite follow his complicated family tree." He lifted the organ from the scales and dropped it into a container, where it landed with a dull plop. "So yes, it's just you and me."

Asha looked around at the recording equipment and cameras on the bench against the wall. "Aaron dropped a sample off with you earlier. I'm here to ask you to move it up the list for priority. I don't care if it's official or unofficial, but I need those results as soon as possible."

He shuffled his feet, avoiding her eye. "I may have sneaked some of the sample in as part of a priority case. It will be listed as unlabelled, but they'll still stick it on the report, which should be back any time now, and I'll know which one it is." He glanced in the direction of his office. "I kept the rest in case you wanted it running officially at any stage for actual evidence."

"Prof, you're the best," Asha said. "I think I owe you a drink, don't you?"

One patrician eyebrow rose up in polite surprise. "Well, well. A date, or work?"

She smiled. Mark Talbot was far older than her, but he was a good-looking man. She imagined the women probably fell at his feet in droves, especially when they heard his Shakespearian tones. "Work, I'm afraid."

He glanced across at the body on the table, the one Asha had been studiously avoiding looking at. "Give me half an hour? The report should be back by then and it'll give me the chance to finish up. Why don't you leave the car here and walk up to the Fort?" He looked at his watch. "At this time, you should be able to get us a snug to ourselves, and you can get a head start on the drinks."

That sounded like a plan. She left the building, pausing to fill her lungs with good, clean, Belfast traffic fumes from the West Link. Better than the heavy scent of death that had seeped into her inside the mortuary. She sent a WhatsApp message to Aaron, on the basis that it was less likely to be intercepted, then she took a moment to doubt her own sanity. This wasn't some Le Carré spy novel. There wouldn't really be people listening in on her phone calls. She was just being paranoid, that was all.

Mark joined her in less than thirty minutes. The barman saw him coming and started pouring the Guinness as soon as the tall figure pushed open the door. By the time his pint had been carefully poured, Aaron had messaged her to say he was on his way, too.

They sat in comfortable silence, sipping their drinks until Aaron arrived and earned himself scorn from the barman by ordering a half of "lager, any lager, whatever's on offer".

As Aaron edged into the seat next to Mark, Asha leaned across and pulled the snug door closed, cocooning them within four walls of rich, red wooden panelling. She took the opportunity to check the booths to either side while she was standing, but they were alone.

"Now," Mark said quietly, "what's all the mystery about?"

Asha told them, beginning with the coincidence of dates for Monica Hearn and William Lee's disappearances and ending with the click on her phone line.

"Perhaps it's a good thing we kept that DNA sample out of the system," Mark said at last. "This way, it'll be harder for anyone to find the results."

"About that . . ." Asha said.

He drew a piece of paper out of his inside pocket. "This came through on the fax machine just before I left."

"You still use a fax?" Aaron asked.

"They have their uses."

"And?" Asha wanted to snatch it from his hand to confirm her own certainty.

He held it out of her reach, smirking. "We have a match. There is sufficient DNA in common for a half-sibling or cousin relationship."

Asha blinked. "So he could, in theory, be Louise's cousin, not her half-brother?"

"In theory, but Sergeant Jacob struck lucky. Will's natural father was forever in and out of prison, serving sentences for affray, criminal damage and a few other drinking-related charges. His DNA was on file from a crime scene in 1996, shortly before he died." Dramatic pause. Asha resisted the urge to deliver a sharp kick to the Prof's shin under the table. "And that's also a match."

CHAPTER 27

"So, what do we have?" Aaron asked. They'd left Mark sipping another pint of the black stuff and were sitting in Aaron's Golf.

"We have an identity for our child skeleton, a date at which he disappeared from the school records — which, by the way, is more than three weeks before he was reported missing by his foster parents." Asha counted off the points on her fingers as she spoke. "We have a link between our little boy and Sue's missing mother. And we have someone in the station trying to confuse us at best and to scupper our investigation at worst."

"*Trying to kill us* at worst." He gave her a sideways glance. "Someone wasn't just attempting to scupper an investigation when they dropped that statue on your head."

She continued thinking aloud. "We need to know more about the foster parents. Were there any other kids living there who might have witnessed anything? And we have Sue's father's story of police involvement when Monica went missing, which could explain why there was no misper report for her."

"We still have all the papers from William Hearn's study to go through," Aaron said. "Perhaps there'll be something in there to explain the background to Monica's disappearance at least."

"What, like a diary saying something along the lines of, 'Today Chief Superintendent Smith abducted Monica. I believe he must have killed her'?"

Aaron's mouth twisted into a wry grin. "Not exactly. But perhaps there might be some reference to Michael Hearn's problems. Didn't you say Sue thought he was a 'druggie', to use her words?"

"That might give someone reason to put the frighteners on him, especially if he owed big money, but where's the link to our fictional policeman? And was it a uniform, a detective, or someone more senior? Or just a figment of the poor man's dementia-fuelled imagination?"

"Probably the latter," he said glumly.

"You can go through William Hearn's papers in the morning. I'll put Lonnie onto tracking down the foster parents and any foster siblings, and I'll have a go at Michael Hearn, if he's well enough to answer questions. If not, I'll have to dig a bit deeper with Sue."

"And what about you?" he asked. Asha blinked at him. Hadn't he been listening to what she was saying? Then she registered the concern in his face.

"I'll be fine. You can't spend another night sleeping in your clothes. If you could drop me off at home on your way, I'd appreciate it. I've left my pool car at the hospital so I'll get a taxi to work tomorrow morning."

"Okay. I'm heading to the station after I drop you home. Need to make a start on those papers before Aiken or some other bugger walks off with them from the evidence room. At least I can take a quick skim through them, so I know what I'm dealing with. Give me your car keys, and I'll send a uniform out to drive it to your place. I'll tell them to stick the keys through the letterbox."

"I really should be going to the station, too, but—"

"Doctor's orders." He grinned and started the engine. "Rest while you can and come back tomorrow with your brain firing on all cylinders, yeah?"

"Yeah."

She found it oddly comforting that he still insisted on checking the place out before he'd let her inside. Aaron wasn't her type, though — not that she didn't find him attractive, but he was more of a wee brother than a lover, and besides, relationships between serving officers, common as they were, often ended in disaster.

After he'd left, she had a bath, then changed into her pyjamas, made herself a mug of hot chocolate and broke out the luxury biscuits someone had given her. She didn't look at the use-by date. If she didn't know, they couldn't kill her, right? The first bite was a bit soft, but they tasted okay, and she helped herself to three more before putting a clip on the wrapper.

She went to bed early, certain she wouldn't be able to sleep, but the next thing she was aware of was her mobile vibrating itself off the wooden chest of drawers next to her bed and onto the floor.

It was as dark as it ever got in central Belfast, where streetlights turned the night orange, but the damn thing had dropped down between the bed and the bedside cabinet and was vibrating across the floorboards. She hung over the edge of the mattress, heart thumping and head spinning as she fumbled for it under the bed.

Just as her fingers closed on it, the doorbell rang — an intrusive, sustained buzz.

A glance at the phone screen showed Aaron's personal mobile. Before she could accept the call, he rang off.

She slid out of bed, skin pimpling at the sudden chill, and headed towards the hall, where the handset for the door mechanism was mounted on the wall. As she stumbled towards it, she called Aaron back. He answered immediately.

"Ash! Where are you?"

"I was in bed, asleep. Where else did you think I'd be?"

"Are you alone?"

Her hand hovered over the handset for the door lock, and she paused, despite the insistent alarm buzzing. "Yes, but there's someone at the door. Is it you?"

149

"Don't open it!" he snapped, sounding so brittle she thought he might explode. "Can you look out of your window and see the door? Don't let them see you."

Asha rushed through to her living room, cursing as she stubbed her toe on the computer desk on the way.

The doorbell stopped.

She ran the last few steps and peered out into the misty, orange night. There was a figure down there, someone bundled up in a dark coat with a shapeless hat upon its head.

"Ash! Can you see anything?"

The figure turned away, without looking up. They moved with a long, masculine stride, disappearing around the hedge that bordered the tiny shared front yard. Soon they were lost in the night, heading towards the Malone Road.

"They've gone, whoever they are. What's going on?"

"I'm nearly at your place. Don't answer the door to anyone until I get there."

"Okay. I'll watch out for you."

"No!" he snapped. "Stay away from the window. I'll let you know when I'm there."

CHAPTER 28

Aaron was there in what felt like moments. Asha was standing in the middle of the front room when she saw the blue lights reflecting on the front of the building opposite hers, and sickness crept over her. If he'd arrived in a squad car, something awful must have happened.

She answered her phone as soon as he rang.

"You can open the door now," he said, sounding older than his years.

He was accompanied by two uniformed officers, both grim-faced. One was the same newly promoted probationer she'd met at Sue's house the day they went to dig up her garden. The other she didn't know. Which was odd, because she thought she knew all the officers working out of her station by name as well as sight. It was a skill she prided herself on.

"I can put the kettle on," she said, vaguely.

Aaron shook his head. "Officer Philips can do it." He turned to the unfamiliar officer. "She'll take a strong, sweet, milky coffee from the machine. If you can't work out how to use it, shout for help."

The uniformed officer nodded and made his way towards the kitchen at the back of the house. A few minutes later, she heard the beep of the coffee machine coming to life

151

and realised that her mouth was so dry, she probably couldn't swallow if she wanted to.

"Okay. What's going on?"

"Did you see who was at your door?" Aaron asked, ignoring her question.

"Not really. It was dark. Male, I'd guess. Bulky, dark overcoat and dark hat. Not a cap or a beanie — one with a brim. He went towards the university."

"SOCO are on the way, but I doubt he'll have left any prints behind."

"Aaron! What. Is. Going. On?"

He let out a deep breath and gestured towards the sofa. They all sat down, the young PC in one armchair and Aaron in the other.

"You know I said I'd send someone to collect your car?"

"Yes," she said warily.

"One of the mechanics went to get it. He hit the remote from a good distance away, then his shoelace came undone and he bent to fasten it. Probably saved his life. There was some sort of incendiary device. We think it must have been rigged to go off a few seconds after the vehicle was unlocked. We won't know for sure until it's been examined, but there's not much car left, and the hospital aren't very happy, either."

A thick cloud descended on her, deadening all sound and smothering rational thought. She was vaguely aware of Aaron taking her hand and rubbing it clumsily, then someone pushed a steaming mug into her free hand and her fingers closed around it in reflex. The first scalding sip brought tears to her eyes. Asha inhaled the rich steam and took another long sip. Neurones fizzed to life, pushing the paralysing fear away. Anger rushed in to fill the vacuum.

"Right," she said, straightening up. She became aware that she was still in pyjamas, the top gaping open to reveal more than she'd ever dream of showing. Aaron hadn't even glanced in that direction. A flash of amusement helped her recover her balance. "First, there'll be CCTV in that area, at least on the approach roads to the hospital. I'm pretty sure

I saw a camera in the mortuary reception area that might have shown part of the car. Constable McAvoy, you can see to that."

McAvoy looked like a rabbit caught in the headlights, but if the killer of William Lee and possibly Monica Hearn was starting to hunt down detectives, they'd need every officer they could get. Besides, it'd be good for her to take some responsibility.

"Philips? Why don't I know you?"

"Seconded from Woodbourne, ma'am."

She wondered who had seconded him and why. Was he a spy for her influential nemesis, or would it be an advantage to have someone from another team? Whichever, if she kept him busy enough, he couldn't spy on her. What could she give him to do that would be useful without giving away her suspicions of police involvement in all this?

"How long will we have you for?"

A glint of surprise, followed by a smile. "If you have a job for me, I can probably make some excuse for staying on for a bit, ma'am."

She turned to Aaron. "Any news on the mechanic? Was he injured?"

"He's not too bad. He had a check-up by a passing doctor who was going off duty, but he got away almost scot-free. Bit of a cut where some shrapnel caught him on the hand, but he seems none the worse for his close shave."

Some of the acid burning her from the inside out evaporated. One less on her conscience.

"Okay, Philips. If you can hang around for a bit, I'd like you to have a chat with the mechanic. He's one of our own, and someone nearly killed him. I want to know why. I can't just leap to the conclusion that I was the target, so we need to make sure he doesn't have any enemies lurking. Check for any links to sectarian organisations . . ." She raised a hand to still his objection that the man would have had a thorough background check before being employed by the PSNI. "It'll be easier for you to get chatting to him — ask him about his

153

family, you know the sort of thing. Any hint of unsavoury connections in any sphere, I want to know."

Philips nodded, frowning. Perhaps he thought he was being given a dead-end job to test him, but it really wouldn't do to leap to conclusions, and the questions needed to be asked by someone. He left, shooing McAvoy in front of him. Asha waited until the door at the bottom of the stairs closed with its customary thump before speaking.

"Aaron, you need to secure the evidence from William Hearn's office as a matter of urgency. I'll liaise with SOCO."

"Already done. That's what I went back to the station for last night, remember? I signed out the evidence and have it safe."

"Where?"

"With Lonnie." Lonnie, whose desk was piled high with files and boxes of evidence dating back decades. No flat surface was safe in her little cubicle, yet she could lay her hands on anything in there at a moment's notice. Plus, the woman never seemed to sleep.

"Good thinking. In that case, you can come with me to the scene. Let's go hunting."

"Maybe put some clothes on first?" he said. "Just a suggestion."

She stalked out of the front room and into her bedroom, letting the door slam behind her. Yesterday's clothes were slung over her chair. She lifted the blouse, then caught a whiff of BO and threw it in the wash basket. A shower would help clear her mind, but walking down the corridor to the bathroom under Aaron's sardonic eye was unthinkable, especially after her dramatic exit.

She squirted deodorant under her arms, then found an older blouse that she rarely wore and slipped it on with yesterday's suit trousers. The jacket was fine, and putting it on felt like donning armour. A quick tidy of her hair, tying it up in a half-ponytail, and she was ready to take on the world.

The clinking of mugs helped her locate Aaron in the kitchen, where he was putting away the mugs he'd washed up. He looked up at her and smiled, but there were lines of worry around his eyes, too.

They took his Golf across to the hospital, Aaron driving in silence. SOCO were still working their way through the ashes and twisted metal that had once been quite a nice car. She was lucky, perhaps, that it had been a pool car and not her own.

CHAPTER 29

The doctors hummed and conferred over scans, but Sue had suffered surprisingly few injuries, considering what she'd been through. The wounds in her side had been sutured, and she'd been given a hefty dose of pain relief and antibiotics. After the morning ward round, they took her off the drip and told her she'd probably get home that day.

Home. She sighed. Would she ever feel safe there again? It had been bad enough when her mum disappeared, but she'd had Grandfather, who'd seemed indestructible to a teenage girl, and even her dad, lost in grief and self-recrimination as he had been, had been some comfort.

Now she recognised that what she'd taken for plain worry had probably been guilt on his part, and it probably explained why relations between Michael and William Hearn had been strained from that time until the old man died. What the hell had he been up to that caused her mum to disappear? She'd considered sectarianism but rejected it. Her family had no connections with either side, no police in their family tree, no military, no religion to speak of. Monica wouldn't have been a likely target for either Nationalist or Loyalist paramilitary abduction. There was always the chance of mistaken identity, of course, but she ruled it out for now.

She'd spent too many years trying to soothe her father, reassuring him, tiptoeing around the subject of her mum's disappearance. All that wasted time, and now it might be too late.

Damn.

When they discharged her, she dressed in the clothes she'd been wearing when she rolled in the gutter, escaping from the van. She refused to examine herself in the mirror before she left the comfortable room, but the expression on the face of the trainee physio at the nurses' station told her what she'd already guessed: she must look like a vagrant.

Her protection had changed. The officer outside was a mature woman with unlikely blonde hair and a face that was all hard planes and lines. As Sue left her room, the woman rose to her feet as if she was about to stop her leaving.

"I've been discharged," she said, wondering why she felt the need to explain herself, "but I'm not leaving the hospital yet. I'm going to see my dad."

The officer gave a sharp nod. "I've instructions to accompany you," she said in a flat voice.

"Okay, but I'll need to be alone with him in his room. He's had a stroke, and there are things we need to talk about, in case he doesn't recover." Her conscience gave a slight twinge at the half-truth.

Another nod. The officer followed a couple of paces behind her all the way through the hospital. Heads turned to follow them, and warmth spread up her neck into her cheeks. She must look like a down-at-heel prisoner.

"Sue?"

Shit. She knew that voice. Orla had been a secretary when she worked in the morgue, an incurable gossip. She was tempted, for a moment, to pretend she hadn't heard, to walk on with her back ramrod straight.

"It *is* you! Sue Hearn. Whatever has happened?"

She stopped and turned, trying to plaster a smile on to her stiff face. "Hello, Orla. What are you doing here?" Attack is the best form of defence — at least, that was what Grandfather always said.

The other woman was staring at her avidly, her eyes scanning the state of Sue's clothes and the dried blood at her waist. "I work here, remember? Are you all right? Can I do anything to help?" The unspoken words hung in the air. *Do you need money?*

"No, but thank you." *Now, piss off.*

Then the police constable surprised her.

"Ms Hearn requires some peace and quiet, if you don't mind. She's been through a lot."

Wow. There must be a heart beneath that flat chest after all. The expressions that raced across Orla's face almost made her laugh.

"Oh. I see." Her eyes darted to Sue's face, and an ugly blush darkened her cheeks. "I'm sorry, Sue. I didn't know."

And nor will you, if I have anything to do with it.

The stroke ward, in the older part of the hospital, was a place of hushed voices and grief. Her father was in a side room, but it wasn't as well appointed as the one she'd just vacated. The officer gave her a tight smile, which Sue now looked on more kindly, and went off to chat at the nurses' station, which was just outside his room.

Her father was sleeping, his breathing stertorous, too loud for the amount of rise his chest was managing. The door closed behind her, cutting off the hushed voices in the main ward. Tears pricked the backs of her eyelids. He looked so peaceful, lying there in the faded striped pyjamas he'd worn on admission — she really must go home, if only to fetch him some clean nightwear — with his grey hair lank and greasy.

She went over to the bed and sat carefully down, so as not to wake him. Now she was here, she had no idea how to ask the questions that had burned in her mind all those years ago and were now making themselves hard to ignore all over again.

She took the thin fingers in hers and stroked them with a thumb. "Dad, I need to know. If I don't ask you now, I might never know. What happened to Mum?" The last word came out as a choking gulp. His hand lay limp in hers, no sign that he'd heard.

"I love you, Dad. I'll always love you, even if you've done something awful, but this . . . this not knowing, it's ripping me apart. I have to know if she's dead."

His breathing had quietened, but there was no other sign that he might have heard her. Perhaps she should ask one of the nurses if he was likely to wake up. But here, in this quiet, peaceful room that smelled of antiseptic and surgical spirit, she found her energy had deserted her. The temptation to lie down next to him, as she had when she was a little girl, feeling the warmth of him as he wrapped her in his arms, was overwhelming.

She shuffled over, moving his arm so it passed around her neck, then gently bent it at the elbow so it came over her shoulder and chest, as if he was hugging her. Hidden beneath the hospital smells was the scent of Dad, a dry muskiness that was uniquely his. Tears sheeted down her cheeks, making wet patches on the pristine white sheets.

All these years, since she left her job to care for him, she'd only seen him as a burden, a responsibility. Why hadn't she hugged him more often when she'd had the chance?

"Monica." The arm around her tightened as the words washed over her.

"No, Dad. It's me. Sue." She nestled in a little deeper, so she could hear the faint, rapid beating of his heart.

"He took Monica, because I couldn't pay. The boy . . ." His voice faded into a mumble.

"Is she dead?"

"I don't know." It came out as a wail, and Sue stiffened, sure it would bring a nurse running, or even the policewoman from outside. "He took her, and I didn't even get to say goodbye."

"Who took her, Dad?" It was as if she was dreaming the scene, seeing it all at one step removed. She felt calm, as if it was an academic question, and the answer didn't matter.

"He was a peeler."

"Did he wear a uniform?"

"Big man in an overcoat. Big shoulders. Eyes that . . ." His chest rose and fell, and Sue's arm rose with it. "Dead eyes. Like a shark."

"Did he have a name?"

"'No names, no pack-drills.' That's what he'd say."

That sounded like a military saying. It had a familiar ring, as if she'd heard it somewhere before.

"If he wasn't in uniform, how did you know he was a peeler?"

"Got driven around by a young fella in uniform. Wee hard man with red hair and a head like a bullet. Nasty piece of work."

"What about the boy?"

But there was no reply this time. His chest fell, then didn't rise. He made a strange choking noise, and she sat up. Too fast. The room spun around her. She dropped her feet to the floor, clinging to the side of the bed for balance. His eyes were half-closed, mouth fallen open. The electronic display showed lines of different colours and beeped randomly, but she had no idea what any of it meant. She'd spent her working years with corpses, or bits of corpses, not the living.

There was a remote with a wire attached. A big orange button had a stylised image of a nurse on it, so she pressed it. An alarm began to beep and the remote flashed orange.

The door opened and a nurse pushed past her. She checked the machine, raised his eyelid and shone a torch in, then ran to the door and shouted for help. Everything became a blur of efficient, professional voices and running feet. Someone wheeled a trolley in, and she lost sight of her father as more and more people crowded around his bed.

She backed away until her shoulders hit the wall. No one had told her to leave, so she stayed, frozen. There was no emotion. No sadness, no hope, no relief. It was as if she was an outsider with nothing invested in the outcome of the battle going on a few feet away.

Then a ripple of change went through the team, like a deep breath. A male voice said, very clearly, "Time of death, 10.43 a.m.," and it was over.

Her fists were clenched tight. Little pinpricks of pain where her nails had dug into her palms were the only things she could feel.

One of the nurses turned and saw her standing there.

"Are you his daughter?"

Sue nodded. Her mouth was too dry to speak.

"I'm so sorry," the nurse said. The words were glib, something she repeated often in this ward where people's lives hung by a thread, but the sympathy in her eyes was sincere. What must it be like, to nurse patients and then watch them die, over and over again?

"Thank you," she managed. She worked some moisture into her mouth. "What happens now?"

The nurse tilted her head. "Could you possibly wait outside for a few minutes? Then you can come back in and spend a bit of time with him. It helps, sometimes. After that, and only when you're ready, there'll be paperwork to deal with. We'll help you with that, so don't be worrying, now."

Sue went out into the hubbub of the main ward. The constable rose to her feet, her face as inscrutable as always, and gestured to the chair she'd been sitting in. Sue sank down into it and closed her eyes.

CHAPTER 30

Asha didn't know the SOCO team at the hospital. What with skeletons, abductions, burglaries and now a bomb under her car, she must be responsible for most of their work these days. She stood with Aaron at the blue tape, watching for a while before someone noticed them.

The uniform in charge of signing people in and out of the scene eyed them warily but he allowed them through once they'd shown their ID. His was an unfamiliar face, too. Where were they digging up these guys from, and why weren't people from her team in charge?

The answer was obvious. A police officer's life had been threatened, and that meant that everything about the investigation had to be able to stand up to scrutiny.

Nowhere did it say that she had to like it, though.

The all-male SOCO team worked away in near-silence, teasing through the wreckage of what was barely recognisable as a car. Everything loose was bagged and labelled, and they looked smoothly efficient. She'd still rather have had Jana and Marley with their grumbling and inappropriate comments.

When it became obvious that no one was going to acknowledge their presence, she cleared her throat. "Found anything?"

Without looking up, the nearest white-suited figure spoke in a gruff voice. "We won't know until we have everything catalogued, ma'am. For now, we're just recording and labelling."

Well. That was her told.

"Come on," she said to Aaron. "We'll learn nothing here. Let's go to the station."

He drove steadily, deep in thought, and Asha was glad of the silence. The smell of burnt upholstery and tortured metal lingered in her nose. It probably wouldn't have smelled much different if it was laced with burnt human. A touch of cooked meat, perhaps? She'd never been called to a fire where lives had been lost, so she could only imagine the stench.

When they drove under the barrier into the compound, and Aaron had nudged the Golf into a free space, she slipped out of the car and set off for the building at a smart pace. He caught up with her as she waited for the desk sergeant to buzz them in, eyes impatiently on the door. Good. If he'd given her sympathy at that moment, she'd have burst into tears. That was a sign of weakness she didn't want anyone to see from her, not even Aaron.

Apart from the desk sergeant, who barely acknowledged them as they passed, they met no one on their way up to Lonnie's little cubicle. A thin line of pale light shone out beneath the door.

The stocky little woman was sitting exactly where she always seemed to be, her nose inches from the old-fashioned CRT monitor she refused to exchange for a flatscreen. She didn't look up as they came in, and Asha had the fleeting thought that she must be invisible. Perhaps she'd died in the explosion, and it was her ghost that was trying to solve this case, unseen and unheard.

"You should get yourselves coffee, and me too while you're at it," Lonnie said without tearing her eyes from her screen. "This is going to take a while, and I need caffeine even if you youngsters don't."

Aaron headed off down the corridor. Asha cleared some papers off a chair and lowered herself onto it, wary of being tipped sideways by the missing castor wheel, and listened to the intermittent tapping of fingers on a keyboard. She'd known Lonnie long enough to recognise the signs. The elderly sergeant had found something, but she wanted to be certain before sharing the information.

When Aaron came back with a tray holding three grubby mugs of brown liquid, she helped him create a space on the corner of the desk. He met her eyes and grinned, then reached into his jacket pocket and drew out a handful of assorted chocolate bars. "Thought these might help, too."

"Boy, you are a wonder," Lonnie said, letting her eyes leave the screen for the first time. She sat up in her chair and eased her back, groaning softly.

"What do you have?" Aaron asked, unable to curb his curiosity any longer.

"You asked me to find out if that poor boy's foster family was still around, and that wasn't too hard." She clicked the mouse. "The foster parents, Gillian and Kevin McCarron, emigrated to Spain about ten years ago, and they took their youngest son, Timothy, with them. The eldest, Joseph, stayed on here. He's got a record: petty theft and possession of cannabis, but he's never served time as an adult. He'd have been around fourteen when William disappeared, so he should remember something, with luck."

"Good work, Lonnie," Asha said. "I take it we have an address?"

"We do." She handed over a note, written in her neat, cramped hand.

Asha rose to leave, but the sergeant stopped her with a gesture. "Aaron also asked me to find out more about Monica Hearn's disappearance. There's no case file anywhere that I can find, but the station call logs were archived, and I found this." She pulled a bound A4 book out from under another pile of paperwork. It had the battered look of a practical diary that had served its time on the front desk. The label stuck on the front cover read: "*Call Logs, Lisburn Road, 1 January 1992 to 31 December 1992*".

A Post-it note had been stuck to one of the pages near the back. Lonnie flipped to that page and turned it around for the others to read, pointing to an entry. *Monday 14 December, 16.35: Call received from Michael Hearn. Wife missing since Thursday.* And a phone number.

"You two will be too young to remember, but winter of '92 was a difficult period in Belfast. This was called in the day after a rocket attack on the Crumlin Road Gaol. We were stretched pretty thin. It doesn't surprise me that no one here followed up on this if the Hearns didn't chase it up."

Someone had initialled it, claiming the case as their own, but Asha didn't recognise the name. She could barely make out the letters. Aaron peered at it, frowning.

"I've seen that same squiggle somewhere recently," he said. Then his face cleared. "The missing case file. Hang on."

He slid his phone out and scrolled to a scan of the missing pages, the foster family's statements. As well as the signatures of the parents, there was a printed name of the officer who took the statements, with a signature under it. Comparing the two, Asha thought she could see letters emerging from the tangled mess that matched the name in the file.

G. A. Aiken.

The diary initials were in the same flamboyant style. Asha could easily convince herself they were G. A. A., but overlaid on each other.

"Well, well. Our old friend, George Aiken again. Well done, Boy Wonder."

He grinned at her. "You do realise that if I'm Boy Wonder, that makes you an old bat?"

CHAPTER 31

Lonnie had wandered off to the archives in search of the call log for the year following the disappearances, 1993, muttering about bad filing. Asha had asked her to go through the paperwork from William Hearn Senior's study but keep it under wraps. She was the only one they could trust, for now at least.

Asha leaned back in the sergeant's chair and closed her eyes. "So, George Aiken was involved with both cases: our murdered boy and our missing woman." She felt queasy, and not all of it was down to injury or exhaustion from her nocturnal excitement. The very thought of a crooked cop made her sick to her core.

"Do you think he was Michael Hearn's bent peeler?"

She shook her head. "I hate this, Aaron. We're looking at one of our own." She held a hand up to silence him. "I know Aiken's a misogynistic, racist, homophobic git, but a killer? I can't wrap my head around that at all."

"I can. And what about Kernaghan, his sidekick? I wish we had a description to go on, but I can't imagine old Hearn's going to be much use, even if he pulls through from this stroke."

"Someone needs to go over to the hospital and ask. No phone calls, not for the moment. Can you follow up the leads

Lonnie unearthed, and I'll head over there now? I'll check in on Sue while I'm there. They said she might be let out today, so I'll run her home and make sure she gets there safely."

"Because that worked out so well last time."

* * *

The officer behind the worn melamine counter eyed her sideways when she checked out another pool car, but had sufficient survival instincts to keep quiet. He gave her the keys to a small Volkswagen hatchback, which she drove with exaggerated care through the busy streets to the Royal Victoria Hospital.

Corridors buzzed with activity as she made her way up in the lift to the floor where Sue had been. The chair outside her room had been moved across next to two others, and now an elderly couple occupied them. Sue's name had been wiped from the whiteboard outside the room, and a glance inside showed a bare bed. She went over to the nurse's station, and a Filipina nurse whose face she recognised looked up from her keyboard.

"You're looking for Ms Hearn, yes?"

"Yes. She's been discharged, I take it?"

"Yes, but she's not gone home yet. She said she was going to see her dad first."

Asha nodded her thanks. "I know where he is. Thank you."

She saw the uniformed constable first, standing outside a room with a closed door. A wheeled trolley sat outside, covered with the debris of some procedure or other: blood-stained swabs and used needles. Her heart sank.

The constable caught her eye and straightened. "Can I help you?"

Asha showed her identification.

"She's inside, taking a wee moment. Her da died just there, now." The Donegal accent was harsh, but the words suggested a compassion the constable's face hid well.

"That's a pity," Asha said without thinking. She felt the heat rise up her neck. "I meant for Sue, of course."

A slight smile came and went. "I think he was talking to her before he died. I couldn't hear what was said, but there was definitely a male voice in there, and they were alone."

Asha took a deep breath. "I'm glad she got talking to him, before he died."

"Hmm."

At last the door opened and Sue appeared in the gap. Her eyes were red-rimmed and swollen, her cheeks shining with damp.

"He's at peace, now. I don't know why I'm crying, because he's wanted to go these ten years or more. He'll be with Mum at last."

That was a small change. It was the first time Asha remembered Sue talking of Monica as if she'd died. What had Michael Hearn said in his final minutes?

"They need me to fill in some paperwork." Sue waved vaguely towards the nurses' station. "But then I think I'm free to leave."

"Where will you go?" Asha asked.

"Home, I suppose. I don't really have anywhere else."

Home, where every room held memories and the silence would eat away at her. And where someone had burgled her grandfather's study and from whence the same person, presumably, had abducted her.

"Do you trust me to drive you there, or would you rather take a taxi?"

Sue let out a breath that was almost a laugh, then her face settled back into grief. "I trust you. It wasn't your fault, last time. Do you trust me as a passenger? What if someone's waiting for us at the other end again, and you get hurt?"

The constable stirred. "As far as I'm concerned, I'm still on escort duty until someone orders me off it. He'd be a bold boyo to take on the three of us."

* * *

The front door of the house looked secure behind its police tape. There was an officer on watch in a marked car.

168

Asha showed him her credentials. "Would you mind checking inside, please? Especially the back door and the gate to the road from the end of the garden."

"Yes, ma'am."

Sue handed over her keys and watched the constable disappear inside.

"I thought we'd both feel better if it was checked out," Asha said.

Sue nodded and swallowed. "I was thinking, in the hospital, that I might sell Carrow Lodge and find somewhere smaller to live, somewhere out of town a bit."

"That sounds like a good idea. I can't imagine you'll have much difficulty finding a buyer, not in this area. Commuter paradise."

Sue sighed. "Yes, but every time I think about it, I imagine generations of Hearns frowning down at me with disapproval. I'm not sure I have the courage to be the Hearn who sold old Tobias's pride and joy."

"You're the last Hearn, aren't you?"

"As far as I know. Dad was an only child, as was my grandfather. If there are distant cousins somewhere, they haven't made any attempt to get in touch."

"Well, then. If you stayed here until a ripe old age and ended your days in Carrow Lodge, it would pass outside your family anyway. All you'd have achieved would be a delay of the inevitable."

A spark appeared in Sue's eyes. "That's a bit of an assumption. I'm only in my early forties. Who's to say I might not marry and have children? That's not unheard of, you know."

Asha was saved from having to reply by the return of the constable. "All clear, ma'am."

"Good." She took the keys from him and handed them to Sue. "After you?"

Sue snorted. "Certainly. After all, what could possibly go wrong?"

Asha followed her inside. Humour, after all Sue had been through, was an excellent sign. She'd need all the resilience she could muster over the coming days.

CHAPTER 32

Joseph McCarron, William Lee's foster brother, lived in an area that even the police were wary of entering alone, especially in marked cars. Aaron pulled up next to the giant tricolour flag painted on the concrete wall at the entrance to the estate, along with some graffiti along the lines of "Brits Out" and something in Irish that he couldn't understand. At least he was in a nice nondescript, unmarked car.

He drove on, searching for house numbers — there weren't many — until his satnav told him he was in the right place.

It was a grey, pebbledashed terrace identical to all the others in the street. A tiny front yard held the rusting remains of a child's bike and discarded packaging from someone's Happy Meal. The curtains were closed, but then so were those of the houses either side. It probably meant nothing.

He opened the car door, and the smell of stale piss assailed his nose. He got out, on the lookout for danger, but the place was quiet. Any kids would be in school, and the adults who were lucky enough to earn a living in this place of despair would be out working. According to Lonnie's information, Joseph was on Universal Credit, so if he did work it was off the books.

Yellow paint hung off the front door in long ribbons, revealing bare wood beneath. The single pane of frosted glass in the upper half of the door had a long crack running across it diagonally.

He knocked, then half-turned to keep an eye open for anyone approaching. In the distance, an elderly man walked an equally elderly Jack Russell. As Aaron watched, the dog squatted and crapped in the middle of the pavement. The old man turned to see what was holding his pet up, saw the mess and jerked on the lead. The little dog continued crapping as it was tugged forwards in short spurts, leaving a trail of little bits of shit as it went.

The door handle creaked, and he snapped his attention back to the task in hand.

Joseph McCarron was in his mid-forties, according to his records, but the bleary, unshaven face that peered out at Aaron through the half-open door could have been in its fifties or even older. His eyelids were baggy, and his skin had the dry, yellowish parchment look of the chain-smoker. A glance down at the hand that held the doorframe confirmed his suspicions. The fingers were stained brown, the nails gnawed and torn.

"Joseph McCarron?" he asked.

The man blinked at him and frowned. "Joe. Who're you?" Then he looked Aaron up and down from his neat tie to his shiny shoes and started closing the door, horror dawning in the bloodshot eyes. "You're a feckin' peeler! I can't talk to you. What the feck are you even doing here?"

Aaron stuck a foot in the door in a practised movement. "It's either here or at the station. Your choice."

"No way. I know my feckin' rights. I've done nothing wrong." His eyes darted from side to side. "Move your foot or I'll break it."

But Aaron held out. "I'm here about William Lee."

"I don't care if you're here about the fuckin' Pope. Get out of here."

A curtain twitched in the window next to the door, but Aaron couldn't see past it into the dark room. It was enough to know that Joseph wasn't alone in the house. He glanced across the street and saw another man watching them from an upstairs window. He had his mobile out and was raising it to his ear. Time to leave.

"We think we've found your foster brother's remains. I need to speak to you about that, that's all. I've no interest in anything else right now." He shoved his card through the letterbox, his action hidden from watchers by his own body. "Call me." Then he withdrew his shoe and the door slammed, the Yale lock snapping home.

He walked steadily to his car and slid inside. In the rearview mirror, two figures appeared from around the corner, both men who any normal person would cross the road to avoid. One held an iron bar, the other had his hands in his jacket pockets. Aaron fired up the engine, put the Golf in gear without bothering with his seatbelt and drove off. Only once he was off the estate completely did he stop to click the seatbelt into place.

His heart was hammering, blood pounding in his ears. And what were the chances of Joseph McCarron calling him? He wouldn't put money on it.

So, what next? He drove slowly towards the Lisburn Road, mulling over the options. By now, Lonnie might have found something in William Hearn's papers. He pulled over to call her, but as he lifted the phone, it rang with an unrecognised landline number. The code was Belfast.

"Detective Constable Birch."

"What did you want to know about Will?" asked a husky voice.

Was it Joseph McCarron? He couldn't be sure.

"I always said the little bastard would come to no good." There was a pause. "Where did you find him?"

"I need to speak to you face to face," Aaron said. "Is there somewhere we can meet?"

Silence, then: "Shaw's Bridge boathouse. One hour." And the line went dead.

Okay. Very cloak and dagger. Still, he wasn't going to go in without telling anyone. He called it in, giving only the

bare minimum of information in case it reached the wrong ears. He just gave a time and a location, and said that he was meeting an informant.

Shaw's Bridge was a popular walking area with its own car park. The towpath ran alongside the River Lagan towards Belfast in one direction and Lisburn the opposite way. Aaron had cycled there as a teenager with his mountain bike club and knew the area well. At this time on a weekday, there'd be a few dog walkers out, some mums with toddlers, but the lunchtime joggers would have mostly gone by now, back to their office desks.

It wasn't a bad place to meet.

He parked up — the place was half-empty, a contrast to weekends, when the cars would be backed right up to the main road — and took a good look around him, checking out the vehicles already there. None of them were occupied.

Someone appeared from the trail with a pair of muddy cocker spaniels and opened the boot of the vehicle next to his to allow the dogs to jump in, stubby tails wagging. He waited for that car to drive off before getting out and stretching, using the opportunity to check the periphery of the car park. No one gave him a second glance.

The boathouse was a square, stone building that housed canoes and kayaks for the local adventure centre. It squatted among trees and bushes right at the edge of the river and wasn't really overlooked, especially at this time of year when the trees were in full leaf. There was no one else there that he could see, but he checked around the back just in case.

Low branches and undergrowth made this spot feel a million miles away from the buzz of the city. From the smell, it seemed the kayakers who used the boathouse had found it a convenient place to relieve themselves, invisible except to anyone lingering on the old bridge, and even then, they'd have spotted any walkers long before they themselves would be noticed.

He turned towards the sunlit path, but a twig cracked between him and the river. He spun, straining to see movement in the shadows, but his eyes had been dazzled by that second of brightness and he could see nothing.

He backed away slowly until he could touch the wall with one hand. It was slimy and gritty to the touch, but its solidity gave him confidence.

"Who's there?"

Joseph McCarron stepped forward, straightening up. He must have been crouching in the gloomy area down by the water's edge. His trainers were black with mud and the bottom of his jeans dark.

"I knew something had happened to Will," he said. "Where did you find him?"

"I can't tell you that. How did you know something had happened?"

"Ma always said he was bad through and through like his no-good parents, but he was kind to our Tim. And he never squealed on me, neither, even when he knew what I was up to."

"Drugs?"

The bloodshot eyes darted around, then came back to him. The older man sighed. "Drugs and booze and ciggies. There was a dealer used to stand outside the school. But Will never had nothing to do with all that. He was squeaky clean, was our wee Will. Teacher's pet and all."

Any bitterness seemed to have faded over the years. The words were flat and unemotional, as if drawn from memory rather than from any real dislike.

"He never stayed out late or played hooky from school. When he didn't come home that night, I knew something had happened to him." He rubbed his nose with a dirty thumb and squinted. "Bu Ma wouldn't hear of it. She said he'd be off robbing someone or in a fight, and that he'd be home to lick his wounds when he got hungry enough."

"But he didn't come home."

"No. She left it as long as she dared, but when school started again after Christmas, she knew there'd be questions asked so she reported him missing then. Must've been a couple of weeks, maybe more. No wonder it took till now to find the wee man." He looked at Aaron, then quickly away. "How'd he die?"

Aaron thought about refusing to answer, but Joseph McCarron seemed genuine enough. "He was murdered and buried in someone's garden."

The eyes flashed towards him again. "So that was him, then? The skeleton in the news? Wee Willie, lying in a posh garden all these years and no one the wiser. D'ye know who did it?"

"The investigation is ongoing."

"Yeah. Not much hope, I reckon. Not after all these years."

There was a hopeful tone, as if he was searching for reassurance that the case would remain unsolved.

"What can you tell me about Will in the days before he disappeared?"

"Happy as a bug. Did his homework, ate his veg, cleaned his teeth. The usual Will." He frowned. "But Tim said something was worrying him. My wee brother — they shared a room. He said something about seeing Will talk to some bloke outside the school one day when he should have been in class. It was just after his teacher went AWOL, I think."

"Mrs Hearn?"

"No. Miss Stewart, her name was. She had a bit of a thing for Will. Even gave him a lift home once or twice. Said it was on her way, but she never lived anywhere near us. Too posh for the estates, was Miss Stewart. She'd have lived in some nice semi somewhere, some new build, I expect."

"So, what happened when he went missing?"

The other man shrugged. "Just didn't come home from school one day. Ma didn't mention it, not at first."

"But Tim must have known? They shared a room."

Joseph shrugged. "S'pose. He didn't say anything, until Ma asked him where Will was. Must've been a few days by then. Reckon he was enjoying having the room to himself, the little bastard."

Joseph was jealous, Aaron realised. Jealous of the wee brother who'd gone with his parents to Spain while Joseph had been left behind.

"Did you not think it strange at the time that your ma didn't report him missing for so long?"

He shuffled his feet, shoulders hunched. "She was hoping he'd just turn up again. Couldn't afford to lose the money."

"Can you remember if anyone came to question your parents about his disappearance?"

"Yeah. Some smart-arse little peeler with hard eyes and red hair."

CHAPTER 33

Asha rubbed her eyes with the heels of her hands before she climbed out of the car after she'd made sure Sue was okay. The disturbances of the night before had caught up with her. Just a dip into the office to check for messages, a quick chat with Lonnie, then she could sneak off home and try to get an early night.

She sleep-walked along the corridors and up the stairs to her office. It was a mixed blessing, this temporary office. Part sanctuary, part millstone around her neck. The pressure to prove herself competent on this, her first case as acting DI, was building inside her head, causing her to trip up and make mistakes, a factor she had underestimated when Chief Superintendent Yvonne Patterson had told her she was giving her a chance to shine on a historical case like this.

She pushed open her door, inhaling the familiar musty smell, and pulled up short.

Yvonne Patterson was sitting in Asha's chair, leafing through a file that must have come from Asha's desk drawer, the drawer she kept locked.

"Ma'am?" Asha said, not sure how to set the tone of the single-word question.

The older woman didn't look up. "Take a seat, Detective."

Just detective. Not detective inspector, nor even detective sergeant. That couldn't be good. Asha pulled up the only other chair in the room, a wooden spindle-back, so it was alongside the desk rather than in front of it. A pathetic attempt at power-play, but she'd be damned before she'd embrace the role of penitent before she even knew what this was about.

Silence was her best weapon. She wasn't going to gabble and give away her nervousness. She sat down and crossed her legs.

The only sounds were the rustle of pages and the distant murmur of voices, harsh Belfast voices that Asha had struggled to get used to when she first arrived from Rostrevor where she'd grown up, only daughter in a family of boys.

How proud her parents had been when she told them she was going to leave the uniform behind and become a detective. Her brothers had teased her, but she'd seen the pride in their eyes, too, and overheard Pratik, her eldest brother, boasting to his friends that his wee sister was going to be a detective like the ones on the TV.

And now, was this bubble going to burst?

Patterson put the file down with a thud, and Asha saw the name on the front: Louise McCoubrey. Where had that come from? Relief that Patterson hadn't broken into her files was tempered by curiosity. How come there was already a file on William Lee's half-sister? Aaron had suspected she might have secrets, but if she'd been arrested for something, surely her DNA would be on the database already?

Patterson put her hand down on the file. "This woman is off-limits," she said in a flat voice. "Is that clear?"

"She's half-sister to our skeleton, ma'am. That's the only interest we had in her." She was sounding defensive. "What should I know that you're not telling me?"

Patterson's face twitched, but whether in a smile or a grimace of disapproval she couldn't tell. "This woman is part of a network of informants. That's all you need to know. I cannot have her compromised."

"Very well."

That would do for now, at least, but Asha made a mental note to dig for more information. She'd learned through experience that what she didn't know could come back and bite her.

"Was there anything else, ma'am?"

Patterson's cold eyes met hers. "Yes. I'd like a verbal progress report now and a written one on my desk tomorrow morning. There's a limit to how long I'm prepared to fund this wild-goose chase. I expected you to have it wrapped up by now and the case closed."

Asha sat up straight, thinking fast. Someone in the force had been interfering with her case, and she had Michael Hearn's claim of police involvement in Monica's disappearance as well, but she was in no position to throw accusations around. Not yet, at least.

"We have identified the skeleton as William Lee, aged ten when he went missing from his foster home late 1992, early 1993."

"Well, which is it? If a ten-year-old goes missing, I'd expect a tighter date than a spread of two years."

That was downright unfair, but Asha kept her face neutral. "Yes, ma'am. He was reported missing by his foster parents in January 1993, but according to his school records, he stopped attending school in mid-December 1992. Before that, he had a hundred per cent attendance. We are attempting to establish the cause of the delay, but it seems likely that the foster parents didn't want to lose the allowance, especially over Christmas. DC Birch is attempting to contact the only member of the foster family left in Northern Ireland to find out more."

Patterson pursed her lips. "Go on."

"The boy was killed by a single stab through the roof of his mouth and into his brain. He'd have died instantly. The garden he was buried in has been in the Hearn family for generations, but the only living family members haven't been able to shed any light on it at all so far."

179

"Then press them harder. You can't tell me someone sneaked in and buried a body in the dead of night in an urban back garden without at least one of the family being aware of it?"

"Yes, ma'am. Sue Hearn, the former path lab technician who found the skeleton, was only in her early teens at the time of the burial, and her father, Michael, who would have been living in the house at the time, had dementia in recent years. Sadly, he took a severe stroke and passed away earlier today before we could question him."

Patterson muttered something. It sounded like, "That's convenient."

"Yes, ma'am." Asha shifted position on the hard chair, still trying to decide how much she felt safe revealing at this stage. Enough to keep the case, but nothing about her suspicions of someone within the force being involved. "We did, however, remove paperwork from William Hearn's study in the house. There was an attempted burglary, which luckily got nothing—"

"Ah yes. The burglary you interrupted. How's the head?" The Chief's voice was still cold, as if she was asking because she felt she ought to rather than because she actually cared.

"Better, thank you." Thumping headaches, bad dreams, exhaustion. "Yes, that burglary. We're hoping we might turn up something in those papers to shed light on the skeleton, and on Michael Hearn's wife, Monica, who disappeared around the same time as the boy was killed."

The pale eyes sharpened. "So, it's possible she killed the boy for some reason as yet unknown and fled, fearing arrest?"

"It's possible, ma'am, but I've not found any evidence as yet to point to that scenario." She sounded stilted, she realised, retreating behind the familiar barrier of police-speak. But the question made sense: William had been in Monica Hearn's class at school, and there'd been child abuse cases in the past where the perpetrator was a teacher. Could Monica Hearn have been abusing William and then killed him when he threatened to report her?

180

Something of her thoughts must have shown in her face, because Patterson looked pleased. "Perhaps you should open your mind to the possibility, my dear."

That casual condescension made Asha's fists twitch, but she kept her hands visible, relaxed, determined not to show that the remark had drawn blood.

She never knew how to take Patterson. The Chief was the one who'd given her the temporary promotion. *Just to let you try your wings. You never know, we might decide to promote from within rather than bring in a new DI from elsewhere. This is your chance to shine, DS Harvey. Don't waste it.*

As the door closed behind her boss, Asha flipped open her laptop and logged in to make a start on that written report. Maybe it was no bad thing. It would help her get her thoughts straight in this confusing, nebulous case. Time was ticking, and she had so many other things to do, but it had to be done.

What Patterson had given, Patterson could take away.

CHAPTER 34

"It was Aiken, I'm sure of it," Aaron said, the next morning. He was perched on the corner of Asha's desk, strung as tight as a bow. "I can't believe those sodding foster parents waited all that time to report William missing. Gits. Good thing for them that they're out of range."

Asha was mildly surprised by his vehemence. He was young, single and didn't have kids, yet he'd become deeply involved in this case from thirty years ago.

"I had the Chief in here yesterday evening," she said, managing to keep her voice even. "She's leaning on me for a quick wrap-up, and she has a theory."

Aaron perked up. "Oh? What's that, then?"

Asha sighed. "She thinks Monica Hearn was abusing William Lee, then she killed him when he threatened to spill the beans and did a runner. She was his teacher in primary school and she did give him lifts home, according to the retired caretaker. It's something we should consider."

Aaron picked up a biro from her desk and began spinning it between his fingers, a sure sign that deep thoughts were being processed. "It could work," he said at last. "But bags not being the one to ask Sue Hearn the question."

Her heart sank. Not that she would have left him with the job. She wasn't that much of a coward. "No, that's one for me, I'm afraid. But you could do a bit more digging about the mysterious Monica. Her background, where she came from, find out if any of the teachers who worked with her then are still around. You can get Lonnie to help you."

"Okay." He slid off the desk and rose to his full height, face troubled. "It just doesn't feel right, though, does it?"

"Yeah. You can tell that to Patterson, if you like. She thinks she's solved it."

* * *

The uniform she'd left outside Carrow Lodge said no one had visited, and that Sue had spent most of the previous afternoon and well into the night stripping out and cleaning the front room, her father's room.

Asha tried not to groan. Everyone dealt with the loss of a loved one differently, and in Asha's experience, the ones who buried themselves in clearing out their dear departed's possessions were often the hardest to work with in the early days.

When she called on Sue, the older woman was in her basement kitchen, cutting up peppers, green beans and carrots. A frying pan spat on the Aga, redolent of herbs and spices. It smelled like spicy chicken. Her stomach clenched.

"Oh hello!" Sue said. "Want to stay for lunch? I've cooked enough for two out of habit, and it doesn't keep well."

"Thank you, but—"

"Now, don't be silly. I'm not trying to ply you with alcohol when you're on duty. A bite to eat can't do any harm, surely? Then we can chat. I've a lot to tell you."

This was a very different woman from the red-eyed, emotionally drained wreck she'd driven home the previous day. She seemed to have a purpose, and the change suited her. She looked a little younger, less vague.

"Okay, then. I'm afraid I have some more questions, too. It's possible some of them might make you quite uncomfortable, but they still need to be asked."

Sue shot her a look but didn't speak as she scraped the prepared veg into the spitting pan and stirred it.

They sat companionably at the scrubbed pine table and ate their lunch from chipped, non-matching plates with non-matching cutlery. Asha decided her questions could wait until after they'd eaten.

Finally, Sue pushed her plate away and stood to fill the kettle at the sink. "Tea or coffee?"

Asha gathered the plates, not a scrap left on either one. "Don't mind. I'll wash up while you make it, shall I?"

With her hands busy, her conscience twinged. She opened her mouth to speak, but Sue got there first.

"My dad told me a bit more, just before he died."

Asha kept her back turned, giving Sue space to think it through.

"I asked him outright what had happened to Mum. In some nasty little recess of my mind, I've always wondered if he had something to do with her disappearance. If he could even have killed her himself. When I found that first finger bone, I was sure it was Mum."

Asha swallowed, but let the silence drag out. Perhaps she wouldn't need to ask the questions she'd been dreading, after all.

"He said it was all his fault. That she'd been taken because he couldn't pay. That it should have been him, not her. I asked him who'd taken her, and he said it was a peeler. I asked him if the man wore a uniform, and he said it was a big man in an overcoat with big shoulders and dead eyes." She swallowed. "Like a shark, he said."

"Did he give you a name?"

"'No names, no pack-drills.' That's what the man would say, according to Dad. I thought it sounded like a military saying."

Yes. Asha had heard the phrase on the lips of her own grandfather, Jaswant Hari, who had volunteered for the British Indian Army in the Second World War. Even her pacifist dad had adopted the phrase, so she'd grown up with it.

"I asked him how he knew the man was a peeler if he wasn't in uniform, and he said the man sometimes had a driver, a uniformed policeman." Sue sighed. "I don't suppose it's much use, not after all these years, but he described the driver as a wee hard man with red hair and a head like a bullet. He said he was a nasty piece of work."

Asha tried not to react, but her body language must have mirrored her emotion.

"You know him, don't you?"

The only serving officer Asha knew who answered that description was George Aiken. And he was definitely a nasty piece of work, too.

"I really couldn't say," she lied. "It's not a lot to go on, but it's a start. We can find out who was working this area in the early 1990s and hopefully that'll give us a lead. Did he mention anything about a boy?"

Sue let her breath out. "No. I did ask, but he died before he could answer. I'm sorry." Her voice sounded leaden, miserable.

Asha dropped the tea towel over the Aga rail and turned to face her. "Don't be. You've given us a great lead, something we can finally get our teeth into. I'm so sorry about your dad, Sue. It must be really hard, coming here again. Have you had any more thoughts about moving out?"

To somewhere less rambling, without a convenient back entrance. Somewhere easier to keep her safe. If word got out that her father had talked before he died, Asha worried that Sue might come to harm. She couldn't rationalise it, but the feeling was overwhelming, that danger stalked Sue Hearn as closely as it did herself.

"No." Sue met her eyes and smiled. "I couldn't sleep last night, thinking about selling up. There's no money to run this place, not at the moment, but now my caring duties are over, I can go out and get a job. I might even go back to the path lab, if they'll have me. Then I can start repairing the old place. I doubt if it'll ever regain its former glory, but at least I can air it out and drag bits of it into the twenty-first century."

Her eyes had a light in them Asha hadn't seen before. It sounded terrible, to swap caring for an elderly father for caring for a rambling old wreck of a house, but perhaps a change was as good as a rest. If it made her feel better about herself, what harm could it do?

"What was it you were going to ask me? You said I wouldn't like it, but I'm much stronger today. Ask away."

"I'm not sure how relevant it is in the light of what you've just told me," Asha temporised.

"Is it about the boy?"

"Well. Yes." Now it had come to the point, she had no idea how to ask the question. "We've been knocking around some potential scenarios to explain how one of your mother's pupils ended up buried in your garden, and—"

"And you're wondering if my mum might have murdered him and then run away, never to be seen again?"

The words were flippant, but the set of Sue's lips when she'd finished speaking, and the glint in her eyes, told a different story.

"That's one of the ideas that came up, yes, but—"

"You never met my mum," Sue said. "She couldn't even bring herself to squash a wasp or a fly, and she'd lift snails and slugs off the vegetables and carry them outside to release them in the park. My mother could no more have murdered a child than she could have flown to the moon."

Asha's cheeks burned, but now the hole had been opened, she might as well keep digging herself in deeper. "I understand she was quite close to William Lee, the murdered boy."

"Yes, she was," Sue said defiantly. "Because she felt sorry for him. She'd talk about him to us, about how he was fostered and how his foster family often didn't seem to know where he was, or care." She took a shuddering breath. "William Lee was incredibly intelligent, and she used to talk about how unfair it was, that a kid like that had been dealt such a terrible hand, and how other kids had no idea how lucky they were."

"You knew him?" Asha asked. Sue sounded too passionate to be talking about a complete stranger.

"No. Not really. But sometimes Mum would give him a lift home on the same days she was collecting me from school. If I was on early finish, she'd pick me up on the way, and I'd hear the two of them chatting. He was a rough wee diamond, but he was interested in everything, always asking questions." She gulped. "I liked him."

"He didn't deserve to be murdered," Asha said neutrally.

"No child deserves to be murdered, and no adult either! I know for certain that the only interest my mum had in William Lee was as a promising pupil, nothing more, and she definitely didn't kill him. Besides, she'd already disappeared before—"

She caught herself. She'd been carried away by her passion, defending her mother, and said too much.

Asha touched her arm lightly with her fingertips, reassuring. "Go on."

The kettle let out its shrill whistle, and they both jumped as if they'd been goosed by someone with very cold hands.

CHAPTER 35

Sue blew out through pursed lips. "All these years. Do you know, I must have blocked it out? I think what I saw that night was so awful I couldn't deal with it, so I pretended it hadn't happened."

Asha had made tea for both of them and Sue had poured some half-covered digestive biscuits onto a plate, but neither of them touched the food. Asha had her fingers wrapped around her mug, taking strength from the heat.

"What did you see?"

"I couldn't sleep. Mum had been missing for almost a week, and no one was doing anything about it. Every time I mentioned calling the police, Dad and Grandfather would just exchange looks. Then that night, I tried to cry myself to sleep like I used to do when I was small, when Mum would hold me and tell me to cry it all out."

Her face was haunted, lost in the past.

"It didn't work. I was lying in bed, staring up at the shadows on the ceiling, when a light moved across the room. It was only very faint, but it moved across the ceiling, down the wall, then disappeared. I got up to see, because it must have come from the garden. I thought it was Mum, come back to us."

A fat tear rolled down her cheek, but her voice was steady as she went on.

"There was someone down in the garden with a torch, moving around. I was going to open the window and call out, but I didn't." She frowned. "I don't know why. Instinct? Instead, I watched, keeping low so I wouldn't be seen. There was someone digging in the garden, in the place where the builders had already laid concrete slabs for the greenhouse. The hedge was only a few feet tall in those days, and I could see over it. He had a couple of slabs up, propped against the fence. He'd put the torch down as he dug. When he moved into the light, I saw who it was. It was Grandfather."

Asha sipped her tea. She should really be recording this, but any sudden movement might break the spell. She'd just have to get Sue to repeat it for a statement later.

"Then he went and fetched something from behind the shed, something I couldn't see, because he'd left the torch by the hole, but now I realise it must have been Will's body." She took another deep breath. "I watched him bury that little boy, and I did nothing to stop him. I don't know what I thought. I was so tired, drained from grief and fear. I convinced myself he was burying a dead dog, but we never had a dog. Dad was allergic, you see."

Asha did see. It wasn't unknown for the brain to provide a more comfortable explanation for something it couldn't cope with.

"But later, as the years went by and there was no trace of Mum, and the police never investigated it, I decided it must be Mum he'd buried there." She raised a haunted face to Asha. "But it never once crossed my mind that he might have killed her. Not once. He was so good and kind and gentle. I thought she must have died in some accident or other, and that he was burying her so someone wouldn't get into trouble. That's the sort of man he was. Caring."

"Did it ever cross your mind that he could have been covering up for your father?" Asha asked carefully.

"Yes. Dad was never like Grandfather. He was weak, lazy. I struggle to say that even now, after all these years. But it's true. He was quite a talented artist, but he hardly ever finished a painting. He'd do so much, then he'd lose interest and move onto another one instead. I always felt that Mum should have been born a Hearn, not Dad. She was strong and clever and industrious and kind. Just like Grandfather."

"Is that why you all lived with your grandfather? Because your dad couldn't earn enough from his paintings to put a roof over your head?"

"I think so, yes — Mum's salary alone wouldn't have been enough to support both a family and an art studio. Not that anything was ever said about it. Grandfather used to say that we were doing him a favour, making the lonely old house sing with our laughter. It might even have been true, at least until Mum went missing."

Asha thought grimly about the stacks of papers from William Hearn's study. As soon as she'd finished here, she'd be back to the station to go through them. There must be something hidden in his diaries or letters to shed light on Monica Hearn's disappearance and William Lee's death.

She stayed long enough to be sure that Sue had nothing else of value to tell her. As the door closed behind her, the lock clicking into place, the vacuum cleaner started up.

The constable outside had finished his shift and been replaced by a female uniform, the same one who'd been at the hospital yesterday. Asha stopped for a word before she left, making sure the new constable knew to do occasional laps of the block, checking that the garden gate was secured, and that she was to be contacted if anything suspicious happened.

The woman nodded. "PC Barnes just did a lap before I arrived, ma'am. I'm planning to do irregular laps, so there's no pattern, in case someone is watching."

"Good thinking."

As she walked to her car, Asha wondered how long Patterson would keep signing off the expenses for a full-time guard on Sue Hearn. Not long, at a guess, and when the guard was lifted, it would leave the field open for an intruder to visit. Maybe, just maybe that might give them the break they needed.

* * *

Lonnie was in her usual position, her squat body seeming to grow out of the computer chair as her fingers flew across her keyboard. She glanced up at Asha when she came in, then glared at her monitor.

Uh-oh. Bad mood.

"Hi, Lonnie. How's it going?"

"It would be better if you didn't use my office as a dumping ground for files," the sergeant said. "I've had to fend off three attempts to steal them so far, and it stopped being funny a while ago."

Asha stiffened. "What? Who's been trying to steal them?"

"I can't be certain. Twice they tried to decoy me away, and once they tried to break in when I was out of the office." She nodded to the door, where fresh wood splinters stood out against the grey paint. Someone had tried to jemmy open the lock.

"Not that clever, or they'd have learned to pick locks." Then she looked closer and saw the fine scratches around the lock. "Or maybe they tried that first and gave up?"

Lonnie didn't smile. "Now you're here, you can take the damn papers away with you and find somewhere else to store them."

"All right. Are you okay for a few minutes if I go and get Aaron to help?"

"Sure."

There were seven file boxes, all neatly labelled in Jana's firm, sloping hand. It took two trips to the car park to stash them in Aaron's little hatchback, barely leaving room for Asha to squeeze into the front passenger seat, which had been slid forward to accommodate the boxes behind it. She tugged the door to close it, but it didn't move.

Patterson had the top of it gripped in her hand, and she must have been strong, because there was no give in it whatsoever.

"Ma'am?" Asha said, surprised.

"What do you think you're doing with those files, Detective?"

Her cheeks warmed. There were protocols about dealing with evidence, a chain of responsibility. Every wet-behind-the-ears rookie knew that, but she'd hoped to sneak the files home without detection and work away at them at her leisure, maybe while sipping a glass of chilled Chablis and listening to something atmospheric through her earphones.

Aaron leaned across her, his patented film star smile on full parade. "I signed them out of evidence, ma'am. There are just too many to work on in that cramped space, and I asked DI Harvey to help me go through them at home."

Asha held her breath. Patterson's eyes narrowed so much that they almost disappeared.

"What case are they from?"

"The cold case we've been working on. The skeleton in the garden. I'm hoping there might be a clue to whatever happened thirty years ago in here somewhere. A shared office space is hopeless if you need to spread out, and I'm unpopular enough as it is, after the last time."

That would be the time he'd tried to rope his fellow DCs and a handful of uniforms into helping him go through a massive pile of betting slips and shop receipts when he was working on a corruption case.

Patterson sucked air between her teeth. Wolf's teeth, Asha thought. I'm glad she's on our side.

"If you've signed them out, then I can see no objection, but with this many files, I'd appreciate you running it past me next time you take it into your head to work at home, DC Birch."

"Yes, ma'am. I should have thought of that. Sorry."

The door was released, and Asha closed it with care, worried in case she caught her superior officer's fingers in the gap. Aaron drove off slowly, giving the bollards a wide berth. As soon as they were out of the main gate and on the road, heavy with slow-moving traffic, Asha let out her breath.

"You didn't need to do that, you know. Those files are my responsibility, not yours."

"Yeah, but I'm not the one looking promotion in the navel," he replied. "If I ever get time to study for my sergeant's exams, you can return the favour."

"Deal," she said, feeling lighter-hearted than she had done in ages.

They reached her terraced house and were lucky enough to find a parking space almost directly outside, too snug for most drivers. Aaron reversed his little hatchback into it in one smooth movement.

"At least you've been keeping your driving skills up to date," Asha said. She'd seen this space a few times since she'd been living in the flat, but thought of it more as a slightly bigger-than-usual gap between cars than as a proper space. She needed something half as big again to get her estate car in.

By the time they'd lugged the boxes up the three flights of stairs to Asha's top-floor apartment, they were both ready for a drink. No Chablis, sadly, but there was a bottle of supermarket plonk in the fridge, so they decided to order a pizza and make the best of it. It was taken without discussion that Aaron would stay to help.

He moved her sofa aside, pushing it to the edge of the room, and they laid out the boxes in a line across the carpet. Jana had labelled each one with a rough guide to contents, so Asha went straight to the one labelled "*Journals and albums*". The journals were beautiful leather-bound books. On the study shelves, they'd have blended in perfectly with all the works the Hearns had collected over the years. No wonder the burglar hadn't spotted them.

She flicked through a couple of photo albums. One contained mostly pictures of Sue as a child playing in the big garden, which had been well cared for in those days. Some showed the whole family: William glowering at the camera

193

from beneath bushy eyebrows, Michael looking off to the side, Sue in a pale blue dress that made Asha think of *Alice in Wonderland*, and a very pretty, dark-haired woman who could only be Monica Hearn.

The second album was filled with bird photographs, some of which were breathtakingly beautiful and had clearly been taken using a long lens from a distance. She wondered if Jana and Marley had turned up William's camera and lenses in their search of the study.

Aaron began with a box labelled "*Letters and Notes*", spreading the contents out in an ever-widening circle around him where he sat on the floor.

They took a break to eat pizza — they didn't want to contaminate the evidence with grease stains — but they both got straight back to it as soon as the last crumb had been chased around the box and eaten.

Asha had the diary for 1992 open to December, but she was struggling to read the beautiful copperplate. The ink had faded from black to pale brown, leaching into the paper where damp had attacked the pages over the last three decades. She rubbed her temples with the tips of her fingers, trying to push away the headache that was making her vision blur.

"Any luck?" she asked, without much hope.

"Not sure," Aaron said, frowning down at a pile of letters. "These are from the school Monica worked at, demanding to know where she is and why she hasn't called in sick. Listen to this."

He spread out one typewritten letter on the carpet and began to read from about halfway down the page, following his finger along the lines.

I know the rumours about your husband have been unpleasant, Monica, but staffroom gossip quickly runs its course. By next term, they'll have moved onto someone else's problems, and Michael's indiscretions will be forgotten. You just need to hold your head up high and pretend you have no idea what they're talking about.

I do wish you'd call me. We could sort this out face to face if you could only bring yourself to meet. Just promise me that you won't do anything foolish.

You have, as always, my full support,

Gavin Barrie

CHAPTER 36

Aaron looked up at her. "Did they mention anything about problems with her husband when you were at the school?"

She shook her head. "No, but then no one who's there now actually knew her, except the secretary, who isn't especially forthcoming, and the retired caretaker, but he didn't mention anything about her marriage."

"He might not have heard the gossip. Do caretakers spend much time with the teachers?"

"No idea." The two childless officers looked at each other helplessly.

"What if Michael was having an affair?" Aaron shook his head, discounting his own suggestion. "No, he doesn't sound like the type. But there must have been something."

"Sue did say she thought he might have been taking drugs when she was a child, around the time her mother went missing."

"Would that sort of thing have got to her workplace gossip mill?"

Asha snorted. "This is Northern Ireland. It runs on gossip, uses it as rocket fuel. You can't sneeze without everyone knowing about it." She took a deep breath. "But apparently you can kill and bury a little boy and make a grown woman disappear without anyone knowing a thing about it. Keep digging."

She went back to the faded diaries, but the words she managed to decipher told of a banal life of birdwatching, golf and dinner parties. She flipped to late November, where the writing was less faded, and a phrase leapt out of the page at her.

> Found Michael comatose again, with an empty vodka bottle lying next to him and white powder around his nostrils. Where the hell does he keep getting this stuff from?

Her attention sharpened, and she scanned the pages before the entry, looking for other occasions.

> Michael is taking cocaine. He denies it, but the signs are there to see. He says it's a cold, just the sniffles, but his pupils are like saucers and he's jiggling around like a toddler at the opera. He's losing weight, too. How did we get to this?

In a December entry she found another reference, and this one made her skin pebble.

> I've seen his dealer. A tall man, massively built. Dark overcoat, expensive. Not at all what I expected. It's pathetic the way Michael squirmed and fawned on the man until he handed over the envelope, then he walked right past me on his way home. He didn't even see me, he was in such a rush to get back and snort the demon powder. What sort of parent have I been? How can I face Monica? Does she suspect? She must. Surely he can't keep this secret from her for long, if she doesn't know about it already.
> No, she can't know. She'd have said something to me. Wouldn't she? She's like the daughter

I never had. She knows she can tell me anything. I can't help her if she doesn't talk to me.

The entry was so different from the ones before that it tore at Asha's heart as she read it. The old man had poured his fears onto the page, never knowing that a stranger would be reading them thirty years later, trying to piece together what had happened.

She leafed through feverishly, trying to find more in the same vein. She had her eye in for the spidery hand now, and reading was becoming easier. On the page for 9 December, she found what she was looking for.

Monica spent the evening with me last night. Michael had gone up to his studio, to paint, he said, but I think we both knew differently. We sipped brandy by the fire, and I let the silence grow. I didn't want to force her into speaking, not now. She told me a man had stopped her at the school when she had a child in the car with her — that wee lad, Will Lee. She said he'd threatened her, threatened Susan, and it's all because Michael owes him money. He didn't say how much, just that if Michael doesn't pay by the end of the week, there'll be trouble, and then he mentioned Susan, in her uniform and that bloody short skirt that worries me so much.

I think it's the same man, from her description. Expensive overcoat, broad shoulders, tall, smells like new money. The one who came to the door, looking for Michael. I knew he was no good.

What will we do? My son is in debt to a drug dealer, and I have no cash to help him. This morning, I called my broker. I'm going to sell my shares, but it takes time. The bloody man almost wept down the phone line. He said I can't sell right now, that I'll lose money, but I told him to sell as fast as he can, losses be damned. I need the money now.

Asha's heart was pounding in counter-rhythm to the throbbing inside her head. She turned the page to the entry for 10 December.

> It's happened. The boy, Will, came to the door this evening with some tale about Monica being kidnapped. I didn't believe him, God forgive me, but I humoured the child for Monica's sake and went with him to see the place he said she'd been snatched from.
>
> He was right. She's been taken.
>
> Bastard! He said we had until the weekend. I could have got the money. I can only pray she won't be harmed, and that we'll get her back as soon as I pay.
>
> Michael has gone to pieces. He keeps sobbing and saying it's his fault, which of course it is, but I've managed not to say that out loud. Give me strength. She's worth ten of him, though I hate myself for thinking it.
>
> Thank God Susan is staying at her friend's house with this choir competition. She wanted to come home today, and I lied to her for the first time in my life. I said that the heating boiler was broken, and the house was freezing. She's such a good girl, and I hate lying to her, but I couldn't bear it if anything happened to her, and her own father is worse than useless.

Asha felt as if she'd just run a marathon, but she couldn't stop now. The next entries were brief, a catalogue of his actions, how he'd argued with his broker for dragging his feet. There were some despairing notes about Michael wallowing in self-pity, but it was clear the old man had tried to avoid his son. Asha could only imagine his state of mind. He must have felt like strangling Michael, but it sounded as if it wasn't in his nature to do violence, as Sue had said. His helpless grief came through clearly, even in the terse phrases.

Then she found another, longer entry for 17 December. Mouth dry, she deciphered his frantic handwriting.

William Lee came by today. I only know because I happened to be coming down the stairs as Michael shut the door in his face. Would he even have told me about the visit if I hadn't been right there? Would it have been better if I hadn't found out? Would that have changed the outcome?

I'm sure Michael saw the anger in my face. I opened the door, but it was too late. The boy had gone. A black car drove past. I caught a glimpse of the driver — it was the same man. I ran outside, but the car was too far away to get the number, and I was wearing my reading glasses, fool that I am. When I looked the other way, I thought I saw the boy slipping down a gap between the houses, the alleyway that leads to the park.

I was afraid for him. I rushed through the house and out into the garden, all the way down to the gate that we hardly ever use. It was locked. Why hadn't I remembered that? I had to go back for the key, and by the time I got it opened, I could hardly breathe. Golfing doesn't prepare one for true exertion.

And there he was, the same man in his dark-blue overcoat, with his shiny black car, right outside my gate. Will was on his toes, poised to run, but then he saw me. I was his saviour, his escape route.

Oh God, how can I even write this? But I have to. If anyone reads this diary, I need them to know that I tried. I tried my best.

He killed that little boy right in front of me. He had dead eyes, cold, merciless. He stuck that knife up inside Will's mouth, right into his brain, and I couldn't do one damn thing to stop him.

I didn't see him leave. I was down on my knees, holding the boy, talking to him, telling him I was sorry. And then it was raining, out of a sky that had been clear just before. A dark cloud and torrential rain that washed the blood away and made his little pinched face look like a waxwork.

I should be grateful for the rain. There was no one in sight at the park, no mothers with children, no dog walkers — the weather had kept everyone inside.

Will was as light as a bird in my arms. I wasn't thinking. Couldn't think. I put his thin body behind the shed and went back to see if there was blood, but if there had been, the rain had washed it all away. So I closed the gate and returned to the house. I'm ashamed to say I finished that bottle of brandy, the one Monica and I had shared, but it didn't make anything better.

I believe I made no sound, aware of Susan sleeping along the corridor from me, but inside my head I railed against fate, against the cold, murdering bastard who'd taken a life without hesitation just to send us a warning, and against my own useless son for causing all this.

And then I calmed down. What was I to do with Will? I knew what I should do. I should call the police and tell them everything, but what if that signed Monica's death warrant?

The boy was with a foster family. Monica used to say that she didn't think they knew or cared where he was. Perhaps it will be a day or two before they report him missing, and by then I will have raised the money, paid that bastard off and got Monica home. If we can be together as a family again, I truly believe nothing could harm us.

Asha turned to the next entry.

Last night I took my torch out to the garden in the early hours, lifted a couple of the slabs where the new greenhouse is to go and dug a hole for Will. I cried as I did it, but I was too late to help him, whereas there may still be time to save Monica.

And now it's done. I have no brandy left to dull the pain, but even if I did, I don't think I'd touch it. It would make me like Michael, deliberately losing myself in oblivion rather than facing up to responsibilities.

Today is a new day. Today, I'll have the money, and then this whole nightmare will be over. After that, I'll face the music and admit to my sins. I'll take my punishment. It can't be any worse than the punishment I'm inflicting on myself, every time I take another breath.

Asha swallowed, then licked her lips, surprised to taste salt on her tongue. Tears were sheeting down her face, and only then did she notice Aaron, watching her with concern written in the lines around his eyes.

CHAPTER 37

Alistair stood hidden in the shadow of a low building by the car park, knowing he'd be invisible to the officer on duty, and watched the remains of the car being winched onto a low loader under the careful supervision of the SOCO team. He didn't recognise the technicians gathering plastic envelopes and boxes of evidence and putting them in the back of their small white van, but that didn't really matter.

Once the low loader had growled its way past him towards the exit of the hospital grounds, he pulled up the collar of his dark woollen overcoat against the chill wind and walked to his car. He needed words with those two. They weren't supposed to get rid of the Indian woman until they'd questioned her. Idiots. He'd given them both a bollocking, but the damage was already done. Still, at least they'd have the chance to find out what she knew now.

He was starting the engine when his phone buzzed with an incoming call.

"Sir, I couldn't get the stuff. That old cow had her office locked up tight, and now they've taken all the papers away in a car. What do you want me to do?"

He thought about it. What could they possibly find, after all these years? Mind you, they'd identified the bones.

He'd never wanted to know the boy's name, but now he wondered if he should have taken a bit more care. He hadn't wanted blood in his car, so he'd left the old man with the body, thinking it would hammer home the lesson.

"Just keep an eye on them. I need you to find out what they know. Isolate them and question them, then get rid of the two of them, but only after you've got the information. Is that clear?"

The snort at the other end made him grip the wheel more tightly. It was that attitude that led to mistakes being made.

"Tell me you at least made sure the device couldn't be traced."

"Kerny swiped it from someone else's evidence locker, and even if they trace it, it'll only lead to a paramilitary group."

"You said they'd never be able to find that misper file, but they did."

"Not this time, boss. We made sure. Wiped the records and all."

"Let me know when it's done."

He turned onto the motorway and engaged the cruise control, revelling in the soft purr from his top-of-the-range Volvo as it carried him north towards his home. His wife was holding a drinks party that evening, and he'd promised to stop on his way back to pick up some finger food from a delicatessen she loved in a cute village not far from their home.

He glanced at the screen that showed his route, a little over an hour's drive through some of the most beautiful countryside in the province. "Hey Siri, text Lorraine."

The virtual assistant acknowledged his request.

"ETA just before seven. Will get food."

When he arrived, Lorraine was dressed as if for a society evening with the *Ulster Tatler* present and ready to take photographs. She'd always put an emphasis on appearance, and he wondered just how lonely she'd been, tucked up here in the wilds of North Antrim since he'd retired.

Still, he had enough pull for the rich and influential to make an effort to visit, and the bloody new house he'd had built could billet an army if it had to. Seeing her shine as she moved between her guests, the perfect society hostess, made everything worthwhile. He still didn't understand why she'd chosen him when she could have had her pick of pretty much any man in the province. He didn't deserve her, but he'd do everything in his power to bring her happiness.

He'd inherited the place years ago, from a senile great aunt, but there'd been no money then to put it right. He'd spent a fortune in the last score of years, extending and improving until they had a home worthy of *Country Life*.

That was an idea. He'd contact the magazine next week, invite them to do a piece on the house. That would cheer Lorraine up, a society journalist doing a photoshoot here, but then he hesitated. Did he really want anyone poking around and asking questions? He'd survived this far by exercising extreme caution, and he wasn't going to ruin everything now by a careless act.

Lorraine had done the house up proper, with soft lighting and music. Hired staff from the village lugged crates of booze in through the front door, and he had to step aside to avoid getting bumped.

"Oh, there you are, darling!" Lorraine said, in that cultured Hillsborough accent that had caught his attention so many years ago. "Some of the guests are here already, so you should change and join us as soon as you can."

"How many are we expecting?" he asked, for something to say. The sight of her always made him feel clumsy and tongue-tied, even after all these years.

"Twenty. Three are staying over."

Oh God, he hated it when her guests spent the night, but he forced a smile onto his face and braced himself to pretend to enjoy it.

"Yvonne's come up from town, too," she said brightly. "I thought you'd enjoy having someone to talk shop with. I know how much you miss the job."

He'd always been careful not to invite too many current officers, lest the size and nature of his estate raised suspicions. He'd put it about that he'd come into an inheritance, which was true as far as it went, but that had been more of a millstone than any help. No. The money to restore this great hulk of a house had come from a different source entirely, and that was the part he couldn't afford to have anyone investigating.

But Yvonne Patterson should be safe enough. For a start, if the rumour mill was correct, she was none too squeaky clean herself, and in any case, she'd never been that effective as a detective. She'd been lucky, that was all, surging up through the ranks in the wake of men who could do the job with their eyes closed but had no survival instincts when it came to women.

Equal opportunities had come at a good time for her, too. She'd been in pole position for promotion just at a time when the politicians needed a few more high-ranking women on the force. Next week, he might start the lads digging into her past, just in case he needed leverage.

As if his thoughts had called her up, Yvonne appeared in the hall behind his wife. He hadn't seen her for years, but there was no mistaking her tall, curvy figure. Her understated dress had probably cost a fortune but looked, on her, as if it could have come from Primark. The blonde hair, the subtle make-up and the flat heels were all designed to make her seem harmless, no threat to the male of the species, but the eyes that flashed beneath those dark brows were hard as flint.

"Hello, Yvonne. How's life in the city these days?"

She walked over, heavy-footed with not a hint of sway to her step, and air-kissed both his cheeks. "Busy, as always. I won't bore you with details."

A stab of irritation, but he kept his face smooth. "You could never bore me, my dear."

"How chivalrous you are, Alistair. A man of your time."

Lorraine, unaware of the atmosphere, went happily back to her preparations.

Yvonne couldn't be much more than ten years his junior. She'd aged well, her face smoother than it ought to be for a woman in her late fifties. Better than he had, for sure.

She gave him a smile that failed to warm those dark, unfathomable eyes. "Wonderful to see the old place looking so good after all these years. I remember it when it was just a derelict farmhouse in an expanse of bog. How many acres do you have? Lorraine didn't know. A body, even several bodies, could get lost in a place as big as this, especially if the sea mist rolled in, don't you think?"

He knew his face hadn't changed, because he'd schooled himself to self-control over the decades. She was trying to rattle him. But how much did she know? Not much, if she thought he'd bury any bodies on this land. This was his safe space, far away from the darkness of the city, and he'd do whatever it took to keep it that way.

CHAPTER 38

Sue could tell from the heaviness in Detective Inspector Harvey's voice when she phoned that something had changed. She glanced at the clock on the kitchen wall: nearly nine o'clock, and it was almost twilight outside, long shadows reaching across the garden.

"Yes. I'm still here," she said. Where else would she be? "Yes, you can come over. I'll put the kettle on."

The kettle had whistled and been moved across to the simmering ring by the time the door knocker sounded. She was mildly surprised to see both Asha Harvey and the tall detective constable whose name she couldn't remember. Something from the Old Testament. If it took two of them to break the news, it couldn't be good.

"Come on in," she said, and they traipsed past her, Asha heading for the stairs down to the kitchen. Sue followed slowly, weighed down by the fear of what they might have to say. She'd wanted answers, but now she was no longer sure she could bear to hear that her beloved grandfather had killed a child and buried him.

On autopilot, she made coffee for them all in the cafetière and laid out mugs, milk and sugar. Both detectives watched her, solemn-faced.

"What's this about?" She set a plate of chocolate biscuits before the constable. Young men were always hungry, and he took two with a murmured thank you.

"We've been going through your grandfather's journals," Asha said. "And we found some entries that go some way towards explaining what you saw that night when you looked out of your window."

Sue didn't know whether she should be relieved or upset, so she just nodded. The lump in her throat left her unable to speak.

"Best if you see for yourself," the detective said. "I've marked the pages." She slid a plastic evidence bag across the table. Sue recognised one of her grandfather's leather-bound diaries inside. The other detective handed her a pair of rubber gloves and she slipped her hands inside with a flash of déjà vu. For a moment, she was back at work, gloving up in preparation to assist at a post-mortem, dread at what might be revealed in a sick mixture with elation at being alone with Mark Talbot.

She took the diary out. Someone had stuck tiny strips of Post-its on the edges of some of the pages to mark certain places, so she began with the one nearest the front.

She had no idea how much time passed before she placed the closed diary inside its plastic bag, but someone had made a fresh pot of coffee and only crumbs were left on the biscuit plate.

Her mouth was bone dry. She worked her lips, trying to force moisture in so she could speak, but then the emotion rolled over her and instead of words, a sob broke loose. Dry-eyed, she shuddered and gasped until there was nothing left inside her to give.

"It wasn't your grandfather," Asha said quietly. "He did his best to protect you all. He was right about William Lee's foster parents: they didn't report him missing until early January."

"And Mum never came back," Sue said. "The man who killed Will must have killed her, too."

"I'm not sure what the man who killed William would have had to gain by killing Monica. Your grandfather was getting his money. The scare worked. But we don't know what happened next."

"Do you know if your father or grandfather ever saw that man again after that?" the constable asked. Aaron, that was his name. She'd known it was something biblical.

Sue shook her head. "I never saw him myself, not that I know of. He must have seen me, if he knew to threaten both Mum and Grandfather with harming me." She frowned. "I do remember there being a car parked on the road outside a few times. I'd see it when I was walking home from school. There was someone in it, but I didn't really look to see who. One of our neighbours gave piano lessons, so there'd often be cars parked outside with parents in them, waiting for their budding Richard Clayderman to finish."

The detectives exchanged a puzzled glance.

"Popular pianist of the eighties and nineties. Mum loved him, and I grew up with his music in the house. You know, romantic stuff. Made piano popular again."

"Can you remember anything about that particular car or driver?" Asha asked. "What made it stand out?"

Sue tried to recall her teenage self's thoughts. She had noticed it more than once. Why? Then the image came into focus and she met Asha's enquiring look.

"It's because it was there on odd days, sometimes while the piano teacher was away. And there was only one man in it. He just didn't look like a dad, somehow." She took a quick breath as the memory sharpened a little more. "No. There was another man with him at least once: younger, with short red hair and a hard face." She flushed. "He stared at my legs, and I didn't like it."

"You're doing brilliantly. Can you describe the older man?"

Sue shook her head, exasperated with herself. "It was thirty years ago. I have no idea how I remember what I've already said, or how accurate it is."

"What about the car?" Aaron asked. "Was it light or dark?"

"Black Volvo," she said, without thinking. "I have no idea how I've remembered that."

He smiled at her across the table. "Memory's a funny thing. What shape was it? Estate, saloon or a hatchback?"

But that was as much as she could dredge up. "I can't even be certain that what I've told you is true. It's been thirty years. My mind could be playing tricks on me."

Asha took her hand, her fingers warm and smooth. "You've done incredibly well. It can't have been easy."

Sue's coffee was cold, a skin of milk on the surface. She rose to her feet. "Are you both coffeed out, or would you like another one?"

"Yes, please," Aaron said. "But I can make it. You sit down. Asha has more to show you."

Sue sat down harder than she intended. More? Could this get any worse?

Asha placed two more plastic bags on the table. One contained another diary, but it was the other that she pushed across to Sue.

"Aaron was going through letters and random papers, and he came across these." She slid them from their envelope. "The top one is a share statement, showing that your grandfather sold all his shares in the family company — at quite a bad time, I might add — so he didn't get as much for them as he would have if he'd managed to hold out for even a few more weeks. The second piece of paper is a covering letter from his sharebroker saying much the same thing and telling him he'd regret this action."

Sue glanced at the papers, but the stacks of figures meant little to her. She couldn't take her eyes off the second diary.

Asha pulled it out and opened it at a page near the front, in mid-January. Sue took it with fingers that trembled. Too much caffeine late at night, she told herself, but that wasn't the only reason.

Her grandfather's hand had weakened in the new entry, the beautiful copperplate turning into a straggling mess. Sue frowned down at the page, then flicked to the beginning of the diary, but the entries were few and far between, not like the previous year where he'd journaled each and every game of golf, dinner and drink with friends. This diary told a tale of a man with no emotional energy left to write and no heart to catalogue his fears.

It has been five weeks since our beloved Monica disappeared. I have paid the man his money, and now I'm sick to my stomach, because he broke his promise. He never brought her back.

Sue swiped away the tears that threatened to splash down onto the page.

I can't even go to the police, not that I can trust them, because they will ask, and rightly so, why it has taken so long for me to report her missing. I can't risk them searching the garden. I read in the paper that they use sniffer dogs for dead bodies, so they would find poor Will and blame me or, worse still, Michael for his death.

As long as Susan is here, under my protection, my hands are tied. I will do nothing that could endanger her, and if Michael were to be taken into custody, she'd have lost not just a beloved mother but also a father. I won't be here to protect her for ever.

Michael does nothing. He mopes around the place, muttering to himself. At least it has ended his addiction to the drugs that lie at the root of this. Before Christmas — Christmas, what a hell on Earth that was — I hunted out all his secret stashes and flushed them down the toilet in front of him. His face, the longing in it, almost made me do something I've never considered doing in my entire life. I had to lock my fingers behind my back to prevent my fists from taking control, but I swore to be a man of peace, and a lifetime of restraint saved me in the end.

Would it have been better to have hit him, I wonder now? Would it have jolted him out of his self-pity and into the world of reality?

I am rambling, but better that than doing something I know I'd regret until the day I die.

Now I have to go downstairs to cook a meal for us all. Susan will be home from school, and I have to be strong for her. She is so much her mother's daughter, I know she will go on to be happy one day, married with a family of her own. But she can never know the truth, not as long as Michael is alive. I fear she would never forgive him.

Sue took a deep, shuddering breath. "I remember that day. I came home from school and found Grandfather in the kitchen with a pinny tied around his waist over his corduroy trousers and checked shirt. It was as though he'd turned a corner, moved on. I was angry at first, but after a few days I began to realise that this was our life now. A life without Mum, and no answers. I couldn't even ask questions, with Dad so fragile, and Grandfather acting as if nothing had happened, as if that was all we'd ever been, a family of three. As if Mum had never existed."

CHAPTER 39

"Have you got any further with the identity of—" Sue stopped. How much had Asha told her constable about the possibility of police involvement?

Asha must have seen the conflict in her face and read it correctly. "The identity of the peeler who we now know probably killed William Lee? It's all right, Sue. Aaron knows about that, but only Aaron. I haven't been able to find out much just yet, I'm afraid. I'm sure it'll turn out to be a red herring, but that doesn't mean I'm not turning over every rock in the force, trying to see if there's a crooked officer hiding under it. You must understand how difficult it is to search for him without alerting him."

"He might be retired, or even dead," Aaron added. "It's a pity you don't have more of a description. The diaries haven't helped us much in that way, either, but maybe there'll be something further on that helps."

Sue nodded. "Knowing my grandfather, I can't imagine he'd have just let this slide. Even if he behaved as if nothing had happened for my sake, I feel sure he'd have been searching for evidence himself."

"We'll keep looking," Asha said. "I promise."

Once they'd left, Sue made herself a mug of warm milk with honey and took it upstairs, intending to go straight to bed with a good book. It was the only way to settle herself for sleep after the emotional roller-coaster of revelations.

Those diaries had been sitting in Grandfather's study for years, and she'd never once opened them. They'd been too imbued with the old man's personality. His study had always been such a private place, his own little refuge. Sue had never been afraid to go in — in fact some of her most treasured memories were of curling up in one of his leather armchairs with a good book — but she'd respected his need for privacy when she was growing up, and the habit had continued even after his death. She hadn't even dusted in there, not that she dusted much anywhere except for her father's room and the kitchen. She wasn't the house-proud type.

Now, she faced the heavy oak-panelled door. She closed her fingers around the cold metal door handle, then huffed out an impatient breath and opened it.

The smell that escaped took her straight to her childhood. Golden Virginia pipe tobacco, old leather, dust. She closed her eyes, so lost in memory that she expected a dry voice to invite her in.

"Choose one book," he would say. "Then read it from cover to cover. Take as long as you need but bring it back in the same condition you found it. No dog-eared pages, d'you hear me?"

The mock severity had always made her giggle. He knew she loved books as much as he did and turning the corner of a page to mark her place would have been like taking a razor blade to her best friend's face.

A wave of loneliness swamped her, coming from nowhere. It wasn't grief for Dad, or even for Grandfather, but for what might have been. They'd been so happy as a family, and then it had all gone wrong. She crossed the room and ran her fingers along the top of Grandfather's favourite chair. It was a wing-backed leather armchair with a soft seat and firm sides that could prop up a head when the user fell asleep while reading a book. On the floor nearby lay the metal camera case he'd kept his long lenses in, and the camera he'd used to photograph birds. Between birdwatching and golf, he'd enjoyed hours in the fresh air.

Three of the walls in here were lined with bookshelves, holding some of her oldest friends. She'd rarely brought school friends to Carrow Lodge. In primary school, she'd felt funny about it because her mum was one of the teachers, and by the time she'd moved up to the grammar school, Dad had started to behave oddly: unpredictable and sometimes irrational.

It must have signalled the beginning of his drug use, but none of them had spotted the signs. Or at least if they had, no one had confided in the youngest member of the family. The books on these shelves had taught her history, geography, philosophy and even anatomy, since some past Hearn had studied medicine and donated his books to the collection.

She pulled down a beautifully bound boxed edition of *The Lord of the Rings*, the one she'd loved most of all the books in this room. She slid the hardback from its box and let it open in the palm of her hand, the scent of old India paper taking her straight back to her childhood.

This thin paper was how the publisher had managed to fit all three volumes into one book, and there were beautiful maps folded up inside the cover. She wanted to lose herself in Middle Earth, away from the terrors of the present. She opened out the map inside the front cover. She expected the familiar names of Mordor, Gondor and Rohan, names that always carried her with them into adventure, but there was something else folded inside the map.

A handwritten note on paper as thin as that used to print the map.

She teased it from the folds, careful not to tear the fragile stuff, and her own name leapt out at her from the page.

Dearest Susan,

I am sure you will find this one day, probably when I am long gone.

These last years have been so difficult for us all, but especially for you, and now I feel my end approaching—

Sue swallowed a sob and sank into the wing-backed armchair.

—I worry how you will manage Michael when I am no longer here to cover up his failings. But you are a kind soul, dearest one, and I am confident you will learn to handle him, for all his fits and starts. I just wish you didn't have to.

You wanted to know what happened to Monica. I'm sorry I kept this from you, and so many other secrets that might, by now, have come to light, but you were so young and so unscarred by life that I couldn't bear to ruin your childhood with the truth. Forgive me?

I tried to find out what happened to her, but I failed. Nevertheless, I have left my notes for you to discover in the hope that you might be able to turn that brilliant mind of yours to the problem and discover the missing links I could not find.

It's hardly a roadmap, dearest Susan, but more of a heavenly path.

Good hunting.

Your friend, always,

Grandfather

Sue folded the paper, her fingers working without any input from her brain, and replaced it where she'd found it.

Hardly a roadmap, he'd said. *More of a heavenly path.*

Her hands shook as she slid the book inside its slipcase and replaced it on the shelf. She knew exactly what he was talking about. The book he'd bought her for Christmas in 1992, when she'd told him she wanted to be an astronaut. *Star Maps for Beginners*.

There was a sliding ladder to reach the upper shelves. Sue moved it along to the section where she'd last seen the book and began to climb.

Are you trying to carry it closer to heaven, Susan? he'd asked, and she had been embarrassed, because that was exactly what she'd been doing when she'd put the new book all the way up here on the top shelf.

And here it was, still in the same place, its slim spine easy to overlook among the leather-bound folios that flanked it. It was weighty for such a slim volume, heavier than she remembered. She tucked it under her arm and descended the ladder.

Back in the chair, legs curled beneath her as she'd sat as a girl, she opened the book.

Except it wasn't a book anymore. The cover was still there with its gold star in the centre, but all the pages were missing. Instead, there was a plain envelope and a stack of loose paper with Grandfather's handwriting covering it.

The envelope was the source of the weight. It was filled with photos, some in colour, some in black and white. She took a sip of cold milk. This was going to be a long night.

CHAPTER 40

The next morning, Asha sent Aaron to the evidence lockers with all the files from William Hearn's study, except for the two diaries and some of Hearn's papers that she didn't want to be available to anyone else for now. Those, she had locked in the glovebox of her car, which was finally out of the impound. She'd touch base with Lonnie, then drive the papers to her parents' house in Rostrevor. Dad could put them in his safe for her.

Lonnie was in a better mood than last time Asha had visited her in her tiny, untidy office. She was sipping at a mug of coffee, a plate of cookies at her elbow.

"They look yummy," Asha said, trying not to send the piles of files around her flying. "Can I nick one?" As she spoke, she reached out to lift one from the plate, and received a sharp smack for her trouble.

"Hands off, lady," Lonnie said, without looking up from her screen. "What are you after, anyway?"

"Maybe I'm just coming in for a wee chat?"

Lonnie snorted, spraying crumbs in a fan across the desk. "Yes, and I believe DCS Patterson has a date tonight with Will Smith."

"Okay. You're right. I just wanted to know if any of our older officers, perhaps retired now, has a military background. Or comes from a military family."

"You are kidding, right? Half the RUC came from the military in the early days. What sort of age are we looking at?"

Asha thought. It wasn't that she didn't trust Lonnie — she'd trust her with her life — but she didn't want to put the elderly sergeant in danger, either. "Oh, I don't know. Would have been active in the late eighties, early nineties, I guess. Plain clothes, probably. Male." Another snort. "Might have worked with our George Aiken sometimes."

Lonnie wiped her lips with a folded paper hanky that appeared from somewhere inside her blouse. "If you're looking for who I think you're looking for, he's retired now. Has a nice place somewhere on the north coast. Inherited it. Must be worth a mill or two these days." She frowned. "And I'm warning you now, Acting Detective Inspector, steer well clear of him. He's dangerous, and he has friends who are dangerous. You don't want to be messing with this guy."

Asha's heart rate accelerated. "Tell me, Lonnie."

"I'm honestly not sure if I should. Some things are best left alone."

Asha leaned on the desk. "A little boy was killed. A woman went missing and still hasn't been found. I can't let this one go." She straightened up. "And besides, if I fail to bring this case to a successful close, I'll be bumped down to sergeant before you can say Joey Dunlop."

"If you're so determined to play with fire, you'll find matches somewhere else."

The analogy made Asha smile. "Yes. There are other people I could ask, but I don't trust them to keep quiet, and I can't afford to alert him that I'm looking for him."

Lonnie lowered her voice until it was barely above a whisper, not that she'd been loud before. "You're after retired Detective Chief Inspector Alistair King."

Asha whistled. "Seriously? Old Walk-on-Water himself?"

"Yes, that one. He took Aiken under his wing when he was a rookie and I think there might have been some sort of family connection, too. King was in the Coldstream Guards before he joined the force. In fact, rumour has it that he was posted here during the Troubles, met his wife and decided to buy himself out of the army. Joined the RUC as a constable and worked his way up through the ranks so fast he was nicknamed 'Everyone's Pal, Al' for a while. Knew how to do favours, get people owing him. Everyone was surprised he stopped at DCI, with all the contacts he seemed to have. We expected to see him as chief constable one day. So, now you know. You need to be careful, Asha. Very careful indeed."

Asha left with her mind buzzing. She'd heard of Alistair King, of course. Everyone had. On his rare calls to the station, it was like royalty was visiting. The only person who didn't grovel and smarm around him was Yvonne Patterson.

She played film music as she drove down to Rostrevor, orchestral stuff that acted as a backdrop to her swirling thoughts. It made sense that it would be someone like Alistair King. He'd have the personal authority to cover up his activities, and with Aiken at his side, he'd have been able to manipulate findings in who knew how many cases.

A blind eye here, a bit of protection there. Of course it had gone on in the bad old days, but it had never occurred to Asha just how far someone like King might have been prepared to go. Drug dealing, threats and the murder of an innocent child just to make a point.

But something still jarred. King was a smooth operator. He was after the money, clearly, so why on earth would he abduct and possibly kill Monica Hearn? Old William was going to pay up. Did pay up, according to his diary. There'd never been any need to abduct Monica, far from it. And why kill William Lee? It could have put his entire operation in jeopardy. If the Hearns had decided to make a stink, it would have put a spotlight on his little scams that even his contacts and tame government officials might have struggled to cover up.

A tiny bell chimed somewhere deep inside her head, but she couldn't quite fathom what it was trying to tell her.

Something about Monica's disappearance threatening King's schemes and the fact that he'd never risen above DCI.

A tractor loomed up ahead of her, taking up most of the width of the narrow road that wound across open moorland. It was towing a trailer full of something that smelled as if it had died a long time ago, bits of which were dropping off to land with a splat in the road. She took her foot off the accelerator and let the car drop back a bit. The last thing she needed was that stinking goo all over her car bonnet.

Her train of thought interrupted, the germ of an idea that had been forming was lost. It'd come back to her, if she didn't force it.

Finally the tractor slowed down almost to a stop and then swung wide to make the turn into a field gateway. She glanced in her mirror, aware of the bend behind her and the risk of collision if someone came around it too fast.

A silver hatchback appeared, swerved as the driver saw her, then braked sharply and came to a stop at an angle across the road, one front tyre on the muddy verge. Sunlight reflected from the vehicle's windows, obscuring her view of the driver. She thought about getting out to see if they were okay, but then the car reversed, shooting towards the blind bend it had just rounded.

The tractor had made it into the field and the road ahead was clear. Asha mentally shrugged and drove on, but she kept an eye in her mirror in case the silver car reappeared.

It didn't, and that bothered her every bit as much as the driver's strange behaviour.

She still didn't spot it as she drove at just under thirty miles per hour through the town and out the other side, where the grey waters of Carlingford Lough glinted in the sun off to her left. There was no silver car in view as she turned in between the stone walls that edged her parents' garden. Her tyres scrunched across the gravel and she pulled her car over to the side, reversing so it wouldn't be easily seen from the road. Then she waited, watching the narrow gateway.

It was a good couple of minutes before the silver hatchback passed, going slower than was usual for this stretch of road. Once again, sun was glinting off the window, but there was an impression of a face in the passenger side, turned towards her. As if they knew she was in here. Knew where her family lived.

Her hand clenched on the wheel until the knuckles ached. She forced herself to relax, but the muscles in her jaw refused to play along.

A sharp tap on the window made her stomach give a sickening twist, but it was her mother, peering in at her with a quizzical expression. She lowered the window and tried to smile back, but there was no fooling her mother.

"Whatever is wrong, Ash? You look as if you've seen a ghost."

"Nothing, Ma, I hope. I was just thinking about a case I'm working on at the moment. It's a tricky one, that's all."

"Okay." There was sympathy in her mum's eyes. "Why don't you do some of that thinking inside? I have the kettle on."

That did make Asha smile. "The old witchy senses still working, then? I didn't tell you I was coming."

"Don't flatter yourself. Your dad always has his coffee at this time of day. Your timing was serendipitous, that's all."

Inside the house, with its familiar smells, she started to relax a little. She perched herself on a raised stool at the breakfast bar and watched her mum making coffee, laying out a tray with slices of fruit cake and some pastries that she'd learned to make on one of her many cookery courses. The scent of spices hung in the air: cinnamon and ginger and nutmeg. It reminded her of Christmas.

"I thought we could take this outside, since it's such a nice day. Bapu's already out there."

They went out onto the patio at the back of the house, where the views along the length and breadth of the lough lifted her spirits. It took moving away, living in an apartment in noisy old Belfast, to make her appreciate the beauty of nature they were lucky enough to have grown up surrounded by. Above her, a gull swooped, its harsh cry sending a ripple of familiarity through her that made her eyes prickle with tears.

She must be more tired than she'd realised.

"Hello, female child," her father said from the depths of a reclining chair. He was wrapped up with fleeces and scarves, and he had a knitted hat pulled down low over his eyes — the OutsideIn hat she'd bought him last Christmas. "How is the big smoke?"

This time, her smile was genuine. "What has he been watching this time? Some futuristic crime film?"

Bapu soaked up sayings and mannerisms from the films and series he watched on the TV. Since he'd retired, his vague interest in film had become more of an obsession, and he was forever quoting random bits that threw the rest of his family into confusion.

"Who knows?" Ma set down the tray on the stone table. "I've given up trying to follow his references."

"The big smoke is as smoky and big as ever. My flat's in a quiet street, though, so it's not too bad."

"If you're ever in it," Ma muttered, but there was pride in her voice. "How does it feel to be an acting inspector? Stressful?"

"You have no idea. I feel as if I'm on trial the whole time."

"At least you have a female boss," Bapu said. "She must understand what it is like to be a woman in the service. Does she support you?"

Asha snorted. "She's worse than the men, sometimes. Don't forget she's still trying to prove *her*self too. She took a chance on me, so if I fall on my face, it will affect her credibility. She doesn't exactly breathe down my neck, but I definitely get the impression she's keeping a close eye on me, waiting for me to trip up so she can plan her own defence." Where had that outburst come from? Her words sounded bitter even to her. "But I haven't been demoted. Not yet. That's good enough for now."

Ma squeezed her shoulder. "You have done so well. Have faith in yourself, my dear. You can do this."

Asha let out a long sigh. "I know I can, Ma. That's part of the problem. I have to be so much better than a man in the same position for anyone to notice. And sometimes, that knowledge makes me do stupid things." Like enter a house without backup when there's an intruder inside.

They sipped their coffee, and Asha nibbled at the fruit cake, relishing the rich sweetness of it. "Have you put alcohol in this, Ma? Am I safe to drive after eating it?"

"Only brandy flavouring. You're safe enough. Would you like me to wrap a couple of slices for you to take with you?"

Asha nodded, her mouth too full to reply, and Ma disappeared into the kitchen, leaving her alone with her father.

She opened her mouth to ask if she could leave the diaries in his safe, then remembered the silver hatchback and closed it again. Surely her parents wouldn't be at risk, would they? But then, a little boy had been killed and a woman had disappeared, not to mention the attempt on her own life and Sue's abduction. Why had she come here? How could she have been so stupid?

"You are worried, Ash. Would it help to unburden yourself?"

She swallowed. "I was about to ask you to keep something for me in your safe, but I'm having second thoughts. It could put you in danger."

He steepled his fingers in the way he'd done when she was a child puzzling over algebra homework.

"What makes you think there is danger?"

"A boy was killed, and a woman disappeared. It was a long time ago, but now I'm raking over the ashes and finding some hot coals still burning after all this time. Whoever did those things is still active, still a threat."

"Are they a threat to you?"

"Yes. But at least I'm aware of it, so I have my wits about me." She huffed out her breath. "I shouldn't have come here. Even this visit might put you in danger."

"You have this thing with you, the thing you were going to ask me to keep for you?"

She tapped the breast of her jacket. She'd tucked the diaries and papers inside and zipped up the front to keep them there, out of sight.

"Then I have an idea. I still have some influence at the bank. How about I accompany you there and we put them in a safety-deposit box? These baddies of yours are hardly likely to raid a bank, are they?"

CHAPTER 41

They *were* followed to the bank, Asha was almost certain of it. The road into Newry was busy, but she thought she spotted the silver hatchback at least once on a long straight stretch. They parked up in a back street and she slowed her pace to match her father's arthritic walk.

She shouldn't have been too surprised at the number of people who nodded and exchanged a word with him as they covered the few hundred yards to his old bank. He'd been a public figure here in the town for decades, and his distinctive appearance, in a country where ethnic minorities were still a novelty, made him stand out from the crowd. More so now, as, since his retirement, he'd thrown off the staid suit and tie and embraced the culture of his forbears, with a loose tunic over trousers and a brightly coloured scarf around his neck.

As they entered the quiet of the bank, faces turned to him with genuine smiles. They were ushered straight through to the back, past the security door and into the inner sanctum of the building.

The current manager, who had been Bapu's protégé, came forward to greet him with outstretched hand. "Welcome, Devendra. It's good to see you. Have you time for a coffee?"

Bapu waved his offer away. "I am swimming with coffee, Jim, thank you. No." He indicated Asha, standing just behind him. "You have met my daughter, have you not? Asha, this is Jim Reed. Jim, Asha."

Jim Reed took her hand and held it perhaps a little longer than he should have. "Of course I remember Asha. You used to come in here after school to do your homework sometimes, when I first started working here."

The man must have a good memory. She didn't remember him at all. "Of course. Good to see you again." She gently disengaged her hand.

"What can I do for you, Devendra?"

"It is a matter of a safety-deposit box, just for a short period."

"Possibly a couple of weeks, but hopefully less," Asha added.

"That shouldn't be a problem. Follow me."

As she left the bank, Asha felt lighter in spirit than she had in days. Weeks, perhaps. And only part of it stemmed from the fact that her evidence was now safe.

She spent another hour at her family's home, enjoying being spoiled. She waited long enough to see Pratik, her eldest brother, when he came in to visit as he did every lunchtime. They sat together around the table in the conservatory, just as they had when she was growing up, and exchanged news. Pratik could speak of little else but the woman he hoped to marry, of whom Asha thoroughly approved. Anyone who made her brother this happy must be a good soul.

"When will I meet her?"

"I was planning to bring her to Belfast in the not-too-distant future." He blushed. "To visit jewellers."

A guffaw of laughter did the rounds, but he took it in good part.

When it was time for her to leave, Asha's defences had been rebuilt, her energy reserves topped up. With a family like hers behind her, she could take on the world.

This positivity lasted all the way into Belfast, surviving the glimpses she kept getting of the silver hatchback, and all the way into the building — right up until the lift doors opened and she emerged onto the grey corridor, with its flickering fluorescent light tubes, and came face to face with Aiken and Kernaghan.

"Oh, here she is, the Chief's pet project," Kernaghan said.

She tried to squeeze past them. Aiken stepped sideways so he was in her way.

Asha drew herself up to her full height and glared down at him. He must have let his hair grow in the years since he'd been King's sidekick, because now he sported a monk's tonsure of ginger curls with a slick of comb-over at the front.

"Sorry. Didn't see you there. I must have been blinded by the glare reflecting from your bald patch."

"Oho! Fighting talk, that," Kernaghan said. "Bullying talk. From a senior officer, too." He sneered the last words, and she was taken aback by the venom in his voice and in his puffy eyes.

"Are you going to let me past," she said, her voice as cold as she could make it, "or am I going to have to put you both on report for harassment?"

Kernaghan's face turned ugly, but Aiken tilted his head and smiled. "Do it. Go on. I dare you. It'll be interesting to see which way the higher-ups jump. A shiny new *acting* inspector's word against the word of two long-serving pillars of the force. Two men who've made a lot of friends over the years."

She wasn't sure what might have happened next, but a voice like vinegar cut through Aiken's threats.

"What is going on here? You two, I thought Inspector Campbell had sent you over to Traffic." Yvonne Patterson glanced at her wristwatch and raised an eyebrow. "Unless you want me to tell him you're hanging around in the corridor, chatting up female officers?"

They took the hint and left, but not before both men shot Asha filthy looks. Kernaghan jostled her as he barged past, causing her to stagger sideways.

She realised she had her fists clenched as if she'd been about to punch one or both of them, and made herself uncurl her fingers. She managed a smile at her senior officer. "Afternoon, ma'am."

Patterson looked her up and down, then nodded and turned on her heel, returning the way she'd come. Just before she turned the corner, she glanced back over her shoulder.

"Good report, that. A bit lacking in detail, but I expect you're going to fill in the blanks momentarily, am I right?"

"Yes, ma'am. Working on it now."

"Very good." And Patterson was gone, leaving Asha shaking, but not sure why.

"Just take care," Bapu had said, before she'd left. She'd promised him she would, but how could she protect herself when the danger came from within?

* * *

About an hour later, her phone rang. She regarded it warily, wondering if it was still tapped, then lifted the receiver to her ear. It was the desk sergeant.

"Got a message here for you to call a Susan Hearn ASAP. Do you want the number?"

"Yes, please."

She took a deep, steadying breath before dialling Sue's home number.

The call was picked up immediately, as if Sue had been sitting by the phone, waiting. Asha wondered why she hadn't phoned her mobile, if it was that urgent. She had Asha's card with her contact details on it.

"Hello, Sue. What can I do for you?"

"Oh, Detective. I *am* sorry to bother you, but I think you left your mobile phone here when you called by yesterday and I was worried in case you needed it. I know how

230

much we depend on these devices these days. I have it here, if you're able to pop over and collect it. There seem to be some missed calls on it."

As Sue spoke, Asha was delving in her handbag. The mobile was right there, where it had always been.

"I don't think—"

"Or it could belong to that nice young constable with the biblical name? Or maybe one of those lovely men and women who were keeping an eye on the house until today?"

A cold feeling seeped through Asha's gut. Sue's voice sounded off. Breathless and gushing, and not one bit like she normally sounded. And *were* they keeping an eye? Something was wrong.

"Oh, thank you. You're quite right, and I hadn't missed it. That must be my personal phone you have there, Sue. My poor mother has probably been going crazy wondering why I haven't answered. I'll send someone over for it shortly."

"Oh, so it is yours? I'm glad to be of assistance." And then the line went dead.

Asha swallowed, her mouth dry. What the hell was going on?

She lifted the phone to call Aaron, then changed her mind and replaced the receiver. Instead, she set off on foot to hunt him down.

He was leaving the canteen, a sandwich in one hand and a plastic cup of the watery brown stuff the canteen optimistically called coffee in the other. She grabbed his elbow and steered him along the corridor towards the lift.

"What's going on? I didn't get my lunch."

"You can eat on the way," she said in a low voice, glancing back to make sure there was no one following them.

As they passed Lonnie's door, Asha had an idea. "Wait here a moment." She left him in the corridor, trying to take a bite of the sandwich without spilling the coffee.

Lonnie looked up, her brows contracting. "Something up?"

"I'm not sure, but I just received a cryptic call from Sue Hearn, and it has me worried. Can you find out who ordered Uniform to cease obs at her house?"

The stubby fingers flew across the keys. "It's been signed off by the Chief."

Asha felt a flood of relief, which was replaced by fresh alarm. If Patterson had signed off on it, why hadn't she mentioned it when they met in the corridor? Did she think it wasn't important? Could someone have signed it in her name?

"Whose actual signature is on it?"

Lonnie frowned. "No signature, just an email from her address ordering the observation to be lifted and citing operational value versus cost. The usual."

"Lonnie, can you think of anyone in this station, or anywhere else for that matter, that you can one hundred per cent vouch for? Someone you know to be straight with no shadow of doubt. Preferably someone with some initiative and a bit of bravery, too. Prepared to stick their neck out."

"What are you planning, *Acting* Detective Inspector?"

"I'm not sure yet, but I think we might be in for some trouble, and I want someone else other than just Aaron to watch my back, even if it's only to give a true, independent report on events." She bit her lip, deciding how much to say. "I was followed this morning, all the way to my parents' house. Then they followed me and my dad to the bank, where I put that evidence in a safety-deposit box. Someone thinks we're close to finding out who is behind this case, and they're not happy."

"You could bring Josh Campbell along with you. He's as solid as they come."

Asha blinked at the elderly sergeant. She knew Inspector Campbell, of course. They all knew each other in the station, and she was sure she must have spoken to him on more than one occasion, but she couldn't for the life of her remember what any conversation might have been about.

"Want me to give him a call? Get him to come here, if he's free?"

"Yes please," Asha said, wondering if she was right to involve someone else. She didn't want to risk anyone getting hurt.

Lonnie put the phone down after a short conversation. "I think he's intrigued. He'll be right over."

"Lonnie, does Josh Campbell have a family?"

"Wife with a bump. Baby due this autumn, I believe. Oh, and he has a bunch of dogs, too. His wife used to be a dog handler, and they have a couple of retired working dogs plus a few other waifs and strays."

Great. She was putting a family man at risk. She was about to say that she'd changed her mind when the door opened, and Campbell walked in.

"That's the most mysterious phone call I've ever had from you, Lonnie," he said. "Cloak and dagger suits you. Whatever it is, DI Harvey, count me in."

CHAPTER 42

Aaron jumped out of Josh's car in the next street across from the house, then tugged the borrowed baseball cap low over his eyes and pulled up the collar of his leather jacket, stooping to hide his height.

They had travelled the short distance to Carrow Lodge in two cars, Asha trailing Josh's ageing Freelander by a good ten minutes. Now he'd dropped off Aaron, Josh would circle around the back and park near the open parkland to the rear of Sue's house. He had one of his wife's ex-police dogs with him, a well-muscled German Shepherd that looked pretty alert despite the grey hairs around its muzzle. He'd be just another dog walker, stopping near the back gate to check his phone while the dog ran around sniffing and marking territory.

Asha had given Josh strict instructions to observe only, and photograph anyone who might emerge from the back gate if he could do so without being spotted. Under no circumstances was he to try to stop anyone or enter the property.

Aaron grinned to himself beneath his collar. Asha might believe that she'd laid down the ground rules, but Josh, quiet man that he was, had had a glint of stubbornness in his eye as he agreed to the instructions.

It had rained recently, and the smell of dog piss and wet grass filled his nostrils as he slouched along, eyes down, until he came to the spot he'd mentally marked as a good place to wait. It was a rundown house with grubby net curtains and weeds growing up in the driveway. The window frames were cracked and rotting — no one lived there. He strode into the driveway as if he belonged, then doubled back to observe the street from the cover of the overgrown privet hedge.

There was no sign of a car outside Sue's house, which was about three doors down on the opposite side of the road, and nothing on the drive that he could see.

No movement in any of the upstairs windows, but then there wouldn't be. It looked totally innocent, just the same as every other house in this well-to-do street with its roomy Victorian detached houses and wide gaps between the entrances. You wouldn't catch modern builders wasting this much space.

He texted a short message to Josh and got an immediate reply, a thumbs-up.

A couple of minutes later, Asha's car drove by. She passed him without a sideways glance and pulled straight into Sue's driveway as if she suspected nothing was wrong.

Aaron waited for her to knock and the door to be answered. He couldn't see the person in the doorway from his vantage point, but Asha went straight in without a backward glance, so it must have been Sue.

Perhaps Asha had overreacted to the odd phone call and was making a meal out of a dry biscuit. He crossed his fingers and hoped, but he'd also learned to trust her instincts. He gave her half a minute to get clear of the doorway, then emerged from his hiding place and crossed the road, slouching along as if he had all the time in the world.

The plan was for Asha to leave the door slightly ajar as she went in, if she could, so he could follow her as soon as it was safe. If not, he'd have to resort to Plan B, picking the lock.

As he passed Carrow Lodge, a glance showed him Asha's car, a closed front door, and no movement from any of the windows. They were probably in the kitchen downstairs. He slipped into the next driveway along.

This house had a gravel path that ran all the way to the back garden. Aaron trod on the grass at the edges so as not to make the gravel crunch, getting wet feet for his pains. The hedge between the two properties was thin and ragged, with gaps near its base, but it was also covered with sharp thorns. *Oh well.*

He found the thinnest section and dropped onto his haunches to examine it. Good thing he'd worn a leather jacket. He pushed his way through, shielding his face with his arms. At the other side, he straightened, checking all around, but there were no windows overlooking this side of the house. He brushed off loose leaves and twigs, registering the snagging thorns stuck into the material with regret. The jacket would never be the same again.

Keeping to the grass, he ducked under the front window and crept up the steps to the door. It was closed. So Asha hadn't been able to stick to the plan. He'd taught himself to pick locks as a teenager, with one of those practice locks you could buy online. He'd never expected to employ this skill as a police detective, but he was glad of it now.

He texted Josh, just one word that they'd agreed, to say that he was going in, and got another thumbs-up in reply.

The lock was a heavy, old-fashioned one. In theory, it should have been easy to pick, just requiring strength to manipulate the levers inside, but he struggled with it. The lock picks he'd brought were too short, so he had to try to turn them using just the very tip that stuck out from the lock. His fingers, sweaty with stress, kept slipping.

It took far longer than he'd calculated before the last one clunked into place, deafening to him in the silence of this quiet street. He said a silent prayer that Asha had been wrong, and that she was just nattering to Sue in the kitchen. She was supposed to have texted him if everything was okay, but he'd felt no vibration from his phone as he worked.

Nothing on the screen, no missed calls or new texts. And he'd been way too long messing around out here when she might need him. He sent a pre-arranged message to Josh to tell him he was inside and pocketed the mobile.

He turned the handle and pushed the door open a few inches, standing to one side just in case, but nothing happened, so he pushed it a bit further. Still nothing. He swallowed and pushed it wide enough to squeeze through the gap.

The hallway was empty and dark after the bright daylight outside. He was grateful for the Victorian tiles on the floor. No boards to creak and betray him.

From downstairs, the buzz of voices sounded.

He was just closing the front door behind him door when a scream ripped through the quiet of the house.

CHAPTER 43

When Sue opened the door, she kept to the shadows, a step inside the dimly lit hallway. Asha smiled and walked up the steps as if she hadn't a care in the world. The door closed behind her. She turned to open it again for Aaron, but Sue was standing in her way. She was trembling.

"I'm sorry," Sue said.

Someone switched the light on, and Asha saw the state of Sue's face. An ugly bruise was already purpling her cheek and one eye was swollen half-shut. Blood trickled down her chin from a cut lip, and she didn't seem to have the energy to wipe it away. Asha's hand was already in her jacket pocket, clutching the heavy Maglite torch she'd cadged from Lonnie before she left, but she didn't get a chance to draw it.

"Don't," said a familiar voice. "I have a gun."

"Aiken. I should have known." She had known. Known it was a possibility, at least. "Was it you who dropped Isaac Newton on my head?"

She turned and met the mean, hard eyes of George Aiken. He did have a gun, too. She'd hoped he was bluffing, but the black hole of a muzzle pointed steadily at her chest. He was frowning, confused. She knew she should take advantage of this but couldn't for the life of her think how.

238

Light dawned. "Oh, that head thing. Yeah, that was me. Pity it didn't finish you." He gestured with the gun and stepped back into the open doorway of Michael Hearn's bedroom, which must have been where he'd hidden until she was safely inside. "Downstairs. You go first, then the woman."

The woman. He didn't even give Sue Hearn a name.

Asha started down the stairs, thinking that if he was alone, there might be a chance to disarm him if she could catch him unawares. Aiken had never been the sharpest knife in the drawer.

"Into the kitchen."

She pushed the door open, and the warmth from the Aga hit her. She stepped aside as she passed inside and reached once more for the Maglite, but then a movement caught her eye. Shit. He wasn't alone. Kernaghan stood at the far side of the room, to one side of the window so he couldn't be seen from outside, and he, too, had a gun. The fact that it was pointing at the floor didn't make it any less dangerous.

Sue came in behind her, her face bleak. She moved like an automaton over to one of the wooden chairs that was pulled out from the table and sat down in it without looking at Asha.

Aiken closed the door behind him. "Hand it over."

"What?" Maybe she could bluff it out. He wasn't that quick.

"Whatever weapon you've got dragging down the pocket of that expensive jacket."

Shit. She pulled out the Maglite, tempted for a moment to swing it at his head, but the barrel of the gun was still pointing straight at her, and he was just far enough away that she'd be off-balance if she tried it. She held it out to him, and he grabbed it with his free hand, weighing it for a moment before putting it on the table. Too far away for her to have any chance of reaching it. Or Sue, for that matter. Not that Sue looked up to trying anything at all.

"Over there." He gestured towards the window. And the Aga, which was burbling away quietly to itself from deep in its innards. The heat from it warmed her chilled skin as she approached it.

"Far enough."

She stopped. Now, she had Kernaghan on one side and Aiken on the other. Not a good place to be.

"What's all this about, George?" she asked, making her voice sound reasonable and calm, despite the sweat that was breaking out on her back and on the palms of her hands.

"It's about finding out what you know." He nodded towards Sue. "She didn't want to help us, so we had to persuade her to make the call."

Asha met Kernaghan's eyes. He seemed the more human of this pair, and she'd always wondered if he just followed the other man's lead.

"You don't need to do this, you know." What the hell was his first name? If she was to get through to him, she needed to connect, but she only knew him as Kernaghan, or Kerny. Some of the younger uniforms called him Kermit behind his back, probably for his large, frog-like eyes. That wouldn't help.

He smiled, genuinely amused. "Oh, but I do, love. You won't get around me that easily."

As he spoke, he edged around the table so he was standing just behind Sue. She didn't seem to be aware, but then that eye was pretty much closed now, so perhaps she was having trouble seeing out of it.

Asha strained to hear any sound from the rest of the house. She hadn't sent the "all clear" text, so by now, hopefully, Aaron would be aware that she was in trouble, but there was no sound through the thick kitchen door.

"So, what do you want to know?" she asked. No point in getting injured if she could fob them off with half-truths.

"It's not so much a matter of what we want to know as how much pain can you take before we ask the questions," Aiken said.

The words were spoken in such a matter-of-fact way that for a moment her brain didn't interpret them, then the meaning sank in.

Aiken moved fast. He was lean and hard, and as his hand clamped around her wrist, she realised he was all muscle beneath that uniform. He dragged her forwards, pulling her off-balance so her hand came down on the top of the Aga to stop herself from falling. She let out a startled yelp as the heat burned her skin, and whipped it away.

His grin widened. "Steady now. No need to rush ahead of yourself." He winked across at Kernaghan. "Got a live one here, mate."

She was taller than him, and she should have been able to resist his pull on her arm, but he still had her off-balance, and he was much stronger than he appeared. He twisted her wrist up in a shoulder lock and she screamed as the tendons strained tight.

She struck out at him with her foot, blinking away the tears. He dodged her kick easily and snatched hold of her free hand, using it as a lever to lift the lid on the left-hand hotplate.

A blast of heat washed over her, and she almost believed she could see the skin blistering on her wrist. Before she could resist, he slammed the hand down onto the hotplate, and now she really could see the flesh bubbling and blistering. The stench of burning meat rose, choking her. Someone was screaming — a high, inhuman sound.

He lifted the hand away from the heat, but the pain still drilled down through her bones, radiating up her arm and into her spine. She squeezed her eyes tight shut, refusing to look at the mess she knew must be at the end of her arm, but she couldn't block out the smell.

"Now I have your full attention," Aiken said, his mouth right by her ear so his breath stirred the hair at the side of her face, "let's start with an easy question. How much do you know?"

She was gasping as if her lungs were as seared as her skin, but pain had always made her angry. "I know you're a white dog turd, stuck to the shoe of a man who kills women and children. You think you're his sidekick, but you're not.

241

You're his scapegoat. You think *he'll* go down, with all his money and influence? No, it's the Aikens and Kernaghans of this world who serve time, not him. And I think you'll just love prison, George—"

He loosed his hold on her burnt wrist and grabbed her by the hair, pushing her face down towards the black hotplate. It looked so harmless, a ring of dark grey metal with some splash stains across the surface, but the heat that hit the side of her face made it seem alive with flames, licking her skin.

Her eyeball dried instantly, even when she closed her eyes to protect it. She didn't want to see this. She didn't think she had any air left in her lungs, yet she managed a scream that could have lifted the roof.

* * *

Aaron raced towards the stairs, pivoting around the newel post without losing momentum, not caring how much noise he made.

The scream came again, a howl of pain. He swore silently. He snagged a black shillelagh as passed the coat rack and threw himself at the kitchen door.

The third scream came as he rocketed into the room, cannoning against someone who grunted as they fell. Someone in police uniform, overweight. Kernaghan.

Aaron kept his feet, staggering to stay upright. Sue was slumped in a kitchen chair, her face a mass of bruises and one eye partially closed with swelling. Over by the range, George Aiken was holding Asha's face down above the left-hand hotplate of the Aga.

He didn't hesitate, but swung the heavy stick in an arc. It made contact with the side of Aiken's head with a sickening thunk. But Aiken was quick. He was spinning even as the blow connected, bringing up a knife that glinted in the harsh electric light.

It felt as if he'd been punched, and not that hard, not hard enough to slow him. Aaron brought the stick up in a

242

backswing, landing an uppercut beneath Aiken's jaw. It should have knocked him out, broken his jaw even, but his arm wasn't as strong as he'd expected. It was like swimming in treacle.

Aiken's snarling face was above him now, blood oozing from a deep gash and dripping down to sizzle with the stench of burnt meat on the hotplate. Then the ground hit. He must have slipped and fallen. He had to get up. Had to help Asha and nail that bastard, Aiken.

Instead, the ground opened up and swallowed him whole, closing over his head in a wave — and then silence.

* * *

The heat was gone, and so was the crippling hold on her arm. She was free. Asha bolted upright, throwing herself as far away from the Aga as she could. She stared all around her, backing up towards the corner, and nursing her injured hand close to her chest. It still throbbed, but the rush of adrenaline was masking some of the pain now. If she was to survive this, she had to move.

Aaron. He and Aiken were locked in a struggle. Aiken's eyes were glazed, and blood ran down the side of his face, but he was still on his feet. Aaron was falling, limp as a ragdoll.

There was a blast of cold air as the back door opened, then Aiken and Kernaghan were gone, leaving only Aaron in her field of vision.

She thought he'd been knocked out, until she saw blood pooling under him, at the base of his ribs. No! Not Aaron.

She pushed herself forward, tried to reach him, but Sue was there before her, already bending over him. She was using a pair of oven gloves to staunch the bleeding in his side.

Asha staggered over to her. Sue thrust a mobile phone at her.

"Phone an ambulance and put it on speaker so I can talk to Control."

Asha fumbled with the unfamiliar phone. She managed to dial 999 and gasped out, "Ambulance. Please hurry."

Then her strength left her. She sank down on the floor next to Sue. Aaron was lying there with his lifeblood pumping out. She was the one who'd got him into this. Her plan had gone so wrong so quickly. How could she ever live with herself if—

A resounding slap brought her back to the present. Sue glared at her with her one good eye. "You were moaning so loud I couldn't hear the emergency operator. Make yourself useful and put some pressure on this while I run up and open the front door."

Asha did as she was told, using her unburnt hand to press down on the wad of cloth, putting her body weight into it. Aaron's skin was corpse grey, his lips pale blue from blood loss and shock.

Her training kicked in. "Aaron. I'm here. The ambulance is on its way, and you're going to be all right. Do you hear me? Don't you dare give up. You fight, do you hear? You fight this and stay with me."

His hand twitched. He was still alive, but how long for?

Then someone pushed her aside and a green uniform blocked Aaron from view.

"All right, lass. We've got him now. Leave him with us."

She shuffled out of the way. Voices spoke across her, registering blood pressure, vital signs, pulse rate, oxygen. The rip of paper tearing as dressings were opened, and the smell of hospitals, cutting through the stench of her own burning flesh.

In no time at all Aaron was on a stretcher, being carried away.

Then a green-clad figure turned to her and a woman's voice, in a harsh English accent, spoke words she didn't understand. Her burnt hand was gently examined, and something cool and wet applied to it. A needle prick in her arm, and coolness flooded her veins, lifting her away from the pain and into a nice, floating, cloudy space.

CHAPTER 44

Aaron awoke in a hospital bed. He knew where he was before he opened his eyes, from the smell of antiseptic and the muffled, hushed voices from somewhere nearby. He'd spent enough time in hospital recovering from a concussion and hypothermia not long ago that he'd recognise those smells anywhere.

He tried to move, but his limbs seemed weighted down and his head was filled with cotton wool. Then he remembered Asha's scream and he gasped.

"It's all right," she said. "I'm here. You're going to be okay, but you have to take it easy for a while."

"Asha?" It came out as a croak. His mouth was dry, despite the drip running into his right arm. Someone pushed a straw to his lips, and he drank the sweet stuff eagerly, then let the straw slide out of his mouth, exhausted.

Cool air wafted over his legs as the sheet was lifted. He opened his eyes, blinking in the bright overhead light, to see Asha peering at his side and frowning. The burnt side of her face was slathered in white cream.

"Just checking to make sure that orange juice isn't leaking straight out through the hole in your side," she said with mock seriousness.

He started to laugh, but it turned into a grimace of pain as something tugged at his skin.

"Steady now. You don't want to undo all the surgeons' good work. Those stitches need time to heal."

He met her eyes, seeing lines around them he hadn't noticed before. "I don't remember—"

"You galloped in and saved the day." She smiled, but that was strained, too.

"You screamed," he said. "That's how I knew where to find you."

"Yes," she said simply.

They stayed like that, quietly taking strength from each other's presence, until a nurse came in and started poking around at Aaron, shining a torch into his eyes and checking the readouts on the machine that bleeped next to his bed.

"Blood pressure's come up a bit," she said, almost to herself, and Aaron realised there was a cuff around his upper arm. It must have been there for a while, but he hadn't noticed it filling and emptying. Still, the machine must have registered that he was alive, at least.

The nurse turned and smiled at Asha. "And you're supposed to be in your own bed in the burns ward. What am I to say when they ask me if I've seen you again?"

Asha smiled back at her. "Tell them the truth. I'm a big girl. I can stand up to those nasty doctors on my own."

When the nurse had gone, Aaron raised an eyebrow.

"Liz was on duty the last time I was brought in here, the time Aiken dropped Isaac Newton on me. She knows there's no point in chasing me back to bed if I don't want to go."

"How bad is it?"

"Doctors say you'll heal quickly enough if you just take it easy for the first week or so. After that, the wound will have begun to knit, so you might be allowed out of bed."

"I meant you," he said.

"Me? I've been better, but I'll heal, too, apparently." She brought her hand up into view from where she'd been hiding

246

it, below the edge of the bed. It was swathed in bandages. He winced. "Does it hurt?"

"Not as much as it did, but I'm topped up with morphine still. What about you?"

"Same. My head feels like a Victorian pea-souper from a Sherlock Holmes story."

"We're a right pair, aren't we?" She sighed. "Aaron, I'm so sorry. I shouldn't have got you into all this."

He laughed, then caught himself again at the twinge of pain. "Got me into it? I'd like to have seen you try to keep me out." He eased his position a little, fighting the early twitch of cramp in his right calf. "Did they get away?"

This time her eyes crinkled in genuine amusement. "Yes, but they won't stay free for long. Josh was a complete star. He kept his head, did exactly as he'd been told and filmed the pair of them leaving through the back gate. He managed to follow them to their car and got them unlocking it, climbing in and driving off. Even got the registration plates. Patterson's ready to burst a blood vessel, apparently, but as far the public's concerned, she's running with a story about a new criminal gang who've got hold of police uniforms. I think she's trying to keep a lid on this as long as she can, but with Josh's camera footage, I don't think it'll stay quiet for much longer. You know what the gossip mill is like."

His spirits lifted, and this was real pleasure, not the false high of opiates. "It was worth it, then. Good for Josh."

"Yeah. Then he came inside to check on us, managed to direct ambulances, put out an alert for the two of them and still get home to his wife in time for dinner. He's a bit of a hero."

"What about Sue?" he asked, the elation fading away. "She looked pretty roughed up."

"She'll be okay. She has some bad bruises. Her police protection is back in place."

"What was that all about, anyway?"

"I'm not sure. Patterson was in earlier, checking up on both of us. She's furious that I've ended up in hospital again

247

— calling me irresponsible and saying that my lack of experience shows — and she was threatening to hand the case over to someone else to finish up, but I think I talked her out of it. As soon as the docs let me, I want to interview Sue and see what she has to say."

"Who removed the police protection? Was it Patterson?"

"She seemed to say it wasn't, but you know how evasive she is. She never gives a straight answer. I keep asking myself if she could be involved, but I just can't see it somehow. What about you?"

"Patterson? No chance. She likes her position too much to get her hands dirty." He shifted again, already bored of lying in bed. "I wish I could come with you."

"So do I. Thank you for having my back. I owe you, big time."

"It was nothing." They both knew that wasn't true. "You'd have done the same for me."

"Still. Thank you."

After she'd gone, he closed his eyes. If he was going to be stuck in bed, healing, he was going to heal as fast as he possibly could. He'd take his meds, obey the doctors, rest up and be back to work as fast as he possibly could.

* * *

The next time he opened his eyes, it was night. The lights in his room had been turned down to their dimmest setting and only the corridor lights outside still glowed at full brightness. Something had woken him, but he wasn't sure what. Everything was as he remembered it, the machine beeping steadily. The drip bag was swinging a little, as if it had just been replaced. Was that what had disturbed him?

But the bag was less than half full, so it couldn't have just been replaced, could it?

A prickle of unease set the hairs on his arms on end. Was paranoia a side-effect of the morphine? But his copper's instincts were screaming at him, and he wasn't going to ignore them.

He reached over with his unattached arm, wincing as the stitches tugged, and spun the little wheel on the side of the drip until the flow slowed and stopped completely.

Then he sank back, cursing himself for a fool. Of course there was nothing wrong with the drip. He thought about opening it up again, but he had no idea how fast it had been set to run, and he didn't want to overdo it.

That warning klaxon in his head was still sounding. Something wasn't right. He examined the place where the drip ran into his vein, in the crook of his elbow. It was itching like crazy, and a dark swelling was bulging out around it, pulling the sticky dressing taut on his skin. Scratching it only made the swelling worse.

In frustration, he hauled at the drip line and pulled the whole thing free. Blood welled up from the site, but he let it run. It took maybe a minute for the machine to start emitting its alarm, an electronic beep that most nurses seemed to be able to tune out.

He was drifting towards sleep when a nurse came bustling in. Her startled cry jolted Aaron awake. He opened his eyes and was shocked at the blood bath drenching the white sheet where his arm lay. The nurse hit an alarm button and in moments, a second nurse responded to the call. Between them, they strapped up his arm with a dressing and taped it in place.

The padding turned scarlet as he watched.

"Is that supposed to happen?" he asked, pointing to the dressing, which was already beginning to ooze.

"Oh, God," the older of the two nurses said. "Hold on."

There was a lull, during which the first nurse put pressure on his arm, but still the blood seeped through the dressing until it dripped onto the bedclothes, stark red against the white.

An exhausted-looking junior doctor came in, his eyes widening at the scene in front of him. Aaron wondered weakly if he'd done a crazy thing, taking that line out of his arm. It only seemed to have made things worse.

Then he shuffled a little and realised his side was also soaking wet. He pulled the sheet up and peered under it. It was soaked in blood, too.

"Nurse?"

CHAPTER 45

Asha hadn't slept at all. She'd been mulling over the events of the last twenty-four hours and trying to make sense of Aiken and Kernaghan's actions. They must have known it would be the end of their careers as serving officers, surely?

But only if they were caught. Only if the spotlight fell on to them. And they had a powerful protector to make sure it didn't. Especially if no witnesses survived to point the finger.

She went cold at the thought. They'd never intended to leave Sue or her alive. They'd set their trap, lured her in, and that's where it would have ended. Had King instructed his minions to question Sue and herself, or had Aiken and Kernaghan been acting out their own nasty little agenda? A bit of fun to stave off the boredom.

She was still lost in thought when a shadow appeared at the glass panel beside the door into her room. It was no more than a silhouette, but there was something familiar about the stocky figure in dark clothes.

She pressed the call button. The familiar soft *doing* sounded outside at the nurses' station, only just loud enough to hear. The figure at the door was trying the handle.

Asha was off the bed and looking about her for a weapon, but there was nothing she could use. No handy drip stand to swing like a cudgel. She gathered up the electrical cord for the call button, hissing as her bandaged hand tried to close on it and failed. She'd have to swing the cord like a South American bola, but it was too light to do much damage.

Then the shadow moved away, disappearing swiftly towards the main entrance. A moment later, a nurse scurried in, looking harassed. She stopped dead at the sight of Asha with the electric cord clutched tight in her good hand and draped over her bad one.

"Is anything wrong?"

"Was there anyone at my door just now, when you came to answer the call button?"

"If there was, he beat a hasty retreat." The nurse frowned. "You must know that visiting hour is long past. It's after midnight! We can't have visitors disturbing other patients in the night." She took the cord from Asha's hand. "Now, why don't you settle yourself down to sleep? I think they're planning to let you out tomorrow, but not if you knock that hand. I know Dr Harrison explained the risk of infection, and how you need to keep it protected to give the fragile new skin a chance to heal."

"Yes," Asha said through dry lips. "Sorry." She climbed into bed, keeping the injured hand lifted clear, and managed to pull the thin sheet over herself, her back to the door. The nurse must have stood and watched long enough to be sure her patient was behaving, because it took a minute before Asha heard the door swish open and shut.

She gave the nurse another couple of minutes to return to her station. Another call button sounded somewhere else in the ward. Good. That would keep the nurse occupied. She scrambled out of bed and began to dress, clumsily and with many muffled curses.

A quick look up and down the corridor showed no one lurking, and her room was quite close to the exit, so it was the work of a moment to slip out, using the automatic open button. Luckily, these fancy new wards let people out in the middle of the night, even if they didn't let anyone in without a pass.

The events of the past few days must have affected her judgement. She was seeing danger everywhere. How could Kernaghan have got into a locked hospital ward in the middle of the night without a pass? It was impossible. She must have been imagining things.

Still, now the fear had taken root, she needed to check on Aaron or she'd never get a wink of sleep. If he was okay and sleeping like a baby, she'd go back to her own ward, apologise to the nurse on duty and sleep the rest of the night away. But the rapid beating of her heart wouldn't allow her to hope that was likely.

She sneaked into the lift just as the doors were closing behind an orderly and pressed the button for Aaron's floor. Her heart was beating a tattoo. She willed the smooth, silent lift to go faster.

The double doors at the entrance to Aaron's ward were wide open. Her chest ached, as if she wasn't getting enough air, but she ran through, eyes locked on the door halfway down, the one with two trolleys parked outside, covered in bloodied dressings.

She grabbed the doorframe, as much to keep herself upright as anything, and froze in the entrance.

A team of doctors and nurses were working on him, setting up a drip, but the bag wasn't clear fluid — it was blood. The medical staff moved around in a choreographed dance to which only they knew the steps, and for one brief moment, a space between two green-clad bodies showed Aaron, as pale and bloodless as he'd been when he'd been stabbed.

She hung back in the doorway, knowing she could do nothing, knowing she'd be in the way if she came any closer.

Terse phrases laced the air around her, swift commands that were followed by scurrying action. All the faces were tight with concern, concentration, disbelief.

"Where's that clotting factor and vitamin K?" cried a doctor, his hair dishevelled and plastered across his forehead with sweat. "We're losing him."

The machine flashed with coloured lines and numbers, but they meant nothing to Asha.

She flattened herself against the wall as a nurse flew past her, clutching two small bottles. The doctor swore again, in relief this time, as he drew the contents of the first one up into a syringe.

"Keep the pressure on. It's all we can do until this stuff kicks in. Vitamin K next. How the hell did this happen?"

"We should pray," said an older nurse with severe features and iron-grey hair pinned into an old-fashioned bun at the nape of her neck. "If anyone here believes, pray. I don't care what God you pray to, so long as he listens. I am not losing this young man, do you hear?"

So Asha prayed. She prayed to the Christian God of her mother and Waheguru, the Sikh god of her father, to Allah and to as many of the pantheon of Greek and Roman gods she could remember.

"It's slowing," someone said. "Am I right?"

Silence, broken only by the squeaking of rubber-soled shoes on the hard floor and the rustling of cloth, then: "I think you're right. Jade, fetch another litre of A positive, and plasma, please. We might have a chance now."

A nurse ran past her and disappeared from view.

"What the hell happened here?" the doctor growled. "When I checked him earlier he was stable, his blood pressure was almost normal, and the wound looked fine." He ran his fingers through his damp hair, eyes bloodshot with tiredness. "What did I miss?"

Asha took a deep, steadying breath and stepped into the room. "I don't think you missed anything, Doctor. I think someone got to him. I think the same someone tried to get into my room just now, but a nurse scared him off."

All eyes turned towards her. The doctor shook his head as if this was a long nightmare and he wanted to wake himself from it. "Who the hell are you?"

"Detective Inspector Asha Harvey. Detective Constable Birch here is my partner, and we were admitted at the same time after we were both attacked. I believe one of the men who did this—" she held up her bandaged hand — "tried to finish his work here tonight. Is there anything he could have given Aaron to make his wounds open up like that again?"

"Do you have any ID?"

Thank God, her wallet was still in her trouser pocket. She tried to reach it, but her bandaged hand wouldn't work. It was too fat.

"Let me," the grey-haired nurse offered. She reached around Asha and drew out the wallet, letting it fall open across her hand. Asha's police photo ID card was prominently displayed.

"Ah. That changes matters," the doctor said. "His wounds didn't break open, they just started bleeding again, and we couldn't stop it. If what you're saying is true, it's possible he was injected with a strong anticoagulant like heparin or warfarin. It had to be something like that. I assumed I'd missed some anticoagulant therapy in his medical history." His sickened expression told Asha he was relieved to find a different explanation.

Aaron groaned. His eyes were open, lips moving, but he was too weak to speak. The frustration showed in his face. He waved his hand in the direction of the drip stand, where a couple of spent bags still hung. The staff must have been too frantic to remove them.

"It was in a drip?" Asha asked as she moved to the drip stand. "Which one?" She pointed to each bag in turn. When she reached the smaller one, still half full, he nodded and a wan smile lit up his face. "This one." She snatched a rubber glove from the box next to the bed and tried to fit it to her good hand, but the other hand was no help, and she grunted her frustration.

The same nurse who'd helped her with her wallet whipped off her own bloodstained gloves and took a new pair from the box, fitting them with the ease of long practice. "I can do that. I take it you'll want it for evidence, Inspector?"

"Yes, please." Relief flooded Asha. If this bag had Kernaghan's or Aiken's prints on it, or, better still, their boss's, it would help their case no end. Aaron's eyes met hers and they both smiled.

CHAPTER 46

Sue wandered around the kitchen the next morning, tired and cross after a night with little sleep. She gathered up the soiled dressings and plastic wrappers left lying around after the chaos in here the night before. The paramedics had taken all their sharps with them, but they'd left almost everything else behind in the rush to get that young policeman to hospital, and the forensics team that had followed them hadn't stopped to help clean up. Not that she blamed them. Besides, it gave her something to do to keep her mind off things.

They'd left a police constable with her to keep an eye on things. This morning, after a shift change, it was PC McAvoy, the same woman who had turned up on her doorstep what felt like months ago now, the day Mark Talbot had called in the police to investigate the skeleton in her garden. She was doing her rounds of the house at the moment, making sure every window and door was secure. She'd already barred the garden gate, blocking it with a heavy teak table from an outdoor set Sue's mother had once been so proud of.

McAvoy came into the kitchen, her face anxious with the responsibility.

"Oh no! You can't clear all that up on your own. Let me help."

Sue didn't have the energy to argue, so the constable put on a spare pair of Marigolds and started tidying, stuffing all the waste into a black plastic bag. When they'd finished and Sue had mopped the floor, the young woman filled the kettle and they sat down together like old friends.

Sue realised she'd avoided sitting in the chair she'd sat in the day before. The flash of memory, the stench of burning flesh, hit her like a punch in the guts, and she put her mug down with a thump before her shaking hand spilled it. McAvoy's face softened in sympathy.

"Are you all right, Miss Hearn?"

She took a deep breath. "Yes. Sorry. It just came back to me. I don't know how my life came to change so much in such a short time. One moment I was a staid, middle-aged daughter, nursing my dad, and the next I'm on my own, tangled up in this mess."

McAvoy took her hand. The comfort of warm skin enveloping her fingers caught her unawares. Her eyes filled, burning with tears, and her breath came in ragged gasps.

"Don't fight it," the young woman said. "Let it go. You've been really brave, and it's time you released the pressure valve."

Her abduction, her dad's death, yesterday's beating . . . even the years of wondering about her mother, all erupted from her. The sobs came from a dark place deep inside her soul, a place she'd kept walled off until now.

She came back to full awareness to find the constable in the chair next to hers, arms wrapped around her. She'd been crying and snottering into the poor woman's neat uniform. She pulled herself free and mined her pockets for a tissue.

"Sorry. So sorry. I don't know what got into me."

"Don't be. It's safer to release grief than to bottle it up." Wise words for one so young. What life experiences had given this woman the depth of character to take such a breakdown in her stride? Or was it all just training?

She sat up straighter, aware that she'd stiffened. "Have you heard anything from the hospital yet? About poor Constable Birch?"

McAvoy took the hint and returned to her own side of the table, sipping at her mug of coffee. "No, but I was thinking of checking in with the station to see if anyone else has heard anything."

Sue smiled encouragement. "I'd feel much better if I knew he was out of danger."

Before McAvoy could radio, the front-door knocker sounded upstairs. She abandoned the radio and leapt to her feet. "I'll get it. You stay here, and don't open the back door for anyone."

Someone had boarded up the glass in the back door and locked it. Sue had no intention of opening it anyway, but she nodded. McAvoy disappeared upstairs, and Sue waited, rigid, straining her ears for the sound of voices.

The tension was too much for her. She darted over to the counter and snatched the biggest of her carving knives from the knife block. *Second biggest*, she reminded herself. The biggest one had been taken away as evidence after that awful little man with the red hair stuck it in Aaron's side.

Footsteps sounded on the stairs, and Sue braced herself, backed into the corner, her knuckles white where they gripped the knife handle. The door opened and McAvoy came in, followed by another woman in an expensive-looking suit that was taut across her broad shoulders and hips but rumpled around her waist.

She stared at Sue, as if she was unaware of the knife or didn't much care about it, and if Sue hadn't known for sure that they'd never met, she might have thought there was recognition in the woman's eyes.

"Hello, Ms Hearn. My name is Chief Superintendent Yvonne Patterson and I'm in charge of this case. I thought I should come and check up on you, see how you're coping."

The voice was deep, almost masculine and very matter of fact. It had a rough edge to it, but there was kindness there, too. Sue's grip on the knife eased a little.

"I have news from the hospital as well. Better to hear it straight from the horse's mouth, as it were, rather than second-hand, huh?"

Sue replaced the knife in the block, still keeping her eyes on this newcomer. "That's very kind of you. There's still coffee in the pot, if you'd like some?"

"Thank you." Patterson sat down in the seat McAvoy had just vacated. The constable took up a position near the door, feet slightly apart, hands behind her back as if she was on military parade and had just been told to stand at ease.

Sue used the excuse of finding a mug and pouring coffee, pushing the milk jug and sugar bowl across, to hide her anxiety. Despite the chief superintendent's relaxed demeanour, there was something about her that set Sue's nerves on edge.

"You have news about Inspector Harvey and Constable Birch?"

"Yes. Some good, some bad, but the summary is that they'll both be just fine."

"Tell me the bad first," Sue suggested, "then the good."

"All right." Patterson took a long gulp of coffee, then set the mug down. "There was an attempt on Constable Birch's life last night, but luckily his own quick wits, as well as some brilliant work by the medical staff, saved him."

Sue sagged, and sat down hard on the nearest chair, only then realising it was the one she'd been avoiding.

"Someone hooked up a warfarin drip to his intravenous line. Without prompt attention, he'd have quickly bled to death from his sutured wound. Thankfully, he was found in time. We have the drip in Forensics, being tested to find out what exactly was in it, and to see if there are any fingerprints on it."

"But he'll be okay?" McAvoy sounded as if she was speaking past a lump in her throat.

Patterson turned and gave her a long look before answering. "I'm assured he'll make a full recovery, and he now has a full-time guard outside his room."

The young constable gave a tight smile. "Thank you, ma'am."

"What about Asha?" Sue asked.

"It seems there might have been an attempt to hurt her, too, but her attacker, or potential attacker, was scared away by the timely arrival of a nurse. I have an officer checking the hospital's CCTV as we speak, to see if we can identify anyone behaving in a suspicious manner."

"So she's okay? How badly was she hurt?"

"Her hand took the brunt of the damage. Luckily it was her left hand, and she's right-handed, so it shouldn't hold her back too badly once it begins to heal. Her face also took some damage, but the doctors say she won't lose her good looks."

The last was said in such a dry voice that Sue wondered if the older woman was jealous.

"Do we know why those two men came here in the first place?" Sue asked. "And who they were?"

They'd appeared from nowhere. She'd seen the police car disappear from the driveway while she was upstairs, and assumed it was just doing its regular rounds until an hour went by and it still hadn't returned. Then she'd heard the front-door knocker and gone to see who it was, all unsuspecting. A fat man in a PSNI uniform, another of her guards, she assumed — until the second man stepped into view, and the pair of them pushed past her to get into the house.

She'd told all this to another officer, a lovely, quiet man whose name she hadn't quite caught. Signed a statement, even. But she hadn't told him everything, not by a long way.

"We're working on the theory that they were members of a local gang. They seem to have acquired police uniforms in order to gain access to residents' homes, but we're not sure what exactly they're after, as nothing has been stolen from the house. Do you have anything they might have been interested in stealing?"

"Well, there are the books," Sue said doubtfully. Thank God she'd hidden the photos where she'd found them. "I grew up with them, so I never really guessed that some of them might be worth money, but when I was cleaning my grandfather's study the other day, I realised he'd been collecting some first editions that might fetch a decent price at auction." She sighed. "I could do with the money, to repair the roof and a few other bits of the house, but I'm not sure I could ever bring myself to part with them."

"Old friends," Patterson said, demonstrating an empathy Sue hadn't expected to find in so controlled a woman. "I'm a bibliophile, too. I can never bear to part with them, either. One day, when you're feeling a little stronger, I'd love to see your grandfather's collection."

Sue tried a tentative smile. "You'd be very welcome to."

Patterson was either being conservative with the truth or she had no idea that Asha and Aaron were already pursuing a member of the PSNI who had killed William Lee and possibly also abducted her mother.

"Did you recognise either of them?"

Yes. The skinny one with greying red hair. She was nearly certain he was the same man she'd seen sitting alongside Will's killer in that black Volvo all those years ago.

"No, I'm afraid not. Is there any reason why I should?"

The policewoman stared at her, unblinking, then smiled. "No reason. I just thought they might have been hanging around the area, waiting for their opportunity."

Really? Sue was almost certain Asha and Aaron wouldn't have shared their suspicions with this woman. They'd told her they were keeping her information to themselves until they got a grasp of how far the rot had spread. She wasn't going to spill the beans.

262

CHAPTER 47

As soon as she was released from the hospital, and after she'd checked on Aaron, who was sleeping but looked a much healthier shade of pink, Asha took a taxi to Sue's house.

She got out a few doors down the street, which was lucky, because she'd just paid off the driver when she noticed a sleek, shiny, top-of-the-range Mercedes in Sue's driveway. Patterson.

She crossed the road and took cover in the same deserted entrance Aaron had used the day before, the one they'd both agreed made a good observation position. She watched until the sun was well over the rooftops. She was on the point of phoning the taxi company and ordering a car to take her home when there was a glimpse of movement and colour through the foliage of the hedge around Sue's front garden.

A car door slammed, then the reverse lights came on and the big car backed out. It drove off with the deep, throaty growl of a powerful engine. She waited until she was certain it was out of sight, then emerged from cover.

Her left shoulder ached from the cold, still strained from the abuse it had received the day before. Inside her bandage, the burnt hand throbbed. She must be due some pain relief anytime now, surely?

Constable McAvoy answered her knock, very sensibly opening the door on the chain until she saw who it was. Her face sagged with relief at the sight of Asha.

"Inspector, am I glad to see you!"

Asha felt a surge of warmth at the greeting. Perhaps she should take some time to get to know McAvoy.

"Everything okay here? I was in the area, so I thought I should check on Ms Hearn."

"All good. You just missed the Chief, though."

"Oh," Asha said as blandly as she could. "That's a shame."

She got a suspicious frown for her pains, then a gurgle of laughter that made the constable appear even younger than she looked. "I'll not ask if you were hanging around outside waiting for her to leave!"

"Very wise."

She descended the stairs while McAvoy secured the locks on the front door. Yale as well as the mortise lock, by the sound of the double click. Good.

Sue wasn't in the kitchen, but steam was beginning to gush from the spout of the big cream kettle on the Aga, and a cafetière stood ready with ground coffee already measured out, so she mustn't be far away.

McAvoy followed Asha in. "Sue's gone upstairs to freshen up."

A moment later, Sue joined them. The bruises on her face were already yellowing at the edges, and the swelling had gone down in her injured eye, leaving it bloodshot and sore-looking, but much healthier than the last time Asha had seen her.

Her face lit up at the sight of the detective. "Asha! I'm so relieved to see you." Then a shadow darkened it. "But it was my fault, what happened to you. How can I ever make it up to you?"

Asha shook her head. "Your quick thinking is the reason I'm still alive today, Sue. What on earth made you think about the mobile phone story?"

"I'd been tidying up Dad's room and left his mobile down here in the kitchen, to remind me to cancel the contract. It's one of those old-people phones designed for dementia sufferers, but I didn't think anyone who hasn't been a carer would know that." She pointed to the phone, which was still sitting in the middle of the table. "They wanted me to string you some tale to get you here, make up some story about having found something useful in Grandfather's papers, but I said I'd been going to call you anyway, to let you know you'd left your mobile here."

"Genius," McAvoy breathed. Asha nodded her agreement.

"I thought that would be enough to put you on your guard. I knew you'd got the message when you played along with the story. I hoped it would keep you away." Her eyes were troubled. "I should probably have known better."

Sue was keeping something back, but Asha wasn't sure what. Presumably, the presence of Constable McAvoy was making her wary, and rightly so. Hadn't Asha drummed into her how few people in the force they could trust?

But McAvoy was far too young to have been involved in the events that had begun all this. She was barely out of probation, and surely hadn't had time to forge any links with undesirable members of the force. Besides, if Aiken and Kernaghan were anything to go by, that little clique was strictly male and aggressively so. A dark-skinned female officer, especially one with no strings to pull, would be of no interest to King or any of his followers.

If only she could be sure. Sue was watching her with wary eyes, letting her make the decision.

Eventually, the silence must have got to the constable. She shuffled her feet. "Maybe I should do another check around. Make sure everything's secure?"

That decided Asha. If McAvoy worked for King, she'd surely want to stay and hear everything she could.

"No, stay. I think you should hear this, too."

Sue's tired smile made Asha think she'd made the right decision.

"You found something, Sue, didn't you? Did you manage to keep it hidden?"

"They didn't even look for it. Seemed to be more intent on hurting me and getting you here." She looked away. "I don't think they were very bright."

"That's Aiken and Kernaghan for you," Asha said.

McAvoy's mouth dropped open. "Those two? The Chief's official story is that it's a local gang, but there are rumours going around." She shook her head. "I still can't believe it. Two. Not one, but two serving police officers involved in serious crime right under everyone's noses. Why didn't any of us guess? How long has this been going on for?"

"Good question," Asha said. "One thing's for sure: Patterson won't be able to keep a lid on it for long. They're hardly going to show up back at the station now Aaron and I can identify them." That must be why they'd tried to kill Aaron, and probably her, too. But how much should she reveal? Nothing more than she had to, for now, at least. The circle was already widening too far, with Josh and now this constable in the loop. "I can't keep calling you Constable, PC McAvoy. You must have a first name?"

McAvoy ducked her head shyly. "Faith. My name is Faith. Religious mum."

"It's a lovely name," Sue said.

Asha had been about to ask if she had sisters called Hope and Charity. She was glad Sue had got in first. "Well, Faith, the reason they've got away with it for so long, and it is a very long time indeed, is that they've had protection from a senior officer."

Faith McAvoy's eyes widened in shock. "Are you serious? Who?" Her voice was tight with stress.

"I don't think it's fair to share that with you just yet, not until we can gather incontrovertible proof that he's guilty. Sorry."

Faith nodded, her face relaxing. "*Him.* That won't rule out too many senior officers, but it's a start."

"Yes. It means we're probably safe with Patterson, at least. Can you imagine how awkward it would have been if she was the one we had to try to bring to justice?" Asha turned to Sue. "What was it you found, Sue?"

"Hang on. I'll go and get it."

Asha sat in companionable silence with the young constable and wondered how well she'd cope with the rough teasing female officers tended to get in the force. Mind you, that might diminish somewhat, now the two main culprits were out of action. How long before they were caught, those two? And where were they now?

Sue reappeared, a little out of breath, clutching a slim paperback.

"Here."

She handed it to Asha. It was heavier than it looked. Bulky, too. She put it down on the table, and all three women pulled up chairs.

"Open it," Sue said.

Ashe flipped the front cover open. And that's all it was, just a cover with all the inner pages removed. Instead, it held one of those old-fashioned envelopes that local photo-developing shops used to send the pictures home in. And some papers. Handwritten notes, in William Hearn's now-familiar flowing letters, but densely written and even harder to read than usual.

She'd look at those in detail later. The photo envelope was stuffed with prints, which had given the book its extra weight. Some in black and white, but most in colour. She stared at each one and took in the details, then passed them on to Faith McAvoy.

Many showed Aiken, young and brash with close-cropped red hair. He did have a bullet-shaped head, and these pictures really showed it. Kernaghan was only in one, but it was an incriminating one. He held the arms of a turbaned man, quite elderly, pinning them together from behind to leave him defenceless while Aiken punched him. There was a series of three, taken in quick succession, showing the line of the punch, straight into the old man's solar plexus.

Faith McAvoy made little distressed noises, and Asha clenched her jaw at the sight. Classic bully trick. Maximum pain and distress, minimum marks, should the victim decide to seek help. And where would he seek help? From the police? The very men who were hurting him?

Could they find the old man, persuade him to testify? There was a shop front in the background, but no name that she could see. Someone might recognise where it was. But this had been nearly thirty years ago. Even if they could find the shop, the old Sikh was probably long dead by now. There were more, and in some there was a third figure, but no clean shots of his face. Just a tall, broad-shouldered man in a dark overcoat. Asha recognised the posture and the way the square head sat low on the shoulders, with not much neck in between. She knew it was King beyond any personal doubt, but not one of these photos would be enough to convince a jury.

"Keep going," Sue said quietly.

It was in the last few photos that Asha found the answer to the prayer she'd been silently sending up to the gods. William Hearn had come up trumps with these ones. A series of images taken close together, these showed another scene with Aiken and Kernaghan. Perhaps the rot hadn't spread any further than those two.

In this series, it was a younger man they were beating up. But they weren't just using their fists this time. Aiken had a knife to the man's throat in one image, and a trickle of blood was making a dark line across the man's pale skin. The victim had his eyes closed, as if he was ready to accept his fate, but then in the next shot, the knife had been taken away leaving just that same small trickle of blood to show it had ever been there. Kernaghan still held him by the arms in the same way he'd held the old Sikh, but the focus of both men was on something outside the frame.

Frowning, Asha moved to the next in the series and gasped. William had caught King full face, but what made her blanch was the child he held.

A little girl, no more, surely, than five or six years old? He had her gripped beneath his left arm, as if he was holding a rugby ball, steadying the back of her head with the same hand while his right hand held a long, thin knife with its tip to the angle of her jaw.

Asha knew in that moment that it was the same knife that had killed Will. She couldn't prove it, not yet, but she knew what King was saying as if she'd been there listening. He was telling the child's father what would happen if he drove that knife home, up through the little girl's jaw, her tongue, the roof of her mouth and into her brain. Just as he had with Will.

How had William Hearn stood there and witnessed this, after what he'd already seen? If it was hitting her so hard, how must it have been for the old man as he took the photograph?

The next picture showed the little girl back on the ground, King holding her by the hand. She was straining to get away, her face crumpled and red with screaming, but her father had capitulated. It showed in the drooping lines of his shoulders and the way his hands hung at his sides. Kernaghan had released him, because they didn't need to hold him anymore. King had him in a grip more powerful than any physical hold.

And that was it. That last image showed all three men, Aiken, King and Kernaghan, together with both victims in the same shot. Enough to convict all three. He'd even written the dates on the back of each one.

Asha let out a long breath and leaned back in her chair. "Sue, you are a wonder. And so was your grandfather. I wish he was here so I could shake him by the hand."

Sue smiled sadly. "You'll read the notes for yourself, but he ends by saying that this scene, the one you've just been looking at, was the last straw for him. He realised he just couldn't contend with that kind of violence, not in the police. He recognised that he was defeated. That was when he gave up trying to find Mum and tried to make the best he could with the family he had left to him.

"He thought that maybe, one day, I'd be able to pick up where he left off and bring those men to justice. He said he hoped times would change sufficiently, by the time I was grown up, that people like these men could be exposed for what they are." She turned tear-filled eyes to Asha. "Was he right, do you think?"

"I truly hope so. I intend to bring them to justice, with your help and the help of a small number of trusted colleagues." She nodded to Faith, who blushed and ducked her head.

Faith had held onto one of the earlier photos and had been scanning it carefully. Asha held out her hand for it, to put it back in the folder with the rest. Faith hesitated for a moment, then handed it over.

Asha glanced at it. It was one from the middle of the bunch, showing just Aiken and Kernaghan as they shook down another shopkeeper, at a betting shop this time.

There were people in the background, but the quality was too poor to recognise faces. A couple with a child, scurrying away with their heads down. A girl on a bike, talking to a woman in a headscarf. An elderly man carrying a shopping bag. They were all too far away to have much idea what was going on outside the betting shop.

She put it away with the rest and closed the envelope. "I think I'll take these to show to Aaron. He'll need cheering up, I reckon."

CHAPTER 48

Aaron woke the morning after the attack with anger burning him up from the inside. When he first opened his eyes, he couldn't remember why he was so furious, but then the memories crept in and the rage flared.

Bastards! They'd tried to kill him while he lay helpless. He attempted to sit up, but the room swirled around him and a buzzing started inside his head. He sank back and fumed silently, willing himself to get stronger.

When the nurse came in, he took his meds docilely — iron tablets, antibiotics and a bunch of others he didn't catch the name of — and downed them with a glass of orange squash.

"Are you up to eating? Doctor says you can as soon as you feel like it."

No! Just let me out of here. "Yes, please," he croaked. He wasn't hungry, but eating would build his strength, and he needed every ounce of that.

Breakfast was a bowl of porridge with a small pot of honey, some toast with butter and jam, and a mug of strong, black coffee, lukewarm and stewed. He forced every last drop down his protesting throat, then closed his eyes. Rest, good food — or as good as he'd get in hospital — and he'd be out of here in no time. Then he could catch those two little shits. Child killers, torturers of women, they deserved to suffer a little of what they'd been dishing out.

Sleep must have overtaken him, because he came to with a start to find Asha bending over him, her face inches from his. Her long, black hair must have woken him when it brushed his cheek. Her eyes were dark brown flecked with gold. He'd never noticed that before.

She drew back, embarrassed. "Sorry. Didn't mean to wake you, but the nurse said it was time for your midday meds, so I said I'd bring them in here for you." She held up the little paper pot with his pills and shook it so they rattled. "Do you need me to support you so you can sit up?"

He grinned, spirits lifted at the sight of her, and pressed a button on the remote he held in his hand under the covers. The back of the bed raised him up. "Magic, see?"

"Oh, very good. What have you prepared for your next trick?"

"Getting out of here, with a bit of luck. How's the hand?"

"Better." She was lying, or so the tightness around her eyes suggested, but he let it pass. "And once you've taken these, I have some good news for you that should speed up your healing no end."

"Oh?" He swallowed down the pills, pulling a face. They'd started giving him oral paracetamol and it tasted vile on his tongue. "Sit and tell me."

"Better still, I can show you." She slid the envelope of photos out from inside the leather document case she used as a handbag and handed them over, then sat down on the horrible visitor's chair as he spread the photos out across the bedclothes.

She was charged with energy, almost vibrating with it.

He wasn't surprised at the first few, the ones of Aiken and Kernaghan, although the sight of the man in the overcoat made him growl.

"There are dates, times and places written on the back," Asha said.

He turned one over and found William Hearn's beautiful copperplate writing on the picture he was holding.

3 July 1993, 9 p.m. Samuel Baumberg's pawn shop off Sandy Row.

That place must be long gone. He'd never even heard of it.

She was still watching him with those intense, brown eyes. He laid out the next set and gasped. "We've got him!"

"We've got all three of them, thanks to William Hearn. He made copious notes, too, so we can probably use those as evidence."

Aaron let the last photo fall from his fingers and closed his eyes. Peace wrapped around him. "Have you told the Chief yet?"

"No. I thought you deserved to know first, since you're the reason I'm still alive today."

He opened his eyes and glared at the bandaged hand. She tucked it behind her, out of sight. "Works both ways," he said.

"I'm taking this to Patterson now, and I've asked Josh to meet me there with the film footage he took from the back gate. We need a watertight case to present to the CPS, especially since it involves two serving officers and one retired senior officer. She won't act unless she's certain the charges will stick."

"True. She didn't get to where she is now by betting on long odds." He shuffled his bum, trying for a more comfortable position, and the dizziness wasn't as bad as it had been earlier. "Hopefully I'll be out of here soon, but let me know how you get on, won't you?"

She nodded and lightly touched the fingers of her good hand to the back of his hand, then she was away, and the room seemed darker.

* * *

After a short nap, he thought he'd have another try at sitting up, and this time he managed it with very little dizziness, so he swung his legs over the edge of the bed and stayed there for a moment.

The change in position had affected his bladder, and bedpans were an invention of Satan, so maybe he could manage the few steps to the en-suite toilet?

Holding tight to the bed frame, he stood up, hunching over to protect the wound in his belly. It felt as if someone had used him as a punching bag. Last night's bleeding had caused internal bruising as well as external blood loss, according to the doctors.

He took two shuffling steps, barely able to reach the bed frame. It wasn't far to the wall, his next support. Deep breath. *You can do this.* He leaned forward, arms wide for balance, and tottered the distance, collapsing against the wall with relief.

Standing to pee seemed like a stupid idea, so he sat down, but the relief of doing this simple act in privacy was overwhelming.

The return journey to his bed was made easier by his sense of achievement. He tucked his feet up, a little shocked at how shaky he was, and pulled the covers over himself. A quick glance at the dressings on his side revealed no tell-tale patches of red, so it seemed he'd got away with it.

But God, he was exhausted. He closed his eyes and slept.

* * *

His next visitor was his brother, Peter, and by then it was getting dark outside.

Five years older than Aaron and his opposite in so many ways, Peter had married his childhood sweetheart almost as soon as he finished at university. Now he had a steady accountancy job, a mortgage and two small children. He was also losing his hair, and grey wings were starting to form at his temples.

"What mischief have you been up to now?" Peter asked as the door closed behind him. "Brought you grapes, by the way. Ellie said it was the right thing to do."

"Good for Ellie. Chocolate-covered dried variety would be even better, but still. Beggars can't be choosers." Aaron took the paper bag and ripped one from the bunch. It burst like sweet nectar in his mouth. "Mm. Good."

"I'm to tell you that you're not discharging yourself until the doctors give the all-clear," Peter said, trying to look stern. But if his brother hadn't learned to recognise a lost cause by now, there'd be no hope for him. Aaron grinned.

"Yes, sir. Couldn't leave if I wanted to yet anyway. Still as weak as a baby, more's the pity."

Peter's face relaxed a little. He'd always been a bit of a sucker.

They chatted for a while about Peter's kids, his plans for the house — an extension with an extra bedroom so Simon wouldn't have to share with his sister. Aaron pretended to be interested, but all he could think of was Asha's meeting with Patterson. It must have happened by now, so why hadn't she been in touch like she'd promised?

Finally, duty done, Peter heaved himself to his feet and stretched, revealing a round belly Aaron didn't remember him having before, but Ellie loved to cook, and Peter loved to eat. Or too many drinks with the "lads from work", perhaps.

In the welcome quiet, he fished his mobile out from under his pillow and checked the screen for texts or missed calls, but it remained stubbornly blank.

Damn Asha. He caught himself. No. If there was anything to tell him, she wouldn't have held back. *Damn Patterson, more like.*

CHAPTER 49

Josh was waiting for Asha in the car park. The sight of his solid frame and steady smile reassured her. He was a good man to have watching your back, and she wondered why it had taken Lonnie to point that out to her.

"Hey," she said. "Have you got the stuff?"

He took a USB pen from his pocket and held it in the air. "The original is with my bank — good advice, that, by the way. Never occurred to me to use a safety-deposit box."

"We shouldn't have to," she replied. "Evidence should be safe in the evidence lockers, but we've never had anything like this to contend with before. Not in our time, anyway."

They walked inside together, into the lift that smelled of stale vomit and piss as it always did. The familiar dread of bumping into Aiken or Kernaghan, with their snide remarks, tightened her chest as the lift doors slid open, until she remembered they were both on the run and couldn't hurt her in the station, not anymore.

She'd had the forethought to book an appointment with Patterson, phoning her assistant from Sue's house earlier, so they only had to wait for a couple of minutes on the hard plastic chairs in her outer office before she buzzed to let them through.

The DCS wore her usual expensive power suit. On her it looked like something off the bargain rack in Oxfam. Patterson just didn't seem to have the right shape for nice clothes.

Guilt stopped Asha in her tracks. That wasn't like her, that bitchiness. It was hard to like the Chief, but if she came up with the goods this time, Asha promised herself that she'd never have a bad thought about her ever again.

"Take a seat," Patterson said, still writing notes at the bottom of a page of printed material. "I'll only be a moment."

She signed with a flourish, stacked the papers and slid the pile into a drawer. "Now, I hope you're bringing me the final report on the skeleton and your cold misper case, Acting Detective Inspector. Although," she added in a pleasant tone, "why you're here, Inspector Campbell, I have no clue."

"I invited Josh to help me, ma'am." Did that sound as if she wasn't capable of doing the job without a male to help her? "If you'll bear with me for a few minutes while I fill in the background, I hope you'll understand why."

Patterson leaned back in her chair. If she'd been a man, Asha thought, she'd have put her size tens up on the desk.

Stop it. Concentrate. You can't afford to get this wrong.

She quickly ran through the facts that Patterson did know: the skeleton, Will's history, Monica's disappearance, but now she filled in the bits she'd glided over in her report. The fact that George Aiken had both signed off the misper report for Will and taken Michael Hearn's call to report Monica's disappearance. The fact that any report on Monica's disappearance had never seen the light of day. Then she went on to tell how Sue remembered the events of that time, about her grandfather burying a body in the garden. Patterson didn't interrupt. She listened with her fingers steepled in front of her, like some elderly university professor.

She told Patterson about William Hearn's diaries, about Michael Hearn's drug habit, about the threats from his supplier. Then she swallowed and dived into the hard part.

"As he was dying, Michael Hearn spoke to Sue several times, and more than once alluded to the dealer being a member of the RUC. A peeler, he called him. He didn't know the man's name. He also said he sometimes had a driver, a skinny, red-haired, little hard man with a head shaped like a bullet. Ring any bells?"

Patterson closed her eyes and let out a long sigh. "Go on."

"Of course, I realised it was possible that his condition, the dementia, had affected his memory. I wasn't about to call out another member of the force on such flimsy evidence, but it did make me wary." She went on to catalogue the times she'd thought her phone might be tapped, the evidence stolen from Aaron's desk, the attempts to break into Lonnie's office. She reminded Patterson of the bomb under the Skoda she'd left parked at the hospital, and told her about her late-night visitor to the flat, the one Aaron and the uniforms had scared off.

"Then we went through William Hearn's diaries."

"The papers you took home with you, that day I caught you with them in the car park." It wasn't a question.

"Yes, ma'am. We found more information in there to incriminate both Aiken and Kernaghan, but still no name for the senior officer, that shadowy figure. At this point, the only people in the loop were me, Aaron and Sergeant Jacob. It was the sergeant who helped me identify our mystery officer. He'd used a phrase, "*no names, no pack-drills*", when he spoke to Michael Hearn, suggesting a military background. When I ran it past Lonnie, and added that he'd probably worked with Aiken and Kernaghan, she knew straight away who I must be talking about. Retired Detective Chief Inspector Alistair King."

Patterson sat up straight and slammed her hands down onto the desk, making Asha and Josh jump. "King, you say?"

There was a light in those calculating eyes that made Asha's skin prickle. Once again, she thought how glad she was that Patterson was on the side of the angels.

"I was at his place up on the north coast only a few days ago. He has a big spread, maybe a couple of hundred acres or more, right up on the coast. Must be worth a fortune." Patterson smiled, and there was pure malice this time in the way those thin lips curled. "Perfect place to hide bodies, don't you think?"

CHAPTER 50

Patterson didn't rush the rest of the meeting. Instead, she buzzed through to her assistant and told her to hold all calls and rearrange any other appointments. She was going to be busy for the rest of the day, and maybe tomorrow as well.

Josh recited his version of the events at Sue Hearn's house, then handed over his video footage, which she played on her giant computer monitor. It showed Aiken and Kernaghan, staggering out of the Hearns' back gate and along the edge of the park. Josh's dog had run at them barking, possibly remembering its police training, and Josh had had to call it to him sharply. The film showed both men jumping into a marked car that had been hidden in a narrow alley beneath overhanging branches. Kernaghan was driving. He spun the wheels in the soft mud and leaf mould, stalling twice before he managed to shoot out backwards into the road.

Josh had filmed all this from around the corner of a hedge, very wisely. Luckily for him, Aiken and Kernaghan retreated onto a different road, so they hadn't passed him on their way out.

"Then Josh came into the house through the back gate and helped me with Aaron, who was wounded."

"Indeed." Patterson frowned at Asha's bandaged hand. "This is the problem with keeping the circle so small. People get hurt. I'd have thought you'd have learned that the last time, Acting Inspector. Was a blow to the head not lesson enough for you?"

"Yes, ma'am. That's why I made sure we had Josh along with us this time, as well as Aaron sneaking into the house as backup for me."

"Hmmm." She was probably thinking about Aaron's lock-picking skills, which Asha had tried to float over without actually drawing attention to them. Hopefully she wouldn't give him too hard a time, once he was out of the hospital.

She went on to describe the attempt on Aaron's life and the possible attempt on hers while they were both in the hospital.

"Even though we had an All Stations alert out for both men, if they turned up at the hospital and flashed their IDs, I doubt anyone would have thought to question them. There are always uniformed officers hanging around in hospitals."

"Have you anything from Forensics on that drip bag yet?"

"Not yet, ma'am. I told them it was urgent, but I don't think they paid much attention. Perhaps if you were to ask?"

Patterson smiled, and this time it did reach her eyes, deepening the crow's feet around them. "Very well. I'll give them a call and see if we can't chase them up."

"So, do you think we have enough?" Josh asked. He'd been quiet, mostly listening, but there was excitement lacing his voice. "Enough evidence to get a conviction?"

Patterson poked at the photos that were spread out on her desk, reshuffling them. "We're almost there, but it would be better if we could find Monica Hearn's body, and the murder weapon, too."

Asha's good hand slipped across the smooth wood of the desk, slick with sweat. She pulled it out of sight so no one would see the way it trembled. "Do you really think he'd be stupid enough to bury them on his own land?"

"Not stupid, no. Arrogant, perhaps. I've known Alistair King for a very long time. He's meticulous in his planning, efficient, calculating. If he has buried evidence on his land, it will be well hidden." She glanced across at Josh. "We'll probably need cadaver dogs. Does Claire still have contacts in the canine division?"

"Yes, ma'am. How much am I allowed to tell her, and how much is she allowed to tell them?"

"Nothing for the moment. Let's keep it between the three of us." She met Asha's eye. "Four of us. I think Constable Birch deserves to know what's going on, don't you? I'll apply for a warrant, chase up the forensics and see if we can't make a move in the next twenty-four hours or so. Until then, total silence, do you hear me?"

"Yes, ma'am," Asha and Josh said at the same time.

They parted ways in the corridor, each lost in their own thoughts and worries. Josh headed to the car park, and Asha wasn't far behind him, once she'd made a call to her father from a phone in an empty office, one that wouldn't be associated with her.

She took another pool car, a battered Ford that no one ever chose to drive if they could avoid it, and drove herself through the dark to the hospital.

Aaron was on his feet, pacing the room, hospital gown flapping open to reveal his white backside.

"Tight buns," she remarked.

Aaron spun around and almost fell. He clutched at his flimsy gown, trying to hold it shut with one hand while he gripped the bed frame for balance with the other one. "Have you never heard of knocking?"

"Have you never heard of pyjamas?"

He grinned at her. "Don't own any."

"Okay. You win. Aren't you supposed to be resting?"

"I'm doing fine," he said through gritted teeth as he eased himself onto the bed. "By tomorrow, I'll be out of here. Want a grape?"

She glanced inside the paper bag. "I'd have loved one, but there are only bare twigs left in there."

"Oops. Did you bring any food with you?"

"Nope. I did better than that. I brought news. And it wasn't easy, getting in at this time of night. The whole hospital is on high alert after what happened last night. I had to make Security phone Patterson to give them the go-ahead to let me in."

"Don't keep me hanging. What news?"

"The Chief's on our side. She's sorting a search warrant for King's place up on the north coast, liaising with the crew up there to clear the ground, and she's chasing up forensics on your drip from last night. Well done with that, by the way. Sounds as if you saved your own life by ripping that out of your arm."

"I thought I'd killed myself when it wouldn't stop bleeding," he said fervently. "So that's good news, then. About Patterson. She can fairly shift when the heat's on."

"Oh, and Josh's wife, Claire, is going to organise us some cadaver dogs to '*hunt down the bodies*', as Patterson puts it." She sighed. "I wish you could be there with us for the finish, Aaron. You always seem to be in hospital for the best bits."

Not so long ago, he'd been knocked unconscious and half-drowned in Lough Neagh during what the more lurid tabloids had dubbed the "Slasher" case. Another pile of guilt for her to carry on her shoulders.

"We'll see," he replied. "Doctor says I can leave as soon as I can walk the length of the ward without support and without my sutures tearing."

"Hence the hospital gown marathon? I hope they make you put some trousers on before they let you loose on the ward."

CHAPTER 51

After a good seven hours' sleep, Aaron was up early and dressed in clean clothes he'd managed to persuade Peter to bring in for him — loose track pants and a soft, baggy shirt, but clothes, nonetheless. His own black leather shoes looked ridiculous with the rest, but this was only an exercise to prove his fitness. Once he'd done that, he could get a taxi home and find something decent to wear.

The uniform outside his door appeared stoical about the whole thing. At Aaron's insistence, he remained in his seat and watched the uneven progress as Aaron lurched, arms akimbo for balance, along the wide corridor.

"Oh, Mr Birch!" called a nurse. "Just look at you!"

A grin spread across his face as one by one, nurses and cleaning staff, orderlies and the woman with the tea tray emerged from rooms and started clapping.

"All the way to the end," growled the doctor who had saved his life a couple of nights ago. "And then I'll check that wound."

He made it the whole way, there and back. Beads of sweat popped out on his skin and trailed fingers down his spine by the time he was back in his own room. The copper had stood up, and now he joined the staff's applause.

"Very good, sir. Now maybe get some rest?" There was warmth in his eyes. He leaned close so only Aaron would hear. "We need you on top form if you're going to catch those nasty little buggers for us and bring some pride back to the Service."

He'd been so wrapped up in his own hatred of the rotten officers that it hadn't occurred to Aaron that others might feel that way. No one liked being made a fool of for thirty years, and one bad policeman reflected on the entire force.

The doctor gave him one last check-up. He made him wait until Pharmacy had sent down his painkillers and anti-biotics to take home, but then he was free.

While he was waiting, he searched through the white plastic laundry bag holding the tattered remains of his clothes, hunting for his wallet, which was a little blood-stained but intact, and his mobile. The screen was cracked diagonally across the centre, and although it powered up, he couldn't get it to respond to anything. Damn. That was his first decent iPhone, too.

The uniform outside smiled as he emerged from his room, still a little hunched over.

"Want a ride anywhere? I'm to stay with you anyway, and I can have a car here in no time."

"I was planning on a taxi, but if you're offering?"

The drive tired him more than he'd expected. Even when he held the seatbelt away from his side, it sent pain radiating through his belly and into his spine. Still, once he'd closed the door to his bedroom, leaving Constable Pirrie opening his kitchen cupboards in search of coffee, he began to relax.

Just five minutes, he promised himself. He let himself fall back gently onto the bed and closed his eyes.

The aroma of coffee woke him. Proper ground coffee, not the bitter instant stuff the hospital called coffee. He half-turned onto his side to sit up without pulling at his sutures and took a deep breath. He felt more rested than he had after a full night of sleep in the hospital.

He dug out some clothes that were smart enough for work but didn't press on the wound: low-slung black jeans that sat on his hips, below the injury, and a checked shirt made from some soft material that fell away from his body if he left it untucked. There was no sign of blood-spotting on the dressing, which was good news.

Pirrie had made a full pot of coffee and was halfway down a mug himself, comfortably ensconced on Aaron's sofa, reading one of the paperback Agatha Christies from the bookshelf. He glanced up and nodded.

"You're looking a whole lot better. Maybe a shave, though?"

Aaron ran a hand over the bristles on his chin. "I thought I'd give designer stubble a try. Might make me look a bit tougher."

"Oh, I reckon that scar will impress the girls enough." Pirrie took another sip of coffee. "There's more in the pot, but you'll have to have it black. The milk in your fridge was turning into cottage cheese."

Aaron poured himself a mug, stuck his nose deep inside and inhaled. It was as refreshing as the morphine they'd flooded his system with the other day. "What do you think of Poirot, then?"

"That poncy little French fella with the moustache? I think he'd last less than a minute over here in Belfast, that's what I think."

"Belgian," Aaron said, and they both laughed. "I take it you're a Christie fan, too?"

"I prefer Miss Marple," Pirrie said. "The wife got me into those books, and I think she's beginning to regret it."

His radio gave a strangled squawk and a beep.

When Pirrie finished on the radio, Aaron asked if he could borrow his phone to send a text. He knew Asha's mobile number by heart, and he only needed to send her a short message.

When and where? My phone's fatally injured, so reply to this one — Constable Pirrie is on guard duty.

It only took her a minute to reply. *I'll have a new phone waiting for you. Come to the station if you're sure you're fit enough. A x*

A kiss? That was unlike Asha. She'd never been one for flowery gestures. Perhaps she'd been more worried about him than he thought.

She was waiting in the car park when he got there, sitting on the bonnet of an ancient Ford that should have been sent to the scrap heap years ago.

He rolled down the window and grinned at her. "Welcoming party? You must have missed me."

"Just needed a gofer. I've had to do all the footwork on my own, so it's good to have you back." But the warmth in her eyes gave the lie to her words.

"Stay in the car for a moment, will you?" he said to Pirrie. The other man nodded and gave him a knowing smile that Aaron ignored. He got out of the car, trying not to wince as he straightened. "What's the story? I take it we're meeting out here so as not to be overheard?"

"Partly that, partly to save you the effort of coming all the way inside only to leave again straight away. You missed the briefing — we were in the middle of it when you texted — but I got Patterson's permission to let you come along with us on the strict understanding that you're to stay inside the car with Constable Pirrie the entire time, and you're not to take any part whatsoever in proceedings. Observation and witness only. Got that?"

"Yes, ma'am." He tried for a mock salute, but the stitches brought him up short before he could complete the movement. "Stay with Nanny. Do not leave the playpen. Got it."

"I mean it, Aaron. Constable Pirrie is under strict orders, too. The slightest hint of idiocy on your part, and he's to drive you straight back to Belfast. In cuffs, if he thinks it necessary."

Aaron turned and glared at Pirrie through the car window. The constable didn't meet his eye, staring rigidly straight ahead through the windscreen. He did have the grace to blush, though.

Asha handed Aaron a new phone, the little plastic screen cover still present as if it was straight out of the box. "This is already charged. Make yourself useful and set it up while you're waiting. If you have any trouble logging in to your iCloud, get Pirrie to call me and I'll have a techie come out here to you."

He waited until she had disappeared into the building before sliding into the passenger seat and firing up the phone. He held his breath while it went through its usual routine until it asked for his password.

"I'm in," he breathed. Then he had to wait while it loaded all his settings. Finally, he checked his photos, and there they were, all the images he'd taken from the case. *Thank God.*

"I think this is them, sir. Looks as if we're on."

Uniformed and plainclothes officers flooded out of the building. Aaron was confused for a moment, because there wasn't a single familiar face among them, but then he realised that Patterson would have drafted in officers from far afield for this operation, in case Aiken and Kernaghan hadn't been King's only stooges.

They climbed into plain, unmarked vans and a couple of four-wheel drives and waited, engines running. Pirrie started his engine, too.

At last, Asha emerged with Josh and Patterson. Asha got into a Jeep with the Chief, but Josh walked over to the unmarked car Aaron was in and ducked into the back seat.

"Mind if I join you?"

"Not at all. Are you here strictly as an observer, too, or are they letting you play?"

"I invited myself along. It's not my case, so technically I'm just another observer." He gave a twisted half-smile that made him look younger. "I wouldn't miss this for the world."

The drive up to King's property on the north coast took well over an hour. Pirrie kept a safe distance behind the two vans, which in turn followed the Jeep with Asha and Patterson inside it. They climbed past housing estates and industrial areas until the ground fell away to their right, giving them a great view of Belfast Lough as it shimmered in the afternoon sunshine.

The constant drone of the engine had a soporific effect on Aaron, combined with the heat of the sun on his window. He let himself sag against the headrest, eyes closed.

The change in note of the engine woke him as they turned onto a bumpy lane with potholes on both sides.

"Back in the land of the living, sir?" Pirrie said. "I think that's the first time anyone's ever slept through my driving."

"All that rolling and swerving rocked me to sleep," he croaked. He tried to work moisture into a dry mouth. His neck was stiff, and he had to ease himself into a new position so he could stretch without pulling at his side, but he did feel refreshed. Must have needed that sleep. "Are we there yet?"

Josh snorted from behind him. "You sound just like my sister's kids. None of them snore as loud as you, though."

"This is the back entrance to the farm," Pirrie said. "We were told to let the van go on ahead and then follow them at a safe distance. If anyone makes a break for it this way, we're the last hurdle."

"Dogs?"

"They went in the front way with the Chief. We've been given a dedicated frequency to listen in on, but there's to be radio silence until the first team give us the all-clear. We don't want to risk alerting them. It's a dead cert they'll be listening for activity." Josh sounded as excited as a schoolboy.

"Are we listening at the moment?"

"Yep," Pirrie said. "We'll know the moment it kicks off."

"Unless the bird has already flown. King must be a crafty one to have survived so long under the radar. He could be long gone by now."

CHAPTER 52

"Where the hell have you been? I expected a report yesterday. Are they dead?" Alistair King gripped the phone with white knuckles.

"Kerny messed up, sir. They're both still alive and kicking."

"What the fuck went wrong?"

"Don't know, sir, not exactly. He says he didn't even manage to get into that bitch's room, but he set up the drip just as you said on Birch. I don't know what went wrong, but the bastard pulled through. My contact in the hospital tells me he's getting out this morning."

"Fuck!"

"Yes, sir. What do you want us to do now?"

"Are you back on your feet? Feeling better?" The words were said sarcastically, but Aiken didn't seem to notice.

"Yes, sir. Ears still ringing a bit, but I'm okay, thanks."

"Glad to hear it. Get your arses up here, but don't come to the house. I'll meet you in the usual place and give you your instructions."

He cut the call and made himself loosen his grip on the satellite phone. He shivered. A sea breeze was picking up, bringing a chill onto the headland, but he had one more call to make before he could go inside.

Leo Kone, his solicitor, was well trained. He didn't ask any questions. He just said he'd be on his way within the next few minutes and to sit tight. Leo had been looking after his legal affairs for the last four decades, and there was little he didn't know, or couldn't guess, about Alistair's work. Still, there were a few secrets. A man needed secrets, if he wanted to stay alive.

Lorraine was in the kitchen, playing at being a chef. She had all the ingredients laid out along the counter in order and was weighing each one into glass bowls of various sizes. That woman was amazing. He couldn't resist going up behind her and wrapping his arms around her waist, planting a kiss on the nape of her neck. She smelled of the expensive perfume he'd bought her for their anniversary, and there was a dab of flour on her shoulder.

"Hands off!" she teased. "And no sneaking a fingerful. You're not to taste this until it's finished."

"What delight are you cooking up for me this time?"

"It's a peach and pistachio tart, but it's not for you, darling. It's my cookery club night, remember? Vanessa's making the starter, Geri's doing the main, and I'm in charge of the dessert."

"Lucky them," he said, and meant it. Lorraine had always been able to take his mind off his worries. "I'll just have to hope they're not too hungry by the time they get to dessert, so you can bring some of it home with you."

He left her to it and went through to the spacious sitting room, with its views out across the clifftops to the sea. In the distance, a low hump of land marked the Mull of Kintyre, and somewhere to his left, out of sight, was Rathlin Island. This place was as remote as it was possible to be in the province. There'd even been a Royal Navy listening station not far away, long abandoned now.

He loved this property, especially now he'd made it so beautiful, but even when he'd visited here as a kid, sweet-talking his Great Aunt Lil until she left the rotting pile to him in her will, he'd always loved the wildness of this cliff-top farm.

He'd never wanted anything to touch the perfection of this place, but that seemed about to end.

He'd been thinking about what Patterson had said about this being a good place to lose bodies. What the hell was that bitch up to?

* * *

He met with Aiken and Kernaghan out at the edge of his property. They'd ditched the marked car and somehow got hold of a short-wheelbase Land Rover with massive, deep-tread tyres and a snorkel to allow it to drive through water. Maybe they had a bit more about them than he'd been giving them credit for. Since he'd retired, he'd had occasional doubts about their commitment, but they hadn't hesitated when he'd sent them to deal with that Indian bitch and the other one, and they were here now, as soon as he called for them. The lure of money still held them.

Aiken jumped down from the passenger seat. "What do you need, sir?"

"I'm going to have company fairly soon. Now they've flushed you two out, it probably won't take long to join the dots and realise that you worked with me back in the day. I hope I'm wrong, but we didn't get this far by acting on hope."

"No, sir."

"So, I'd like one of you on the back lane, one up on the hill there, where you can see pretty much the whole spread. There's a gateway about halfway up the lane that gives good cover. Call the house soon as either of you see anything. Just let it ring four times. I won't answer."

"Want us to slow them down or anything?" Kernaghan asked.

"Not unless you're seen. I'd rather have you undiscovered, at least at first." He tugged at the strap that passed across his shoulder and swung the long bag around in front of him. "Which of you got the highest marks with a long gun on the range?"

"That'd be George, sir," Kernaghan said.

"Very well. Aiken, take this. You'll be at the top of the hill." He patted the canvas affectionately. "She's not young, not like these modern sniper rifles, but she fires true and I put a new scope on her last year. You should be able to hit anything you aim at."

"Sir?" Aiken didn't reach for the gun. "What do you want me to aim at?"

"I've a bad feeling we might have DCS Patterson out here shortly. She's been sniffing around the place recently, and I don't trust her one little bit. If it looks as if she's found anything incriminating, take her out of the equation."

"Sir?"

"Kill her," he snapped, and turned to start the long walk to the house so he could hug Lorraine and give her a last kiss before she left.

CHAPTER 53

The main entrance to King's place was at the end of a brilliant white concrete driveway with tall stone walls flanking a pair of wrought-iron gates. Nothing overly ostentatious, but they must have cost a fair bit. No sign of CCTV, but the gates were closed and there was a numerical code pad on the wall to the right-hand side.

"What now, ma'am?"

"We open them," Asha said, and tapped the uniform in the passenger seat on his shoulder.

"Hold on, ma'am," he said, pointing. The gates were swinging inwards. Perhaps there was CCTV after all, in which case this was a pretty ballsy move.

But then a car appeared at the top of the hill, a sporty Mercedes convertible in gleaming white.

"That's his wife, Lorraine. What excellent timing," Patterson said. She waited for the car to reach the gates, then stepped out of the Jeep and flagged down the driver. There was recognition in the other woman's face, and a guarded welcome.

After a couple of minutes, King's wife drove her car onto the verge and parked it, shutting down the engine. She passed her keys, her mobile and a small remote control out to Patterson, then huddled down into the driver's seat inside a knitted wrap that all of a sudden looked far too big for her.

Patterson got into the Jeep, looking smug. "Lorraine King has always been so fucking condescending. That gave me far more pleasure than it ought to have."

The convoy drove on, with the van full of police in the lead now, then Patterson and Asha, and finally the dog handlers' van bringing up the rear. Asha's pulse hammered in her ears and her palms were slippery with sweat. This was on her. If it went wrong, which it very easily could, she was under no illusions about where the blame would fall.

As they topped the rise, a substantial range of modern buildings came into view on the backslope, with an archway through to an enclosed gravelled yard. The van slewed to the right as soon as it was through the arch, leaving room for Patterson's Jeep to stop behind it, blocking the exit in case any of the three cars parked there should try to leave.

"Black Volvo," Asha murmured. "A leopard doesn't change its spots."

"Stay in the car for now," Patterson said. "I'm going to speak to him alone first."

Asha didn't like it. "What if they're all there together? We know Aiken won't hesitate to stick a knife in a fellow officer, and you've seen the evidence on King himself. Are you sure it's safe?" Then, as an afterthought: "Ma'am."

"I'm wearing a stab vest," Patterson said, "but I don't think he'll want to start anything, not as long as he thinks he might still be able to talk his way out of this."

Patterson walked up to the main door and rang the bell. Asha opened her car door a little so she could hear what was going on.

King answered it himself. The sight of him, standing there with a welcoming smile, made her feel nauseous. His silk shirt and designer shoes, the house, everything, all built on the suffering of others. This was the man who had stabbed little William Lee, the man who had taken a young girl's mother from her.

"Hello, Yvonne. To what do I owe this surprise visit?" He didn't seem to notice the van full of armed police, but he could hardly have missed it. "You've just missed Lorraine, I'm afraid. She's gone into Ballycastle to some cookery club or other. She'll be sorry to have missed you."

Patterson said something in a low voice that Asha couldn't catch, and King's whole demeanour changed from one of affable host, surprised but still prepared to be hospitable, to indignant householder, ready to stand on his rights.

"What the hell are you talking about? I'm retired, I know, but surely I still have some rights as a former officer? Even common courtesy demands a bit of warning, or an invitation to come in voluntarily for questioning. To turn up on my doorstep and demand to be let in? That's overstepping the mark, my good woman."

Asha winced. *My good woman* wouldn't go down well with the Chief.

Holding her composure, Patterson produced a warrant from an inner pocket.

King snatched it from her and waved it in her face. "I have my solicitor here with me. A social call, but lucky, don't you think? Let's see what he has to say about this!" He stormed into the house.

As soon as he turned, Patterson made a sign behind her back. The van doors slid open to release half a dozen armed officers. They fanned out, guns ready, and began a search of the outbuildings.

A skinny, balding man in a suit appeared in the open doorway, pushing his glasses up the bridge of his nose with a forefinger. He reminded Asha of a startled rabbit. He spoke too quietly for Asha to hear, so she got out of the car and moved closer.

Patterson leaned in, her lips near the solicitor's ear. If Asha hadn't been so close, she'd never have heard her words.

"Tell your client I know where the bodies are buried. Just that."

He blinked at her, then took a step back, and another, before turning tail and running into the house.

Patterson took the radio from her shoulder pocket and spoke into it. "All right. Full search. Leave no stone unturned. Dogs, with me." She spotted Asha. "I thought I told you to stay in the car?"

"I was worried about you. Sorry, ma'am."

Patterson narrowed her eyes but didn't argue. "Then since you're here, I'll put you in charge of searching the house. We won't arrest Mr King, not quite yet. We'll let him sweat it out for a while first, don't you think?"

"Yes, ma'am."

"Carry on."

The house was like something from one of those shiny celebrity magazines you found in the dentist's waiting room, all soft leather and deep-pile carpets. The open-plan kitchen was bigger than Asha's entire flat. King's solicitor perched on a cream leather couch with his knees together and hands clasped between them. King stood with his back to the room, staring out of the window as if all this had nothing to do with him, but as she entered, he was just replacing a mobile in his trouser pocket. Who had he called?

Her team didn't need much direction. They were from a station in County Fermanagh, if the culchie accents were to be believed — a place as far away from King's influence as possible. They turned the house upside down with experienced hands, leaving everything tidy behind them but missing nothing. Asha watched as they removed the contents of drawers, shook everything out, then checked for false backs and bases. If there was anything to be found, they'd find it, she was certain.

She was equally certain there'd be nothing to find. King wouldn't keep anything incriminating in his house, under his wife's nose. He'd have a hidey-hole somewhere else, somewhere only he knew about.

But if Patterson's dog team was successful, they might not need to worry about finding paperwork. Just one body buried on the farm and traceable back to crimes dating anywhere from the late eighties to when King retired in 2016 and they'd have him. Even without a body, the evidence they'd already accumulated should be enough to convince a jury.

Not that this would be an ordinary trial. King was known to have connections in every public office, every government department, every walk of life. Maybe if they could round up his two sidekicks and get one of them to talk in exchange for a plea bargain—?

"Ma'am?" It was one of the uniformed constables. "I may have found something."

King swung around and glared at her, then he pulled his mobile out of his pocket. He must have had the person on speed dial, because he got through almost immediately, before Asha could stride across the room and wrest the phone from his grasp with a firm, "I'll take that, sir, if you please."

"You, young woman, are overreaching," King snarled.

Asha held the phone to her ear, listened to the aggressive voice on the other end — a voice she heard almost daily on a local BBC Radio discussion show — and cut the call off.

"Seriously, sir? You're really scraping the barrel now, aren't you?"

She thought for a moment that King would strike her, but he turned those blazing eyes away from her and went back to staring out of the window. Asha followed the direction of his gaze. The dog team was quartering the ground on a hill about three hundred yards away.

She dropped the mobile into an evidence bag and went over to the constable who had called her. The woman held up a bloodstained bandage.

"Found this at the bottom of the bathroom bin, ma'am. It was wrapped inside a sanitary towel wrapper."

"Good work. Bag it and label it, and we'll send it off to the lab to see whose blood that is."

"I can tell you whose blood it is. Mine." King held up a bandaged hand. "Cut myself with the axe when I was chopping wood for the stove, and I didn't want to worry Lorraine. That's why I hid the dressings." His tone was scathing, but Asha thought he looked a bit paler than he had.

"Very good, sir. I'm sure it'll turn out to be your blood, but we still have to keep it as evidence."

Another uniform called out from the upper landing. "Found something, ma'am. Master bedroom."

She went upstairs, along the bright landing area, where roof windows let in enough light for an artist's studio, and into the main bedroom. The officer searching there had removed all the drawers from a set in the dressing room, an annexe that was nearly the size of her kitchen.

"Found this taped to the underside of a drawer, ma'am." He held out a folded sheet of paper.

No, not paper. Canvas, like an artist might use. The edges were frayed as if it had been there for a while. She unfolded it and an unfinished portrait smiled up at her, as vibrant and alive as Monica Hearn must have been thirty years ago. Sue had her eyes, though not that thick, dark hair. Why had he kept this, after all these years?

"Good work, Constable. Bag it and label it, please."

She wandered out onto the balcony and let her eyes adjust to the failing light. This would be the best place for watching the dogs work.

A table and two chairs were placed where they'd get the sun most of the day in this high-up position, as well as the best view out across the darkening sea, but she went to the edge and leaned on the glass wall, straining to see the figures darting around on the hill.

The sun was low in the sky, silhouetting the dogs and their handlers, with Patterson a distinctive figure, even in silhouette against the evening sky, directing the search.

What had she meant by "*Tell him I know where the bodies are buried*"? Did she actually know where to look, or had she just been trying to frighten King into saying something to condemn himself?

The sound of excited barking reached her, and all the little stick figures in the distance congregated in one spot, just over the brow of the hill where she couldn't see them. What she wouldn't give for a closer look. Then the sound of a gunshot split the night, and everyone froze.

CHAPTER 54

The sun was beginning to sink down in the sky, and it took Aaron's energy with it. His side was throbbing, and he had a headache. How long since he last had a drink? The coffee Pirrie had made earlier. Was he dehydrated? He'd left his tablets sitting by the bathroom sink in his house, fool that he was.

"Do you have any paracetamol on you?" he asked Josh. "A drink?"

The inspector shook his head. "Sorry. Didn't the hospital give you something?"

"Yeah. A packet of painkillers and a load of other stuff, and they're all in a safe place, back in my house."

"No, they're not," Pirrie said. "Hang on."

He got out and went around to the boot, returning a moment later with a blue plastic bag labelled "*Hospital Pharmacy*".

"Thought you might need these before the day was done." From the other hand, he produced a canvas satchel that bulged in places. "Thought we might need something to keep us going, too."

"Pirrie," Aaron said fervently. "You are a god among men. Whichever division Patterson stole you from, please consider jumping ship and coming to Lisburn Road."

"I understand there might be a couple of vacancies in the near future, sir. I'll think about it." He sat back in the driver's seat and closed the door. "But I should probably tell you that this wasn't my idea. DI Harvey told me to bring this stuff."

Aaron swallowed his pills and sipped at the hot, strong coffee. Already, the world felt like a better place.

"I'm getting out for a minute," Josh said. "Need to see a man about a dog."

"Don't go too far, sir," Aaron said. "Shadows are getting long, and we don't want to lose you."

"Just as far as the nearest bush," Josh assured them. He loped off through a gap in the drystone wall, about fifty yards in front of them, and disappeared from sight.

"Done many of these stakeouts?" Pirrie asked.

"I'm not sure I'd call what we're doing a stakeout, but yes. Spent a few long nights of boredom waiting for a criminal to do something stupid. Why? Fancy the detective line of work yourself?" Although Pirrie was a bit old to come in as a detective. These days, it was the bright young sparks that were tapped on the shoulder rather than experienced men like Pirrie.

"I've thought about it once or twice, sir, I will admit."

"It's never too late. Want me to put in a good word with Patterson for you?"

"That would be very good of you, sir. Yes, please."

They sat in silence for a while, watching the shadows lengthening even more, until it was almost fully dark.

"Inspector Campbell's been a long time, sir. Think he's all right?"

Aaron had been asking himself the same question.

"I should get out and take a look around."

"No you don't, sir, with respect. I have orders to keep you in the car. I'll have a quick look, give him a shout. Maybe he's decided to get a closer look at the search."

"All right." His side was still stiff and sore, and he had to admit to himself that he'd be pretty useless if it came to

301

any sort of action. "Leave me the car keys. I'll run the engine to get some heat on."

Pirrie slid out of the driver's seat and set off up the track, his solid, square form soon blending into the darkness. Aaron locked the doors from inside, then climbed painfully across into the driver's seat. He glanced at his watch, so he'd know how long since Pirrie set off. Despite his trust in both Josh and Pirrie, something was making his skin twitch, and he didn't think it was just the painkillers.

The engine roared into life, blasting out into the silence of a country twilight, and the automatic headlights came on, sending a white beam along the track all the way to the top of the hill.

There was something lying on the track, a hump, not thirty yards away. His adrenaline surged. A second figure straightened up from the first and stared straight into the headlights, eyes wide and scared. It was Josh. There was blood running down the side of his face.

What the hell had happened? Had Josh attacked Pirrie? Because that must be Pirrie, lying there on the track. Or had Josh been attacked himself, and was only now able to stand and warn Aaron?

In the fraction of a second those thoughts took to flash through his mind, he had the car in gear and bumping up the track towards the figure on the ground. It *was* Pirrie. His uniform cap was lying a few feet from him. He was either dead or out cold. Josh held his hands out in front of him, as if to fend off the car. Aaron swung the wheel to the right, away from the drystone wall, and the tyres mounted the grassy edge of the track where it opened into boggy fields.

The wheels spun, spitting out loose gravel and mud, then found purchase again. The car bounced onto the track the other side of the unconscious constable. Something hit the side with a soft thump, but he kept going, gunning the engine. He was in no fit state to take on an attacker. He needed to fetch help. Somewhere up ahead were a dozen armed officers.

Then the rear window of the car shattered with a deafening crash. A dusty explosion sent the stuffing of the passenger seat back mushrooming out in a spray of fluff and cloth. He ducked down as well as he could and kept his foot to the floor until he saw the lights of the main house ahead, along with bobbing torches.

He careered into the yard, wheels skidding, slamming on the brakes just in time to avoid a startled dog handler and his furious canine partner.

He flung open the door and half-fell out, twisting his body to save himself. Flames licked up his side, and his lungs seemed to empty of air. It was as if he'd been punched in the solar plexus.

"Hold on," a familiar voice said urgently. "Sit down and let me take a look at that. Are you hit?"

Asha's cool hand pushed him back until he was sitting on the cold gravel, clutching his side. He managed a breath, another one.

"Not shot. They missed," he gasped. "There's no time. Pirrie and Josh. Pirrie's unconscious. Josh is covered in blood." He pointed back the way he'd come. "Don't know if Josh is a victim or—"

"Take three men and find out what's going on," she snapped at the nearby uniforms. "And be careful. We still have at least two armed men unaccounted for."

The men jumped into one of the jeeps and roared off up the hill. One of their own was injured, so they'd be ready for anything.

Another officer helped Aaron to his feet. Between his shoulder and Asha's steadying arm, he managed to get inside the house. They helped him down onto an armchair in a room with a giant TV screen. He blinked in the dim light, confused, until he realised this must be a cinema room, with reclining armchairs and a projector at the back of the room.

How the other half lived.

"I've got to go," Asha said apologetically. "The dogs have found something." She turned to the constable who'd helped him in. "Don't take your eyes off him for one moment. And radio for the medic. Patterson said we had a first-aider with us. I think we'll have at least one more casualty for him to look at shortly."

"Yes, ma'am."

CHAPTER 55

Leaving Aaron felt like betrayal, especially as control seemed to be slipping from Asha's grasp. He should have been safe, far away from all the action, yet somehow Pirrie had been attacked. She couldn't even think about Josh.

The dogs were beside themselves with excitement now, and she needed to see what was happening. But she had orders to keep an eye on King.

Perhaps she could kill two birds with one stone?

In the sitting room, King was still at the window, but his head was hunched in a posture of defeat. At the sound of the door closing, he spun round to glare at her.

"Whatever those dogs have found out there, it's been planted. Do you really think I'd be stupid enough to leave evidence on my own land?"

"Why don't you come out there with me and we can see for ourselves?"

He stared at her, eyes wide in disbelief. "Are you serious? I'm not going out there so someone can take a pot shot at me, and you can't make me."

Asha's thoughts spun like a dog chasing its tail. *He* was worried about being shot? *King?* The man behind all this? That made no sense at all.

Or did it? Aiken and Kernaghan were still on the loose somewhere out there. Perhaps they'd been in touch with King, let him know they were feeling betrayed. Did they think King had cut them loose to take the blame?

Another thought crept in like a burglar at night, leaving her cold. What if King *wasn't* the man at the top? What if he answered to someone else?

Her face must have betrayed her thoughts, because he gave her a sardonic smile. "Worked it out, have you?"

No. He was playing her. He had to be.

"Okay. You can stay here and stew. I'm going outside to see what's happening."

"Hope you're wearing a vest," he said as she closed the door behind her.

She was, and he would have seen the way it made her bulky beneath her jacket. She left strict instructions that King was not to be left alone: he was not to leave the room. The sergeant who was leading the search team nodded his understanding.

"I'm going to find out what the dogs have turned up, but I'll be straight back. If you're worried about anything, radio me." She tapped her shoulder.

As she stepped outside, even the tightness around her chest caused by the stab vest didn't reassure her. It protected her chest and upper abdomen — the vital organs, they were always told — but left her head and lower abdomen uncovered. During training, they'd joked that the PSNI didn't consider the brain to be a vital organ. It didn't seem so funny now, with the cold night air pinching at her nose and a low mist creeping in across the rocky ground that surrounded the house and outbuildings.

The dogs were quiet at last. They must have been called off, once they'd completed their work, but a flickering halo of yellowy light showed where the action was as torches moved around.

Then the night sky lit up in an arc. Someone had set up a generator and working lamps. In that moment before her night vision fled, Asha was almost certain she'd seen a running figure off to the right, bent double, moving away from the lights.

Too quick on his feet to be Kernaghan. Could it be Aiken? One of the search team appeared from around the side of the house. He was staring up at the hill, too, his face turned to lines and flat planes by the distant lights.

"Did you see that?" she asked.

"I think so, ma'am. A man running?"

"Yes. Put the word out, will you? We have company, possibly one of the two rogue officers we've been looking for."

"Yes, ma'am." He turned away and began to talk into his radio.

She took half a dozen steps when another light caught her eye. It was the car she'd sent down the lane, returning slowly as if they didn't want to jolt their passengers.

Josh was sitting in the back seat with Pirrie's head on his lap. Pirrie was unconscious, and it didn't take a doctor to see why. He had a lump the size of a pigeon egg on the back of his head, visible through his thinning hair now his cap was off. Someone had hit him from behind, and hit him hard.

"What happened?" she asked.

Josh's eyes were wide. "I have no idea. I went for a leak, and next thing I knew, I was throwing up into the heather. Then I heard someone calling my name, so I went to see what was happening and I found Pirrie in the road, like this. Then some bastard tried to run us both over. Oh, and there was a gunshot, I think. Unless it was a tyre blowing out. Sorry. Someone's playing the drums inside my head so I'm not sure what I heard."

Asha weighed his words. "No, there was a gunshot. You don't have any memory of what happened between you taking a leak and throwing up?"

"No." He touched his forehead. "I must have fallen and hit my head on a rock. There were several lying around where one of the drystone walls had collapsed. There's a cut here that really hurts—" he touched his temple — "but I don't remember how I came to fall. Must have tripped."

The officer who had been driving the car tugged at her sleeve and she followed him a short way into the darkness, out of the car headlights.

"I think he was knocked out by someone, ma'am, and that's why he fell and hit his head on the stone. He has a lump on the back of his head, too, and there's some blood there as well. His story has the ring of truth. I found the rock he must have hit his head on when he fell. It's covered in blood, and there are tracks in the damp grass, coming in from across the fields."

Shit. "Pass the word. I think Aiken and Kernaghan might be around here somewhere. They could well still be in uniform, so give every officer you see a second look. Make sure you can identify them — and watch your backs."

There was a slow-burning anger in his eyes. "They'll not get past us, ma'am."

"Good. Now, I'm going to see what they've found up there. Take these two to the house. There's a first-aider up there who can take a look at them and at DC Birch."

She'd stashed a pair of boots in the car, so she swapped her shoes for the stout, rubber wellingtons and finally set off up the hill. As she topped the rise, she could see a hive of activity. A SOCO team in white paper overalls were excavating a hole in the ground, and there were a couple of yellow markers to indicate the next areas to be searched.

She slithered down the slope, careless of the potential for a sprained ankle, and landed in bog. She had to know. For Sue's sake, if nothing else, she hoped they had found the resting place of Monica Hearn. Her boots sucked and squelched as she made her way across the wet tussocks.

Patterson stood off to one side from the dig, the hood of her white suit pulled back to reveal her untidy hair. She was smoking a thin French cigarette, letting the ash fall around her like confetti.

"I'm far enough away from the scene, Inspector. I won't contaminate it."

"Thought hadn't crossed my mind, ma'am."

Patterson smiled. Or it might have been a grimace. Hard to tell, really.

"At least three sites, according to the dogs. We're excavating them one at a time until I can get some extra manpower drafted in. First body is almost certainly a woman, so it could be your historical misper, but the ground is waterlogged around here, and that's making it hard."

"Any identifying marks? Jewellery?"

"Not that they've told me. It might be a case of dental records, after all this time."

Another delay for Sue, but then she'd waited this long for answers. A few more days wouldn't hurt her.

Someone called Patterson's name. She stubbed out her cigarette and pulled her hood back up, sliding a mask over her nose and mouth. "There are spare suits there." She pointed to a uniform officer with a clipboard and a cardboard box at his feet, posted at a gap in the police tape.

Asha signed in and struggled into a suit, made extra clumsy by the added bulk of her stab vest and bandaged hand. She wasn't about to take the vest off, not with those two on the loose.

As she approached the dig, someone straightened up and handed Patterson something. She called Asha over.

"I think this clinches it, don't you?"

The object she held was a gold watch, still gleaming despite the dirt embedded in the woven metal band. The workmanship was exquisite. There was an engraving on the back:

To Monica, on our wedding day.
Forever, Michael.

CHAPTER 56

Asha swallowed. She'd hoped they would find Monica's body, but hadn't really expected it to be identified so soon. She'd have to break the news to Sue as soon as she could.

"Thank you, ma'am. That solves my old misper case. Not the best outcome for her daughter, but at least she'll know now."

"Indeed." Patterson's voice sounded unusually gentle, and even that hint of sympathy made Asha's eyes fill up.

She couldn't let the Chief see her moment of weakness. "Anything else?" she asked the dig team. "Any idea how she died?"

"Nothing yet, ma'am. We might know more after the PM, but there's nothing leaping out at us so far. The good news is that this acidic soil, the wet and the cold up here has meant the body has been preserved surprisingly well, so we should be able to get some meaningful results, with luck."

"And there's the possibility of more bodies?"

"Yes, ma'am. We'll be opening the next potential site as soon as we have this one recorded and lifted."

"Walk with me," Patterson said.

They stripped off their overshoes, gloves and suits at the edge of the taped area and went back towards the house.

"Ma'am. I think you should know that Aiken and Kernaghan might be around here somewhere." She brought Patterson up to date with the attacks on Josh and Pirrie, and Aaron's flight to the house. "King is trying to imply that he's in danger. I think he was hinting that there could be someone else he answers to. That he's not the one in charge of all this."

"He might do that to muddy the waters, but that doesn't mean we should ignore the idea. Have you any thoughts on the matter?"

"Not yet, ma'am. I think we need to see what further evidence is turned up. He's also claiming that whatever we find up here on the hill has been planted. He asked if I really thought he was stupid enough to hide evidence on his own land." They walked another few paces. "He may have a point."

"As I said before, he's arrogant. I've known Alistair King for more years than I care to remember, and he's always been a meticulous planner, but his arrogance is what kept him out of the very top positions in the service. He put people's backs up. He wasn't always someone his fellow officers were comfortable working alongside."

That could be the explanation. He'd struck Asha as supremely confident whenever she'd met him. Except for tonight. The dogs' discovery had shaken him, that was for sure.

"We'll bring him in and question him anyway," Patterson said. "The evidence you've accumulated, along with the bodies, should be enough to send him down for a very long time."

"What about the other two? His sidekicks?"

"We'll get them, believe me. This is a small country. Strangers are still noticed around here, and their faces will be splashed across every news outlet by tomorrow. We'll get them."

It sounded like the Chief was trying to convince herself as much as anyone else. At least she seemed to have let go of her earlier plan, to try to blame it on a criminal gang. The sooner those two were behind bars, the better Asha would sleep.

Since Asha had been up the hill, two ambulances had drawn up in front of the house, their rear doors open.

"We've done all we can for now. Let's get these injured men to hospital for a check-up and that bastard, King, locked up somewhere safe for the night, and then we can all get some well-deserved rest. Briefing at, oh, let's say 0900 tomorrow. Give us all a lie-in."

"Ma'am."

Asha went to find Aaron. He was on his feet, pale but steadier than she'd have expected. He turned towards her as she came in, the unspoken question clear on his face.

"I thought you might want to see King being arrested," she said.

"Hell, yeah." He followed her through to the lounge.

Patterson must have dismissed the other officers because she and King were alone in the room. Patterson's cheeks were flushed, and her eyes sparked, but King looked smug. Whatever had been said while they were alone had rattled her.

Patterson looked around, visibly controlling her emotions, but her voice was brittle. "Want to do the honours, Inspector?"

As she read him his rights, King's knowing smile set Asha's hackles up. Even now, he was arrogant, the git.

"Take him away. He can stay in the local lock-up for tonight, and we'll move him to Belfast tomorrow, once we've arranged secure transport."

As he passed Asha, King paused to whisper in her ear. The words were barely more than a breath, stirring her hair. "It'll never come to trial, you wait and see. I know too much about certain people."

"We'll see," she replied and led him outside, leaving Patterson talking on the phone to someone with rapid, urgent words.

The van that was to take him to Ballymena stood about twenty paces away, its rear doors open and engine running.

312

Armed police stood around, watchful, as if fingers were on triggers.

She'd gone a few paces towards the van when she realised that Alistair King had stopped. He was looking around him, as if saying a final goodbye to the place. Even with his hands secured, he still had the air of the lord of the manor surveying his lands. In the headlights from the vehicles, his cheeks were glistening.

A shot rang out. He staggered, only to straighten again, as if determined to stand and face the hidden enemy. Asha dived towards him, but was yanked back by one of the armed officers, who pulled her into cover behind the van. "Don't be so stupid. You think he wouldn't shoot you, too?"

Orders were being shouted. Patterson appeared in the doorway, her mobile still in her hand. Her eyes were shining as if she was carried away by the drama unfolding in front of her.

Asha peered around the edge of the van. Police ran towards the sound of the report, torches bobbing, zigzagging across the rough ground. There were far too many hiding places out there. Hollows and dips, rocky outcrops. It'd take an army to find one lone sniper.

A second shot rang out. Asha couldn't be sure, but it sounded as if it had come from further east, as if the sniper had changed positions.

This time, King was knocked off his feet by the force of the bullet. He fell sideways, facing Asha as she crouched by the van.

His eyes locked onto hers. *I told you. No trial.*

Then the light went out of them and he was gone.

EPILOGUE

Aaron flicked through the report from the forensics team that had been working on the farm for the last couple of weeks.

There had been four bodies buried on King's estate. All women. All young. Apart from Monica, strontium analysis of teeth and bones suggested they originated in Eastern Europe and came to Northern Ireland when they were still in their early teenage years.

He leaned back in the visitor's chair in Asha's office, which now had a shiny new nameplate on the door since her temporary appointment had been converted to a full promotion. It felt good to be able to stretch without sending fire through every nerve ending, but he was still being careful. "I wish we'd had the chance to question King further. Do you suppose he was involved in human trafficking, among his other crimes?"

"I don't know. I just can't see it somehow, and I'm still not sure he took Monica."

He picked up the other report, Monica's post-mortem. "Apparently she had undetected hypertrophic cardiomyopathy — that's an enlarged heart, for those without a degree in jargon. Prof suggests that the shock of being abducted might have stressed her heart to the extent that she died of sudden cardiac failure. Whoever took her might not have intended to harm her, but it must have been a bit of a blow when she dropped dead."

"King was right, though. Why would he bury her, or the other women for that matter, on his own land?"

"He wouldn't," Aaron agreed, and threw the report down in disgust. "So we still have someone else out there, some shadowy figure we haven't yet identified."

"There is some good news," Asha said. "Sue is making a new life for herself. She's going back to the path lab on a part-time basis. I think romance might be in the air."

"I thought Mark Talbot was looking happy."

"He's started wearing some gross aftershave. Have you noticed? I can hardly breathe when I'm in the same room as him, but at least it masks the other smells in there."

"What's gross about it?" Aaron asked. "I use the same one, and you've never complained. In fact, it was me who told him which one to buy."

She just laughed.

"Still no word on those two gits?" he asked.

"Nope, which makes me think they must be getting help from somewhere. There's no way those two managed to leave the country without someone turning a blind eye, and if they're still here, someone must be providing them with a safehouse."

"What does the Chief think?"

"She isn't saying, but I expect she must be thinking along the same lines. I'm hoping she's working away, trying to get to the bottom of it. I hate wondering who's been fooling us all these years."

"So all we can do is watch each other's backs. Trust no one else. Except Patterson. And Josh."

"And that PC, Faith McAvoy," Asha said. "She's too new to have been recruited by anyone, and she seems pretty sharp. I see a bright future ahead for her."

Asha's phone rang and she picked it up.

"Yes, ma'am. Yes, he's been cleared as fit for duty. We'll be right there, ma'am."

315

"Work to do?"

"Nothing too exciting, I'm afraid. A mugging, but the victim is the daughter of a local politician, so it gets the full work-up. Helps the argument for more government funding if we keep her daddy on side. He's one of our most outspoken critics."

* * *

Patterson put the phone down and smiled at the young woman at the other side of her desk. "Everything's looking good. You're already making friends, earning people's trust." Her face hardened. "So don't mess this up. Don't lose sight of the reason I recruited you. You will be my eyes and ears."

"What about George and Larry?"

"Let me worry about them. They shouldn't be coming anywhere near you, but if you do happen to see either of them, you won't recognise them. Is that clear?"

"Yes, ma'am." And thank God for that. They both made her skin crawl.

"Now you'd better get back on the beat, like the good little peeler you are. Keep your head down and your nose clean, and we'll make a detective of you soon enough."

Faith McAvoy left the office, closing the door behind her. Once she was through the outer office, where Patterson's assistant barely spared her a glance, she stopped to lean against the wall, closed her eyes and took a deep breath. Then she pulled the crumpled photo from her pocket and looked at it again. The figures in the foreground had captured Asha's attention, but it had been the side profile of a woman in the background that had caught her eye. A lock of pale hair had escaped from the headscarf. The build and the way the woman wore her clothes was familiar.

She put it away again. It was her insurance. Her ticket out of here if things became unbearable. Because there were going to be hard years ahead. In the meantime, anything was better than lying on her back for a living like her mum, and risking God knows what STDs. Besides, she wasn't doing any real harm, was she? Patterson hadn't given her anything to do that jarred with her conscience.

Not yet, anyway.

THE END

ALSO BY KERRY BUCHANAN

HARVEY & BIRCH
Book 1: KNIFE EDGE
Book 2: SMALL BONES

Thank you for reading this book.

If you enjoyed it please leave feedback on Amazon or Goodreads, and if there is anything we missed or you have a question about, then please get in touch. We appreciate you choosing our book.

Founded in 2014 in Shoreditch, London, we at Joffe Books pride ourselves on our history of innovative publishing. We were thrilled to be shortlisted for Independent Publisher of the Year at the British Book Awards.

www.joffebooks.com

We're very grateful to eagle-eyed readers who take the time to contact us. Please send any errors you find to corrections@joffebooks.com. We'll get them fixed ASAP.

Made in the USA
Columbia, SC
18 June 2021